The
Darkest Evening
of the Year

Dean Koontz

The
Darkest Evening
of the Year

Bantam Books

THE DARKEST EVENING OF THE YEAR
A Bantam Book / December 2007

Published by Bantam Dell
A Division of Random House, Inc.
New York, New York

Book design by Virginia Norey

A signed, limited edition has been privately printed by Charnel House.
Charnelhouse.com

Bantam Books is a registered trademark of Random House, Inc.,
and the colophon is a trademark of Random House, Inc.

Library of Congress Cataloging-in-Publication Data
Koontz, Dean R. (Dean Ray), 1945-
The darkest evening of the year / Dean Koontz.
p. cm.
ISBN 978-0-553-80482-9
1. Dog rescue—Fiction. 2. Golden retriever—Fiction.
3. California, Southern—Fiction. I. Title.

PS3561.O55D287 2008
813'.54--dc22
2007040255

Printed in the United States of America
Published simultaneously in Canada

www.bantamdell.com
BVG 10 9 8 7 6 5 4 3 2 1

To Gerda, who will one day be greeted
jubilantly in the next life by the
golden daughter whom she loved so well
and with such selfless tenderness in
this world.

AND TO

Father Jerome Molokie, for his many
kindnesses, for his good cheer,
for his friendship, and for his
inspiring devotion to what is
first, true, and infinite.

The

Darkest Evening
of the Year

PART ONE

"The woods are lovely, dark, and deep"
—Robert Frost
Stopping by Woods on a Snowy Evening

Chapter

1

Behind the wheel of the Ford Expedition, Amy Redwing drove as if she were immortal and therefore safe at any speed.

In the fitful breeze, a funnel of golden sycamore leaves spun along the post-midnight street. She blasted through them, crisp autumn scratching across the windshield.

For some, the past is a chain, each day a link, raveling backward to one ringbolt or another, in one dark place or another, and tomorrow is a slave to yesterday.

Amy Redwing did not know her origins. Abandoned at the age of two, she had no memory of her mother and father.

She had been left in a church, her name pinned to her shirt. A nun had found her sleeping on a pew.

Most likely, her surname had been invented to mislead. The police had failed to trace it to anyone.

Redwing suggested a Native American heritage. Raven hair and dark eyes argued Cherokee, but her ancestors might as likely have come from Armenia or Sicily, or Spain.

Amy's history remained incomplete, but the lack of roots did not set her free. She was chained to some ringbolt set in the stone of a distant year.

Although she presented herself as such a blithe spirit that she appeared to be capable of flight, she was in fact as earthbound as anyone.

Belted to the passenger seat, feet pressed against a phantom brake pedal, Brian McCarthy wanted to urge Amy to slow down. He said nothing, however, because he was afraid that she would look away from the street to reply to his call for caution.

Besides, when she was launched upon a mission like this, any plea for prudence might perversely incite her to stand harder on the accelerator.

"I love October," she said, looking away from the street. "Don't you love October?"

"This is still September."

"I can love October in September. September doesn't care."

"Watch where you're going."

"I love San Francisco, but it's hundreds of miles away."

"The way you're driving, we'll be there in ten minutes."

"I'm a superb driver. No accidents, no traffic citations."

He said, "My entire life keeps flashing before my eyes."

"You should make an appointment with an ophthalmologist."

"Amy, please, don't keep looking at me."

"You look fine, sweetie. Bed hair becomes you."

"I mean, *watch the road*."

"This guy named Marco—he's blind but he drives a car."

"Marco who?"

"Marco something-something. He's in the Philippines. I read about him in a magazine."

"Nobody blind can drive a car."

"I suppose you don't believe we actually sent men to the moon."

"I don't believe they *drove* there."

"Marco's dog sits in the passenger seat. Marco senses from the dog when to turn right or left, when to hit the brakes."

Some people thought Amy was a charming airhead. Initially, Brian had thought so, too.

Then he had realized he was wrong. He would never have fallen in love with an airhead.

He said, "You aren't seriously telling me that Seeing Eye dogs can drive."

"The dog doesn't drive, silly. He just guides Marco."

"What bizarro magazine were you reading?"

"*National Geographic.* It was such an uplifting story about the human-dog bond, the empowerment of the disabled."

"I'll bet my left foot it wasn't *National Geographic.*"

"I'm opposed to gambling," she said.

"But not to blind men driving."

"Well, they need to be *responsible* blind men."

"No place in the world," he insisted, "allows the blind to drive."

"Not anymore," she agreed.

Brian did not want to ask, could not prevent himself from asking: "Marco isn't allowed to drive anymore?"

"He kept banging into things."

"Imagine that."

"But you can't blame Antoine."

"Antoine who?"

"Antoine the dog. I'm sure he did his best. Dogs always do. Marco just second-guessed him once too often."

"Watch where you're going. Left curve ahead."

Smiling at him, she said, "You're my own Antoine. You'll never let me bang into things."

In the salt-pale moonlight, an older middle-class neighborhood of one-story ranch houses seemed to effloresce out of the darkness.

No streetlamps brightened the night, but the moon silvered the leaves and the creamy trunks of eucalyptuses. Here and there, stucco walls had a faint ectoplasmic glow, as if this were a ghost town of phantom buildings inhabited by spirits.

In the second block, lights brightened windows at one house.

Amy braked to a full stop in the street, and the headlights flared off the reflective numbers on the curbside mailbox.

She shifted the Expedition into reverse. Backing into the driveway, she said, "In an iffy situation, you want to be aimed out for the fastest exit."

As she killed the headlights and the engine, Brian said, "Iffy? Iffy like how?"

Getting out of the SUV, she said, "With a crazy drunk guy, you just never know."

Joining her at the back of the vehicle, where she put up the tailgate, Brian glanced at the house and said, "So there's a crazy guy in there, and he's drunk?"

"On the phone, this Janet Brockman said her husband, Carl, he's crazy drunk, which probably means he's crazy from drinking."

Amy started toward the house, and Brian gripped her shoulder, halting her. "What if he's crazy when he's sober, and now it's worse because he's drunk?"

"I'm not a psychiatrist, sweetie."

"Maybe this is police business."

"Police don't have time for crazy drunk guys like this."

"I'd think crazy drunk guys are right down their alley."

Shrugging off his hand, heading toward the house once more, she said, "We can't waste time. He's violent."

Brian hurried after her. "He's crazy, drunk, and *violent*?"

"He probably won't be violent with me."

Climbing steps to a porch, Brian said, "What about me?"

"I think he's only violent with their dog. But if this Carl does want to take a whack at me, that's okay, 'cause I have you."

"Me? I'm an architect."

"Not tonight, sweetie. Tonight, you're muscle."

Brian had accompanied her on other missions like this, but never previously after midnight to the home of a crazy violent drunk.

"What if I have a testosterone deficiency?"

"Do you have a testosterone deficiency?"

"I cried reading that book last week."

"That book makes everyone cry. It just proves you're human."

As Amy reached for the bell push, the door opened. A young woman with a bruised mouth and a bleeding lip appeared at the threshold.

"Ms. Redwing?" she asked.

"You must be Janet."

"I wish I wasn't. I wish I was you or anybody, somebody." Stepping back from the door, she invited them inside. "Don't let Carl cripple her."

"He won't," Amy assured the woman.

Janet blotted her lips with a bloody cloth. "He crippled Mazie."

Mouth plugged with a thumb, a pale girl of about four clung to a twisted fistful of the tail of Janet's blouse, as if anticipating a sudden cyclone that would try to spin her away from her mother.

The living room was gray. A blue sofa, blue armchairs, stood on a gold carpet, but a pair of lamps shed light as lusterless as ashes, and the colors were muted as though settled smoke from a long-quenched fire had laid a patina on them.

If Purgatory had formal parlors for the waiting multitudes, they might be as ordered and cheerless as this room.

"Crippled Mazie," Janet repeated. "Four months later, he . . ." She glanced down at her daughter. "Four months later, Mazie died."

Having begun to close the front door, Brian hesitated. He left it half open to the mild September night.

"Where is your dog?" Amy asked.

"In the kitchen." Janet put a hand to her swollen lip and spoke between her fingers. "With him."

The child was too old to be sucking her thumb with such devotion, but this habit of the crib disturbed Brian less than did the character of her stare. A purple shade of blue, her eyes were wide with expectation and appeared to be bruised by experience.

The air thickened, as it does under thunderheads and a pending deluge.

"Which way to the kitchen?" Amy asked.

Janet led them through an archway into a hall flanked by dark rooms like flooded grottoes. Her daughter glided at her side, as firmly attached as a remora to a larger fish.

The hall was shadowy except at the far end, where a thin wedge of light stabbed in from a room beyond.

The shadows seemed to ebb and flow and ebb again, but this phantom movement was only Brian's strong pulse, his vision throbbing in time with his laboring heart.

At the midpoint of the hallway, a boy leaned with his forehead against a wall, his hands fisted at his temples. He was perhaps six years old.

From him came the thinnest sound of misery, like air escaping, molecule by molecule, from the pinched neck of a balloon.

Janet said, "It'll be okay, Jimmy," but when she put a hand on the boy's shoulder, he wrenched away from her.

Trailed by her daughter, she proceeded to the end of the hall and pushed the door open, and the stiletto of light became a broadsword.

Entering the kitchen behind the two women and the girl, Brian could almost have believed that the source of the light was the golden retriever sitting alertly in the corner between the cooktop and the refrigerator. The dog seemed to shine.

She was neither pure blond nor the coppery hue of some retrievers, but clothed in many shades of gold, and radiant. Her undercoat was thick, her chest deep, her head beautifully formed.

More compelling than the dog's appearance were her posture and attitude. She sat erect, head lifted, alertness signified by a slight raising of her pendant ears and by the ceaseless subtle flare-and-quiver of her nostrils.

She didn't turn her head, but she shifted her eyes toward Amy and Brian—and at once refocused on Carl.

The man of the house was at the moment something less than a man. Or perhaps he was only what any man eventually might become when guided by no hand but his own.

When sober, he probably had a neighborly face or at least one of those faces that, seen by the thousands in city streets, is a bland mask of benign indifference, with lips compressed and eyes fixed on a distant nothing.

Now, as he stood beside the kitchen table, his face was full of character, though of the wrong kind. His eyes were watery with drink and blood, and he looked out from under a lowered brow, like a bull that sees on every side the challenge of a red cape. His jaw hung slack. His lips were cracked, perhaps from the chronic dehydration that afflicts an alcoholic.

Carl Brockman turned his gaze on Brian. In those eyes shone not the mindless aggression of a man made stupid by drink, but instead the malevolent glee of a chained brute who had been liberated by it.

To his wife, in a voice thick with bitterness, he said, "What've you done?"

"Nothing, Carl. I just called them about the dog."

His face was a snarl of knotted threats. "You must want some."

Janet shook her head.

"You must really want some, Jan. You do this, you know it's gonna get you only one thing."

As though embarrassed by the evidence of her submissiveness, Janet covered her bleeding mouth with one hand.

Crouching, Amy called to the dog. "Here, cutie. Come here, girl."

On the table stood a bottle of tequila, a glass, a salt shaker in the shape of a white Scottish terrier, and a plate holding slices of a fresh lime.

Raising his right hand from his side and high above his head, Carl revealed a tire iron. He gripped it by the pry end.

When he slammed the tool down hard upon the table, slices of lime leaped from the plate. The bottle of tequila wobbled, and the ice rattled in the glass.

Janet cringed, the little girl stoppled a cry with her thumb, Brian winced and tensed, but Amy just continued to coax the retriever to come to her. The dog was neither startled nor made fearful by the crash of iron on wood.

With a backhand swing of the tool, Carl swept everything off the table. At the farther end of the kitchen, tequila splashed, glass shattered, and the ceramic Scottie scattered salt across the floor.

"Get out," Carl demanded. "Get out of my house."

Amy said, "The dog's a problem. You don't need a problem dog. We'll take her off your hands."

"Who the hell are you, anyway? She's my dog. She's not yours. I know how to handle the bitch."

The table was not between them and Carl. If he lurched forward and swung the tire iron, they might be able to dodge a blow only if the tequila made him slow and clumsy.

The guy didn't *look* slow and clumsy. He seemed to be a bullet in the barrel, and any wrong move they made or wrong word they spoke might be the firing pin that sent him hurtling toward them.

Turning his malevolent gaze upon his wife, Carl repeated, "I know how to handle the bitch."

"All I did," Janet said meekly, "was give the poor thing a bath."

"She didn't *need* a bath."

Pleading her case but careful not to argue it, Janet said, "Carl, honey, she was filthy, her coat was all matted."

"She's a *dog*, you stupid skank. She belongs in the yard."

"I know. You're right. You don't want her in the house. But I was just, I was afraid, you know, afraid she'd get those sores like she did before."

Her conciliatory tone inflamed his anger instead of quenching it. "Nickie's *my* dog. I *bought* her. I *own* her. She's *mine*." He pointed the tire iron at his wife. "I know what's mine, and I keep what's mine. Nobody tells me what to do with anything that's *mine*."

At the start of Carl's rant, Amy rose from a crouch and stood staring at him, rigid and still and moon-eyed.

Brian saw something strange in her face, an expression he could not name. She was transfixed but not by fear.

Pointing the tire iron at Amy now, instead of at his wife, Carl said, "What are you staring at? What're you even doing here, you dumb bitch? I told you *Get out.*"

Brian put both hands on a dinette chair. It wasn't much of a weapon, but with it, he might be able to block the tire iron.

"Sir, I'll pay you for the dog," Amy said.

"You deaf?"

"I'll buy her."

"Not for sale."

"A thousand dollars."

"She's mine."

"Fifteen hundred."

Familiar with Amy's finances, Brian said, "Amy?"

Carl transferred the tire iron from his right hand to his left. He flexed his free hand as if he had been gripping the tool with such ferocity that his fingers had cramped.

To Brian, he said, "Who the hell are you?"

"I'm her architect."

"Fifteen hundred," Amy repeated.

Although the kitchen was not too warm, Carl's face glistened with a thin film of greasy perspiration. His undershirt was damp. This was a drunkard's sweat, the body struggling to purge toxins.

"I don't need your money."

"Yes, sir, I know. But you don't need the dog, either. She's not the only dog in the world. Seventeen hundred."

"What're you—crazy?"

"Yeah. I am. But it's a good crazy. Like, I'm not a suicide bomber or anything."

"Suicide bomber?"

"I don't have bodies buried in my backyard. Well, only one, but it's a canary in a shoe box."

"Somethin's wrong with you," Carl said thickly.

"His name was Leroy. I didn't want a canary, especially not one named Leroy. A friend died, Leroy had nowhere to go, he had nothing but his shabby little cage, so I took him in, and he lived with me, and then I buried him, though I didn't bury him until he was dead because, like I said, I'm not that kind of crazy."

Under his brow, Carl's eyes were deep wells with foul water glistening darkly at the bottom. "Don't mock me."

"I wouldn't, sir. I can't. I was pretty much raised by nuns. I don't mock, don't take God's name in vain, don't wear patent-leather shoes with a skirt, and I have such an enlarged guilt gland that it weighs as much as my brain. Eighteen hundred."

As Carl transferred the tire iron from his left hand to his right, he turned it end for end, now gripping it by the lug socket. He pointed the pry end, the sharp end, at Amy, but said nothing.

Brian didn't know if the wife-beater's silence was a good sign or a bad one. More than once, he'd seen Amy talk an angry dog out of a snarl, into a belly rub; but he would have bet his last dollar that Carl wasn't going to lie on his back and put all four in the air.

"Two thousand," Amy said. "That's as much as I have. I can't go any higher."

Carl took a step toward her.

"Back off," Brian warned, raising the dinette chair as if he were a lion tamer, although a lion tamer would also have had a whip.

To Brian, Amy said, "Take it easy, Frank Lloyd Wright. This gentleman and me, we're building some trust here."

Carl extended his right arm, resting the tip of the pry bar in the recess between her collarbones, the blade against her throat.

As though unaware that the point of a deadly weapon was poised to puncture her esophagus, Amy said, "So—two thousand. You're a tough negotiator, sir. I won't be eating filet mignon for a while. That's okay. I'm more a hamburger kind of girl, anyway."

The wife-beater was a chimera now, only part angry bull, part coiled serpent. His gaze was sharp with sinister calculation, and although his tongue was not forked, it slipped between his lips to test the air.

Amy said, "I knew this guy, he almost choked to death on a chunk of steak. The Heimlich maneuver wouldn't dislodge it, so a doctor cut his throat open there in the restaurant, fished the blockage out."

As still as stone, the dog remained alert, and Brian wondered if he should take his lead from her. If the bottled violence in Carl was about to be uncorked, surely Nickie would sense it first.

"This woman at a nearby table," Amy continued, "she was so horrified, she passed out facedown in her lobster bisque. I don't think you can drown in a bowl of lobster bisque, it might even be good for the complexion, but I lifted her head out of it anyway."

Carl licked his cracked lips. "You must think I'm stupid."

"You might be ignorant," Amy said. "I don't know you well enough to say. But I'm totally sure you're not stupid."

Brian realized he was grinding his teeth.

"You give me a check for two thousand," Carl said, "you'll stop payment on it ten minutes after you're out the door with the dog."

"I don't intend to give you a check." From an inside jacket pocket, she withdrew a wad of folded hundred-dollar bills held together by a blue-and-yellow butterfly barrette. "I'll pay cash."

Brian was no longer grinding his teeth. His mouth had fallen open.

Lowering the tire iron to his side, Carl said, "Something's for sure wrong with you."

She pocketed the barrette, fanned the hundred-dollar bills, and said, "Deal?"

He put the weapon on the table, took the money, and counted it with the deliberateness of a man whose memory of math has been bleached pale by tequila.

Relieved, Brian put down the dinette chair.

Moving to the dog, Amy fished a red collar and a rolled-up leash from another pocket. She clipped the leash to the collar and put the collar on the dog. "Nice doing business with you, sir."

While Carl was conducting a second count of the two thousand, Amy tugged gently on the leash. The dog rose at once and padded out of the kitchen, at her side.

With her little girl in tow, Janet followed Amy and Nickie into the hallway, and Brian went after them, glancing back because he half expected Carl to find his rage again and pick up the tire iron.

Jimmy, the keening boy, was silent now. He had moved from the hallway to the living room, where he stood at a window in the posture of a prisoner at his cell bars.

Leading the dog, Amy went to the boy. She stooped beside him, spoke to him.

Brian couldn't hear what she said.

The front door was open, as he had left it. With the dog prancing smartly at her side, Amy soon joined him on the porch.

Standing on the threshold, Janet said, "You were . . . amazing. Thank you. I didn't want the kids to see . . . see it happen again."

Her face was sallow in the yellow light of the porch lamp, and the whites of her eyes had a jaundiced tint. She looked older than her years, and tired.

"You know, he'll get another dog," Amy said.

"Maybe I can prevent that."

"Maybe?"

"I can try."

"Did you really mean what you said when you first answered the door?"

Janet looked away from Amy to study the threshold at her feet, and shrugged.

Amy reminded her: "You wished that you were me. 'Or anybody, somebody.'"

Janet shook her head. Her voice lowered almost to a murmur. "What you did in there, the money was the least of it. The way you were with him—I can never do that."

"Then do what you can." She leaned close to Janet and said something that Brian could not hear.

Listening intently, Janet covered her split and swollen lip with her right hand.

When Amy finished, she stepped back, and Janet met her eyes once more. They stared at each other, and although Janet didn't say a word or even so much as nod, Amy said, "Good. All right."

Janet retreated into the house with her daughter.

Nickie seemed to know where she was going, and moved forward on her leash, leading them off the porch, to the Expedition.

Brian said, "You always carry two thousand bucks?"

"Ever since, three years ago, I wouldn't have been able to save a dog if I hadn't had the money on me to buy it. That first one cost me three hundred twenty-two bucks."

"So sometimes to rescue a dog, you have to buy it."

"Not often, thank God."

Without command or encouragement, Nickie sprang into the cargo space of the SUV.

"Good girl," Amy said, and the dog's plumed tail swished.

"That was crazy, what you did."

"It's only money."

"I mean letting him put the pry bar to your throat."

"He wouldn't have used it."

"How can you be sure?"

"I know his type. He's basically a pussy."

"I don't think he's a pussy."

"He beats up women and dogs."

"You're a woman."

"Not his type. Believe me, sweetie, in a pinch, you'd have whupped his ass in a New York minute."

"Hard to whup a guy's ass after he embeds a tire iron in your skull."

Slamming shut the tailgate, she said, "Your skull would be fine. It's the tire iron that would've been bent."

"Let's get out of here before he decides he should have held out for *three* thousand."

Flipping open her cell phone, she said, "We're not leaving."

"What? Why?"

Keying in three numbers, she said, "The fun's just getting started."

"I don't like that look on your face."

"What look is that?"

"Reckless abandon."

"Reckless is a cute look for me. Don't I look cute?" The 911 operator answered, and Amy said, "I'm on a cell phone. A man here is beating his wife and little boy. He's drunk." She gave the address.

Nose to the glass, peering from the dark cargo hold of the SUV, the golden retriever had the blinkless curiosity of a resident of an aquarium bumping against the walls of its world.

Amy gave her name to the operator. "He's beaten them before. I'm afraid this time he's going to cripple or kill them."

The breeze stirred faster, and the eucalyptus trees tossed their tresses as if winged swarms spiraled through them.

Staring at the house, Brian felt chaos coming. He had much hard experience of chaos. He had been born in a tornado.

"I'm a family friend," Amy lied in answer to the 911 operator's question. "Hurry."

As Amy terminated the call, Brian said, "I thought you took the steam out of him."

"No. By now he's decided that he sold his honor with the dog. He'll blame Janet for that. Come on."

She started toward the house, and Brian hurried at her side. "Shouldn't we leave it to the police?"

"They might not get here in time."

Vague leaf shadows shuddered on the moon-silvered sidewalk, as if they were a thousand beetles quivering toward sheltering crevices.

"But a situation like this," he said, "we don't know what we're doing."

"What we're doing is the right thing. You didn't see the boy's face. His left eye is swollen. His father gave him a bloody nose."

An old anger rose in Brian. "What do you want to do to the sonofabitch?"

Climbing the porch steps, she said, "That's up to him."

Janet had left the front door ajar. From the back of the house rose Carl's angry voice and hammering and crystalline shatters of sound and the sweet desperate singing of a child.

At the core of every ordered system, whether a family or a factory, is chaos. But in the whirl of every chaos lies a strange order, waiting to be found.

Amy pushed open the door. They went inside.

Chapter

2

Ceramic salt and pepper shakers, paired dogs—sitting Airedales, quizzical beagles, grinning goldens, prancing poodles, shepherds, spaniels, terriers, noble Irish wolfhounds—waited in orderly rows on shelves beyond open cabinet doors, and others stood in disorder on a kitchen counter.

Shaking, face pale and wet with tears, Janet Brockman moved two sheep dogs from the counter to the table.

The tire iron swung high as the woman moved, descended as she put the shakers on the table, and barely missed her snatched-back hands. Salt and ceramic shrapnel sprayed from the point of impact, then pepper and sharp shards.

The double crack of iron on wood was followed by Carl's demand: "Two more."

Watching from the dark hallway, Amy Redwing sensed that the collection must be precious to Janet, the one example of order in her disordered life. In those small ceramic dogs, the woman found some kind of hope.

Carl apparently understood this, too. He intended to shatter both the figurines and his wife's remaining spirit.

Clutching a ragged pink rabbit that might have been a dog toy, the little girl sheltered beside the refrigerator. Her jewel-bright eyes were focused on a landscape of the mind.

In a small but clear voice, she sang in a language that Amy did not recognize. The haunting melody sounded Celtic.

The boy, Jimmy, evidently had taken refuge elsewhere.

Alert to the fact that her husband would as soon shatter her fingers as break the salt and pepper shakers, Janet flinched at the *whoosh* of arcing iron. She dropped a pair of ceramic Dalmatians on the table.

Crying out as the weapon grazed her right wrist, she cowered back against the ovens, arms crossed over her breasts.

When the lug wrench rang off oak, sparing both the salt and pepper, Carl snatched up a Dalmatian and threw it at his wife's face. The figurine ricocheted off her forehead, cracked against an oven door, and fell dismembered to the floor.

Amy stepped into the kitchen, and Brian pushed past her, saying, "Leave her alone, Carl."

The drunkard's head turned with crocodilian menace, eyes cold with a cruelty as old as time.

Amy had the feeling that something more than the man himself lived in Brockman's body, as though he had opened a door to a night visitor that made of his heart a lair.

"Is she *your* wife now?" Carl asked Brian. "Is this *your* house? My Theresa there—is she *your* daughter now?"

The sweet song rose from the girl, her voice as clear as the air and as strange as her eyes, but mysterious in its clarity and tender in its strangeness.

"It's your house, Carl," said Brian. "Everything is yours. So why smash any of it?"

Carl started to speak but then sighed wearily.

The tide of foul emotion seemed to recede in him, leaving his face as smooth as washed sand.

Without the anger he had shown previously, he said, "See . . . the way things are . . . nothing's better than smashing."

Taking a step toward the table that separated them, Brian said, "The way things are. Help me understand the way things are."

The hooded eyes looked sleepy, but the reptilian mind behind them might be acrawl with calculation.

"Wrong," Carl said. "Things are all wrong."

"What things?"

His voice swam up from fathoms of melancholy. "You wake in the middle of the night, when it's blind-dark and quiet enough to *think* for once, and you can feel then how wrong it all is, and no way ever to make it right. No way ever."

As clear and silvery as the music of Uilleann pipes in an Irish band, Theresa's small voice raised the hairs on the nape of Amy's neck, because whatever the girl's words meant, they conveyed a sense of longing and loss.

Brockman looked at his daughter. His sudden tears might have been for the girl or for the song, or for himself.

Perhaps the child's voice had a premonitory quality or perhaps Amy's instincts had been enriched by the companionship of so many dogs. She was suddenly certain that Carl's rage had not abated and that, concealed, it swelled toward violent expression.

She *knew* the iron would swing without warning and take the broken wife in the face, breaking her twice and forever, shattering the hidden skull into the living brain.

As if premonition were a wave as real as light, it seemed to travel from Amy to Brian. Even as she inhaled to cry out, he moved. He didn't have time to circle the kitchen. Instead he scrambled from floor to chair to table.

A tear fell to the hand that held the iron, and the fingers tightened on the weapon.

Janet's eyes widened. But Carl had drowned her spirit. She stood motionless, breathless, defenseless under a suffocating weight of despair.

As Brian climbed toward confrontation, Amy realized that the bludgeon might as likely be flung at the child as swung at the wife, and she moved toward Theresa.

Atop the table, Brian seized the weapon as it ascended to strike a blow at Janet, and he fell upon Brockman. They sprawled on the floor, into broken glass and slices of lime and puddles of tequila.

Amy had left the front door open, and from the farther end of the house came a voice: *"Police."* They had arrived without sirens.

"Back here," she called, gathering Theresa to her as the girl's song murmured to a whisper, whispered into silence.

Janet stood rigid, as if the blow might yet come, but Brian rose in possession of the tire iron.

Braided leather gun belts creaking, hands on the grips of their holstered pistols, two policemen entered the kitchen, solid men and alert. One told Brian to put down the tire iron, and Brian placed it on the table.

Carl Brockman clambered to his feet, left hand bleeding from a shard of embedded bottle glass. Once burning bright with anger, his tear-streaked face had paled to ashes, and his mouth had gone soft with self-pity.

"Help me, Jan," he pleaded, reaching out to her with his bloody hand. "What am I gonna do now? Baby, help me."

She took a step toward him, but halted. She glanced at Amy, then at Theresa.

With her thumb, the child had corked her song inside, and she had closed her eyes. Throughout these events, her face had remained expressionless, as though she might be deaf to all the threats of violence and to the crash of iron on oak.

The only indication that the girl had any connection to reality was the fierceness of her grip on Amy's hand.

"He's my husband," Janet told the police. "He hit me." She put a hand to her mouth, but then lowered it. "My husband hit me."

"Oh, Jan, please don't do this."

"He hit our little boy. Bloodied his nose. Our Jimmy."

One of the officers took the tire iron off the table, propped it in a corner beyond easy reach, and instructed Carl to sit in a dinette chair.

Now came questions and inadequate answers and gradually a new kind of awfulness: the recognition of lost promise and the bitter cost of vows not kept.

After Amy had told her story to the police, and while the others told theirs, she led Theresa out of the kitchen, along the hallway, seeking the boy. He might have been anywhere in the house, but she was drawn to the open front door.

The porch smelled of the night-blooming jasmine that braided through the white laths of a trellis. She had not detected the scent earlier.

The breeze had died. In the stillness, the eucalyptus trees stood as grim as mourners.

Past the dark patrol car at the curb, in the middle of the moon-washed street, boy and dog seemed to be at play.

The tailgate of the Expedition was open. The boy must have let Nickie out of the SUV.

On second look, Amy realized that Jimmy was not playing a game with the retriever, that instead he was trying to run away. The dog blocked him, thwarted him, strove to herd him back to the house.

The boy fell to the pavement and stayed where he dropped, on his side. He drew his knees up in the fetal position.

The dog lay next to him, as though keeping a watch over him.

Settling Theresa on a porch step, Amy said, "Don't move, honey. All right? Don't move."

The girl did not reply and perhaps was not capable of replying.

Through a night as quiet as an abandoned church, breathing eucalyptic incense, Amy hurried into the street.

Nickie watched her as she approached. Under the moon, the golden looked silver, and all the light of that high lamp seemed to be given to her, leaving everything else in the night to be brightened only by her reflection.

Kneeling beside Jimmy, Amy heard him weeping. She put a hand on his shoulder, and he did not flinch from her touch.

She and the dog regarded each other across the grieving boy.

The retriever's face was noble, with at this moment none of the comic expression of which the breed was so capable. Noble and solemn.

All the houses but one remained dark, and the silence of the stars filled the street, disturbed only by the boy's softly expressed anguish, which grew quiet as Amy smoothed his hair.

"Nickie," she whispered.

The dog did not raise its ears or cock its head, or in any way respond, but it stared at her, and stared.

After a while, Amy encouraged the boy to sit up. "Put your arms around my neck, sweetheart."

Jimmy was small, and she scooped him off the pavement, carrying him in the cradle of her arms. "Never again, sweetheart. That's all over."

The dog led the way to the Expedition, ran the last few steps, and sprang through the open tailgate.

While Amy deposited the boy in the backseat, Nickie watched from the cargo space.

"Never again," Amy said, and kissed the boy on the forehead. "I promise you, honey."

The promise surprised and daunted her. This boy was not hers, and the arcs of their lives likely would have only this intersection and a short parallel course. She could not do for a stranger's child what she could do for dogs, and sometimes she could not even save the dogs.

Yet she heard herself repeat, "I promise."

She closed the door and stood for a moment at the back of the SUV, shivering in the mild September night, watching Theresa on the front-porch steps.

The moon painted faux ice on the concrete driveway and faux frost on the eucalyptus leaves.

Amy remembered a winter night with blood upon the snow and a turbulence of sea gulls thrashing into flight from the eaves of the high catwalk, white wings briefly dazzling as they oared skyward through the sweeping beam of the lighthouse, like an honor guard of angels escorting home a sinless soul.

Chapter

3

Brian McCarthy and Associates occupied offices on the ground floor of a modest two-story building in Newport Beach. He lived on the upper floor.

Amy braked to a stop in the small parking lot beside the place. Leaving Janet, the two children, and the dog, Nickie, in the SUV, she accompanied Brian to the exterior stairs that led to his apartment.

A lamp glowed at the top of the long flight, but here at the bottom, the darkness was unrelieved.

She said, "You smell like tequila."

"I think I've still got a slice of lime in my shoe."

"Climbing the table to jump him—that was reckless."

"Just trying to impress my date."

"It worked."

"I'd sure like to kiss you now," he said.

"As long as we don't generate enough heat to bring the global-warming police down on us, go ahead."

He looked at the Expedition. "Everybody's watching."

"After Carl, maybe they need to see people kissing."

He kissed her. She was good at it.

"Even the dog's watching," he said.

"She's wondering—if I paid two thousand for her, how much did I pay for you."

"You can put a collar on me anytime."

"Let's leave it at kisses for now." She kissed him again before returning to the Expedition.

After watching her drive away, he went upstairs. His apartment was spacious, with Santos-mahogany floors and butter-yellow walls.

The minimalist contemporary furnishings and serene Japanese art suggested less a bachelor pad than a monk's quarters. He had gutted, rebuilt, and furnished these rooms before he met Amy. He didn't want to be either a bachelor or a monk anymore.

After stripping out of his tequila-marinated clothes, he took a shower. Maybe the hot water would make him sleepy.

Still feeling as alert and wide-eyed as an owl, he dressed in jeans and a Hawaiian shirt. At 2:56 A.M., he was awake for the day.

With a mug of fresh-brewed coffee, he settled at the computer in his study. He needed to get work done before sleep deprivation melted the edge off his concentration.

Two e-mails awaited him. The sender was *pigkeeper*.

Vanessa. She hadn't contacted him in over five months. He had begun to think he would never hear from her again.

For a while, he stared at the screen, reluctant to let her into his life once more. If he never again read her messages, if he never answered them, he might be rid of her in time.

Hope would be gone with her, however. Hope would be lost. The price of freezing Vanessa out of his life was too great.

He opened the first e-mail.

Piggy wants a puppy. How stupid is that? How can a piggy take care of a puppy when the puppy's smarter? I've known houseplants smarter than Piggy.

Brian closed his eyes. Too late. He had opened himself to her, and now she was alive again in the lighted rooms of his mind, not just in the dark corners of memory.

How are you doing, Bry? Do you have cancer yet? You're only thirty-four next week, but people die young of cancer all the time. It's not too much to hope for.

After printing a hard copy of her message, he filed the e-mail electronically under *Vanessa*.

To avoid slopping coffee out of the mug, he held it with both hands. The brew tasted fine, but coffee was no longer all that he needed.

From the sideboard in the dining room, he fetched a bottle of cognac. In the study once more, he added a generous portion of Rémy Martin to the mug.

He was not much of a drinker. He kept the Rémy for visitors. The visitor tonight was unwelcome, and here in spirit only.

For a while he wandered through the apartment, drinking coffee, waiting for the cognac to take the edge off his nerves.

Amy was right: Carl Brockman was a pussy. The drunkard reeked of tequila, but even at a distance, Vanessa smelled of brimstone.

When Brian felt ready, he returned to the computer and opened the second e-mail.

Hey, Bry. Forgot to tell you a funny thing.

Without reading further, he pressed the PRINT key and then filed the e-mail under *Vanessa*.

Silence pooled in the apartment, and not a sound ascended from the office below or from the dark depths of the street.

He closed his eyes. But only genuine blindness would excuse him from the obligation to read the hard copy.

Back in July, the pigster built sandcastles all day on the little beach we have in this new place, then wound up with a killer sunburn, looked like a baked ham. Old Piggy couldn't sleep for days, cried half the night, started peeling and then itched herself raw. You might expect the smell of fried bacon, but there wasn't.

He was a swimmer on the surface of the past, an abyss of memory under him.

Piggy is pink and smooth again, but there's a mole on her neck that seems to be changing. Maybe the sunburn made some melanoma. I will keep you informed.

He put this second printout with the first. Later he would read both again, searching for clues in addition to "the little beach."

In the kitchen, Brian poured the contents of the mug down the drain. He no longer needed coffee and no longer wanted cognac.

Guilt is a tireless horse. Grief ages into sorrow, and sorrow is an enduring rider.

He opened the refrigerator, but then closed it. He could no more eat than sleep.

Returning to the study and working on one of his current custom-home projects had no appeal. Architecture might be frozen music, as Goethe once said, but right now he was deaf to it.

From a kitchen drawer, he extracted a large tablet of art paper and a set of drawing pencils. He had stashed these things in every room of the apartment.

He sat at the dinette table and began to sketch a concept for the building that Amy hoped he would design for her: a place for dogs, a haven where no hand would ever be raised against them, where every affection wanted would be given.

She owned a piece of land on which hilltop oaks spread against the sky, long shadows lengthening down sloped meadows in the early morning, retracting toward the crest as the day ripened toward noon. She had a vision for it that inspired him.

Nevertheless, after a while, Brian found himself turning from sketch to portrait, from a haven for dogs to the animal itself. He had a gift for portraiture, but never before had he drawn a dog.

As his pencils whispered across the paper, an uncanny feeling overcame him, and a strange thing happened.

Chapter

4

After dropping Brian at his place, Amy Redwing called Lottie Augustine, her neighbor, and explained that she was bringing in three rescues who were not dogs and who needed shelter.

Lottie served in the volunteer army that did the work of Golden Heart, the organization Amy founded. A few times in the past, she'd risen after midnight to help in an emergency, always with good cheer.

Having been a widow for a decade and a half, having retired from a nursing career, Lottie found as much meaning in tending to the dogs as she had found in being a good wife and a caring nurse.

The drive from Brian's place to Lottie's house was stressed by silence: little Theresa asleep in the backseat, her brother slumped and brooding beside her, Janet in the passenger seat but looking lost and studying the deserted streets as if these were not just unknown neighborhoods but were the precincts of a foreign country.

In the company of other people, Amy had little tolerance for quiet. Enduring mutual silences, she sometimes felt as though the other person might ask a terrible question, the answer to which, if she spoke it, would shatter her as surely as a hard-thrown stone will destroy a pane of glass.

Consequently, she spoke of this and that, including Antoine, the dog driver who served blind Marco, out there in the far Philippines. Neither the two troubled children nor their mother would take the bait.

When they came to a stop at a red traffic light, Janet offered Amy the two thousand dollars that she had given to Carl.

"It's yours," Amy said.

"I can't accept it."

"I bought the dog."

"Carl's in jail now."

"He'll be out on bail soon."

"But he won't want the dog."

"Because I've bought her."

"He'll want me—after what I've done."

"He won't find you. I promise."

"We can't afford a dog now."

"No problem. I bought her."

"I'd give her to you anyway."

"The deal is done."

"It's a lot of money," Janet said.

"Not so much. I never renegotiate."

The woman folded her left hand around the cash, her right hand around the left, lowered her hands to her lap as she bowed her head.

The traffic signal turned green, and Amy drove across the deserted intersection as Janet said softly, "Thank you."

Thinking of the dog in the cargo area, Amy said, "Trust me, sweetie, I got the better half of the deal."

She glanced at the rearview mirror and saw the dog peering forward from behind the backseat. Their eyes met in their reflections and then Amy looked at the road ahead.

"How long have you had Nickie?" Amy asked.

"A little more than four months."

"Where did you get her?"

"Carl didn't say. He just brought her home."

They were southbound on the Coast Highway, scrub and shore grass to their right. Beyond the grass lay the beach, the sea.

"How old is she?"

"Carl said maybe two years."

"So she came with the name."

"No. He didn't know her name."

The water was black, the sky black, and the painter moon, though in decline, brushed the crests of the waves.

"Then who named her?"

Janet's answer surprised Amy: "Reesa. Theresa."

The girl had not spoken this night, had only sung in that high pure voice, in what might have been Celtic, and she had seemed to be detached in the manner of a gentle autistic.

"Why Nickie?"

"Reesa said it was always her name."

"Always."

"Yes."

"For some reason . . . I didn't think Theresa said much."

"She doesn't. Sometimes not for weeks, then only a few words."

In the mirror, the steady gaze of the dog. In the sea, the sinking moon. In the sky, a vast intricate wheelwork of stars.

And in Amy's heart rose a sense of wonder that she was reluctant to indulge, for it could not be true, in any meaningful sense, that her Nickie had returned to her.

Chapter

5

Moongirl will make love only in total darkness. She believes that her life has been forever diminished by passion in the light, when she was younger.

Consequently, the faintest glow around a lowered window shade will burn away all of her desire.

A single thread of sunshine in the folds of drawn draperies will in an instant unravel her lust.

Light intruding from another room—under a door, around a crack in a jamb, through a keyhole—will pierce her as if it is a needle and cause her to flinch from her lover's touch.

When her blood is hot, even the light-emitting numerals of a bedside clock will chill her.

The luminous face of a wristwatch, the tiny bulb on a smoke detector, the radiant eyes of a cat can wring a cry of frustration from her and squeeze her libido dry.

Harrow thinks of her as *Moongirl* because he can imagine her loose in the night, silhouetted naked on a ridge line, howling at the moon. He doesn't know what label a psychologist might apply to her particular kind of madness, but he has no doubt that she is mad.

Never has he called her Moongirl to her face. Instinct tells him that to do so would be dangerous, perhaps even fatal.

In daylight or dark, she can pass for sane. She can even feign wholesomeness quite convincingly. Her beauty beguiles.

Especially in purple, but also in pink and white, bouquets of hydrangea charm the eye, but the plant is mortally poisonous; so, too, the lily of the valley, the blossoms of bloodroot; the petals of yellow jasmine, brewed in tea or mixed in salad, can kill in as little as ten minutes.

Moongirl loves the black rose more than any other flower, though it is not poisonous.

Harrow has seen her hold such a rose so tightly by its thorny stem that her hand drips blood.

Her pain threshold, like his, is high. She does not enjoy the prick of the rose; she simply does not feel it.

She has total discipline of her body and her intellect. She has no discipline of her emotions. She is, therefore, out of balance, and balance is a requirement of sanity.

This night, in a windowless room where no starshine can reach, where the luminous clock is closed in a nightstand drawer, they do not make love, for love has nothing to do with their increasingly ferocious coupling.

No woman has excited Harrow as this one does. She has about her the ultimate hunger of the black widow, the all-consuming passion of a mantis that, during coitus, kills and eats its mate.

He half expects that one night Moongirl will conceal a knife between mattress and box springs, or elsewhere near the bed. In the blinding dark, at the penultimate moment, he will hear her whisper *Darling* and feel a sudden stiletto navigate his ribs and pop his swelling heart.

As always, the anticipation of sex proves to be more thrilling than the experience. At the end, he feels a curious hollowness, a certainty that the essence of the act has again eluded him.

Spent, they lie in the hush of the blackness, as silent as if they have stepped out of life into the outer dark.

Moongirl is not much for words, and she always speaks directly when she has something to say.

In her company, Harrow follows her example. Fewer words mean less risk of a mere observation being misconstrued as an insult or a judgment.

She is sensitive about being judged. Advice, if she dislikes it, might be received as a rebuke. A well-meant admonition might be interpreted as stinging criticism.

Here in the venereal aftermath, Harrow has no fear of any blade she might have buried in the bedding. If ever she tries to kill him, the attempt will be made between the motion and the act, at the ascending moment of her fulfillment.

Now, after sex, he does not seek sleep. Most of the time, Moongirl sleeps by day and thrives in the night; and Harrow has reset himself to live by her clock.

For one so ripe, she lies stick-stiff in the darkness, like a hungry presence poised on a branch, disguised as bark, waiting for an unwary passerby.

In time she says, "Let's burn."

"Burn what?"

"Whatever needs burning."

"All right."

"Not her, if that's what you're thinking."

"I'm not thinking."

"She's for later."

"All right," he says.

"I mean a place."

"Where?"

"We'll know it."

"How?"

"When we see it."

She sits up, and her fingers go to the lamp switch with the unerring elegance of a blind woman following a line of Braille to the end punctuation.

When he sees her in the soft light, he wants her again, but she is never his for the taking. His satisfaction always depends on her need, and at the moment the only thing she needs is to burn.

Throughout his life, Harrow has been a loner and a user, even when others have counted him as friend or family. Outsider to the world, he has acted strictly in his self-interest—until Moongirl.

What he has with her is neither friendship nor family, but something more primal. If just two individuals can constitute a pack, then he and Moongirl are wolves, though more terrible than wolves, because wolves kill only to eat.

He pulls on his clothes without taking his eyes from her, for she makes getting dressed an act no less erotic than a striptease. Even coarse fabrics seem to slide like silk along her limbs, and the fastening of every button is a promise of a future unveiling.

Their coats hang on wall pegs: ski jacket for him, black leather lined with fleece for her.

Outside, her blond hair looks platinum under the moon, and her eyes—bottle-green in the lamplight—seem to be a luminous gray in the colorless night.

"You drive," she says, leading him toward the detached garage.

"All right."

As they pass through the man door, he switches on the light.

She says, "We'll need gasoline."

From under the workbench, Harrow retrieves a red two-gallon

utility can in which he keeps gasoline for the lawn mower. Judging by the heft of the can and the hollow sloshing of the contents, it holds less than half a gallon.

The fuel tanks of both the Lexus SUV and the two-seater Mercedes sports car have recently been filled. Harrow inserts a siphon hose into the Lexus.

Moongirl stands over him, watching as he sucks on the rubber tube. She keeps her hands in the pockets of her jacket.

Harrow wonders: If he misjudges the amount of priming needed, if he draws gasoline into his mouth, will she produce a butane lighter and ignite the flammable mist that wheezes from him, setting fire to his lips and tongue?

He tastes the first acrid fumes and does not misjudge, but introduces the hose into the open can on the floor just as the gasoline gushes.

When he looks up at her, she meets his eyes. She says nothing, and neither does he.

He is safe from her and she from him as long as they need each other for the hunt. She has her quarry, the object of her hatred, and Harrow has his, not merely whatever they might burn tonight, but other and specific targets. Together they can more easily achieve their goals, with more pleasure than they would have if they acted separately and alone.

He places the full utility can in the sports car, in the luggage space behind the two bucket seats.

The single-lane blacktop road, with here and there a lay-by, rises and falls and curves for a mile before it brings them to the gate, which swings open when Moongirl presses the button on the same remote with which moments ago she raised the garage door.

In another half-mile, they come to the two-lane county road.

"Left," she says, and he turns left, which is north.

The night is half over but full of promise.

To the east, hills rise. To the west, they descend.

In lunar light, the wild dry grass is as platinum as Moongirl's hair, as if the hills are pillows on which uncountable thousands of women rest their blond heads.

They are in sparsely populated territory. At the moment, not a single building stands in view.

"How much nicer the world would be," she says, "if everyone in it were dead."

Chapter

6

Amy Redwing owned a modest bungalow, but Lottie Augustine's two-story house, next door, had spare rooms for Janet and her kids. The windows glowed with warm light when Amy parked in the driveway.

The former nurse came out to greet them and to help carry their hastily packed suitcases into the house.

Slender, wearing jeans and a man's blue-and-yellow checkered shirt with the tail untucked, gray hair in a ponytail, eyes limpid blue in a sweet face wizened by a love of the sun, Lottie seemed to be both a teenager and a retiree. In her youth she had probably been an old soul, just as in her later years she remained a young spirit.

Leaving the dog in the SUV, Amy carried Theresa. The child woke as they ascended the back-porch steps.

Even awake, her purple eyes seemed full of dreams.

Touching the locket Amy wore at her throat, Theresa whispered, *"The wind."*

Carrying two suitcases, followed by Janet with one bag and with Jimmy in tow, Lottie led them into the house.

Just beyond the threshold of the kitchen door, still in Amy's arms and fingering the locket, Theresa whispered, *"The chimes."*

Cast back in time, Amy halted. For a moment, the kitchen faded as if it were only a pale vision of a moment in her future.

The child's trance-casting eyes seemed to widen as if they were portals through which one might fall into another world.

"What did you say?" she asked Theresa, though she had heard the words clearly enough.

The wind. The chimes.

The girl did not blink, did not blink, then blinked—and plugged her mouth with her right thumb.

Color returned to the faded kitchen, and Amy put Theresa down in a dinette chair.

On the table stood a plate of homemade cookies. Oatmeal raisin. Chocolate chip. Peanut butter.

A pan of milk waited on the cooktop, and Lottie Augustine set to making hot chocolate.

The clink of mugs against a countertop, the crisp crackle of a foil packet of cocoa powder, the burble of simmering milk stirred by a ladle, the soft knocking of the wood ladle against the pan . . .

The sounds seemed to come to Amy from a distance, to arise in a room far removed from this one, and when she heard her name, she realized that Lottie had spoken it more than once.

"Oh. Sorry. What did you say?"

"Why don't you and Janet take their bags upstairs while I tend to the children. You know the way."

"All right. Sure."

Upstairs, two secondary bedrooms were connected by a bath. One had twin beds suitable for the kids.

"If you leave both doors open to the shared bath," Amy said, "you'll be able to hear them if they call out."

In the room that had one bed, Janet sat on the arm of a plump upholstered chair. She looked exhausted and bewildered, as if she had walked a hundred miles while under a spell and did not know where she was or why she had come here.

"What now?"

"The police will take at least a day to decide on charges. Then Carl will need to make bail."

"He'll come looking for you to find me."

"By then, you won't be next door anymore."

"Where?"

"Over a hundred sixty people volunteer for Golden Heart. Some of them foster incoming dogs until we can find each one's forever home."

"Forever home?"

"Before we make a permanent placement of a rescued dog, we have a vet make sure it's healthy, up-to-date on all its shots."

"One day when he was gone, I took Nickie for her shots. He was furious about the cost."

"The foster parents evaluate the dog and make a report on the extent of its training—is it housebroken, leash friendly. . . ."

"Nickie's housebroken. She's the sweetest girl."

"If the dog has no serious behavioral problems, we find what we hope will be its forever home. Some of our fostering volunteers have room for more than visiting dogs. One of them will take in you and the kids for a few weeks, till you get on your feet."

"Why would they do that?"

"Most golden-rescue people are a class apart. You'll see."

In Janet's lap, her hands worried at each other. "What a mess."

"It would have been worse to stay with him."

"Just me, I might've stayed. But not with the kids. Not anymore. I'm . . . ashamed, how I let him treat them."

"You'd need to be ashamed if you stayed. But not now. Not unless you let him sweet-talk you back."

"Won't happen."

"Glad to hear it. There's always a way forward. But there's no way back."

Janet nodded. Perhaps she understood. Most likely not.

To many people, free will is a license to rebel not against what is unjust or hard in life but against what is best for them and true.

Amy said, "It might be too late to help the swelling, but you ought to try putting some ice on that split lip."

Rising from the arm of the chair, moving toward the bedroom door, Janet said, "All right. But I heal fast. I've had to."

Putting one hand on the woman's shoulder, staying her for a moment, Amy said, "Your daughter, is she autistic?"

"One doctor said so. Others don't agree."

"What do the others say?"

"Different things. Various developmental disabilities with long names and no hope."

"Has she had any kind of treatment?"

"None that's brought her out of herself. But Reesa—she's some kind of prodigy, too. She hears a song once, she can sing it or play it note-perfect on a child's flute I bought her."

"Earlier, was she singing in Celtic?"

"Back at the house. Yes."

"She knows the language?"

"No. But Maev Gallagher, our neighbor, loves Celtic music, plays it all the time. She sometimes baby-sits Reesa."

"So once she's heard a song, she can also sing it word-perfect in a language she doesn't know."

"It's a little eerie sometimes," Janet said. "That high sweet voice in a foreign tongue."

Amy removed her hand from Janet's shoulder. "Has she ever . . ."

"Ever what?"

"Has she ever done anything else that strikes you as eerie?"

Janet frowned. "Like what?"

To explain, Amy would have to open door after door into herself, into places in the heart that she did not want to visit. "I don't know. I don't know what I meant by that."

"In spite of her problems, Reesa's a good girl."

"I'm sure she is. And she's lovely, too. Such beautiful eyes."

Chapter

7

Harrow drives, and the silver Mercedes conforms to curves with the sinuous grace of free-flowing mercury, and Moongirl simmers in the passenger seat.

No matter how good the sex has been for her, Moongirl always rises in anger from the bed.

Harrow is never the cause of her rage. She is furious because she can only have carnal satisfaction in a lightless room.

She has put this condition of darkness upon herself, but she does not blame herself for it. She imagines herself to be a victim and instead blames another, and not just another but also the world.

Drained of desire by the act, she remains empty only until the last shudder of pleasure has passed through her, whereupon she fills at once with bitterness and resentment.

Because she has the capacity for ruthless discipline of the body and the intellect, her undisciplined emotion can be concealed. Her face remains placid, her voice soft. Always she is lithe, graceful, with no telltale twitch of tension in her stride or gestures.

Occasionally Harrow swears that he can *smell* her fury: the faintest scent of iron, like that rising from ferrous rock scorched by relentless desert sun.

Only light can vaporize this particular anger.

If they lie together in the windowless room in the daytime, she wants afterward to be in the light. Sometimes she goes outside half clothed or even naked.

On those days, she stands with her face turned to the sky, her mouth open, as if inviting the light to fill her.

Although a natural blonde, she takes the sun well. Her skin is bronze even into the creases of her knuckles, and the fine hairs on her arms are bleached white.

By contrast to her skin, the whites of her eyes are as brilliant as pure arctic snow, and the bottle-green irises dazzle.

Most often she and Harrow make loveless love at night. Afterward, neither the stars nor the moon is bright enough to steam away her distilled fury, and though she sometimes refers to herself as a Valkyrie, she does not have wings to fly into the higher light.

Usually a bonfire on the beach will reduce her anger to embers, but not always. Occasionally she needs to burn more than pine logs and dried seaweed and driftwood.

As though Moongirl can will the world to meet her needs, someone ideal for burning may come to her at the opportune moment. This has happened more than once.

On a night when a bonfire is not enough and when fate does not send her an offering, she must go out into the world and find the fire she needs.

Harrow has driven her as far as 120 miles before she has located what requires burning. Sometimes she does not find it before dawn, and then the sun is sufficient to boil off her rage.

This night, he drives thirty-six miles on winding roads through rural territory before she says, "There. Let's do it."

An old one-story clapboard house, the only residence in sight, sits behind a well-tended lawn. No lamps brighten any window.

The headlights reveal two birdbaths in the yard, three garden gnomes, and a miniature windmill. On the front porch are a pair of bentwood rocking chairs.

Harrow proceeds almost a quarter of a mile past the place until, prior to a bridge, he comes to a narrow dirt lane that slants off the blacktop. He follows this dusty track down to the base of the bridge and parks near the river, where sluggish black water purls in the moonlight.

Perhaps this short path serves fishermen who cast for bass from the bank. If so, none is currently present. This is an hour made more for arsonists than for anglers.

From the two-lane county road above, the Mercedes cannot be seen here at the river. Although few motorists, if any, are likely to be abroad at this hour, precautions must be taken.

Harrow retrieves the two-gallon utility can from the luggage space behind the seats.

He does not ask her if she has remembered to bring matches. She always carries them.

Cicadas serenade one another, and toads croak with satisfaction each time they devour a cicada.

Harrow considers going overland to the house, across meadows and through a copse of oaks. But they will gain no advantage by taking the arduous route.

The target house is only a quarter-mile away. Along the county road are tall grasses, gnarls of brush, and a few trees, always one kind of cover or another to which they can retreat the moment they glimpse distant headlights or hear the faraway growl of an engine.

They ascend from the riverbank to the paved road.

The gasoline chuckles in the can, and his nylon jacket produces soft whistling noises when one part of it rubs against another.

Moongirl makes no sound whatsoever. She walks without a single footfall that he can hear.

Then she says, "Do you wonder why?"

"Why what?"

"The burning."

"No."

"You never wonder," she presses.

"No. It's what you want."

"That's good enough for you."

"Yes."

The early-autumn stars are as icy as those of winter, and it seems to him that now, as in all seasons, the sky is not deep but dead, flat, and frozen.

She says, "You know what's the worst thing?"

"Tell me."

"Boredom."

"Yes."

"It turns you outward."

"Yes."

"But toward what?"

"Tell me," he says.

"Nothing's out there."

"Nothing you want."

"Just nothing," she corrects.

Her madness fascinates Harrow, and he is never bored in her company. Originally, he had thought they would be done with each other in a month or two; but they have been seven months together.

"It's terrifying," she says.

"What?"

"Boredom."

"Yes," he says sincerely.

"Terrifying."

"Gotta stay busy."

He shifts the heavy gasoline can from his right hand to his left.

"Pisses me off," she says.

"What does?"

"Being terrified."

"Stay busy," he repeats.

"All I've got is me."

"And me," he reminds her.

She does not confirm that he is essential to her defenses against boredom.

They have covered half the distance to the clapboard house.

A winking light moves across the frozen stars, but it is nothing more than an airliner, too high to be heard, bound for an exotic port that at least some perceptive passengers will discover is identical to the place from which they departed.

Chapter

8

Having moved the Expedition from Lottie's driveway to her own carport next door, Amy opened the tailgate, and Nickie leaped out into the night.

Amy remembered coming out of the Brockman house and finding the tailgate open, Jimmy trying to run away and the diligent dog herding him toward home.

He must have freed Nickie with the expectation that they would escape together. Having endured four months with Carl Brockman as its master, any other dog might have led the boy in flight.

As Nickie landed on the driveway, Amy snatched up the red leash, but the dog had no intention of running off. She led Amy around the vehicle, into the backyard. Without any of the usual canine ritual, Nickie squatted to pee.

Because Amy had two golden retrievers of her own—Fred and Ethel—and because often she kept rescue dogs for at least a night or two before transporting them to foster homes, she assumed that Nickie would want to spend some time sniffing around the yard—reading the local newspaper, so to speak.

Instead, upon completion of her business, the dog went directly to the back porch, up the steps, and to the door.

Amy unlocked the door, unclipped the leash from the collar, stepped into the house, and switched on the lights.

Neither Fred nor Ethel was in the kitchen. They must have been asleep in the bedroom.

From the farther end of the bungalow arose the thump of paws rushing across carpet and then hardwood, swiftly approaching.

Fred and Ethel did not bark, because they were trained not to speak without an important reason—such as a stranger at the door—and they were good dogs.

She most often took them with her. When she left them at home, they always greeted her return with an enthusiasm that lifted her heart.

Usually Ethel would appear first, ebullient and grinning, head raised, tail dusting the doorjamb as she came into the room.

She was a darker red-gold than Nickie, although well within the desirable color range for the breed. She had a thicker undercoat than usual for a retriever and looked gloriously furry.

Fred would probably follow Ethel. Not dominant, often bashful, he would be so thrilled to see Amy that he'd not only wag his tail furiously but also wiggle his hindquarters with irrepressible delight.

Sweet Fred had a broad handsome face and as perfectly black a nose as Amy had ever seen, not a speckle of brown to mar it.

At Amy's side, Nickie stood alert, ears lifted, gaze fixed on the open hall door from which issued the muffled thunder of paws.

A sudden drop in the velocity of approach suggested that Fred and Ethel detected the presence of a newcomer. She checked her speed first, and Fred blundered into her as they came through the doorway.

Instead of the usual meet-and-greet, including nose to nose and tongue to nose and a courteously quick sniff of butts all around, the Redwing kids halted a few feet short of Nickie. They stood panting, plumed tails swishing, with cocked-head curiosity, eyes bright with what seemed like surprise.

Keeping her own tail in motion, Nickie raised her head, assuming a friendly but regal posture.

"Ethel sweetie, babycakes Fred," Amy said in her sweet-talk voice, "come meet your new sister."

Until she said "new sister," she hadn't known that she'd decided beyond doubt to keep Nickie rather than placing her with an approved family on the Golden Heart adoption list.

Previously, both kids had reliably been suckers for their master's squeaky sweet-talk voice, but this time they ignored Amy.

Now Ethel did something she always did with a visiting dog but never until the meet-and-greet was concluded. She went to the open box of squeeze toys and pull toys and tennis balls inside the always-open pantry door, judiciously selected a prize, returned with it, and dropped it in front of the newcomer.

She had chosen a plush yellow Booda duck.

The message that Ethel usually managed to deliver with the loan of a toy to a visitor was this: *Here's one that's exclusively yours for the length of your visit, but the rest belong to me and Fred unless we include you in a group game.*

Nickie studied the duck for a moment, then regarded Ethel.

All the protocols were being revised: Ethel made a second trip to the box in the pantry and returned with a plush-toy gorilla. She dropped it beside the duck.

Meanwhile, Fred had circled the room to put the breakfast table between him and the two females. He lay on his belly, watching them through a chromework of chair legs, tail sweeping the oak floor.

If you are a dog lover, a true dog lover, and not just one who sees them as pets or animals, but are instead one who sees them as one's dear companions, and more than companions—sees them as perhaps being but a step or two down the species ladder from humankind, not sharing human exceptionalism but not an abyss below it, either—you watch them differently from the way other people watch them, with a respect for their born dignity, with a recognition of their capacity to know joy and to suffer melancholy, with the certainty that they suspect the tyranny of time even if they don't fully understand the cruelty of it, that they are not, as self-blinded experts contend, unaware of their own mortality.

If you watch them with this heightened perception, from this more generous perspective, as Amy had long watched them, you see a remarkable complexity in each dog's personality, an individualism uncannily human in its refinement, though with none of the worst of human faults. You see an intelligence and a fundamental ability to reason that sometimes can take your breath away.

And on occasion, when you're not being in the least sentimental, when you're in too skeptical a mood to ascribe to dogs any human qualities they do not possess, you will nevertheless perceive in them that singular yearning that is common to every human heart, even to those who claim to live a faithless existence. For dogs see mystery in the world, in us and in themselves and in all things, and are at key moments particularly alert to it, and more than usually curious.

Amy recognized that this was such a moment. She stood quite still, said nothing, waited and watched, certain that forthcoming would be an insight that she would carry with her as long as she might live.

Having dropped the plush-toy gorilla beside the Booda duck, Ethel made a third trip to the toy box in the pantry.

Nickie peered at Fred, where he watched from behind a bulwark of chair legs.

Fred cocked his head to the left, cocked it to the right. Then he rolled onto his back, four legs in the air, baring his belly in an expression of complete trust.

In the pantry, Ethel bit at toys, tossed them aside, thrust her head deeper into the collection, and at last returned to Nickie with a large, plush, eight-tentacled, red-and-yellow octopus.

This was a squeaky toy, a tug toy, and a shake toy all in one. And it was Ethel's favorite possession, off limits even to Fred.

Ethel dropped the octopus beside the gorilla, and after a moment of consideration, Nickie picked it up in her mouth. She squeaked it, shook it, squeaked it again, and dropped it.

Rolling off his back, scrambling to his feet, Fred sneezed. He padded out from behind the table.

The three dogs stared expectantly at one another.

Uniformly, their tail action diminished.

Their ears lifted as much as the velvety flaps of a golden are able to lift.

Amy became aware of a new tension in their muscular bodies.

Nostrils flaring, nose to the floor, head darting left and right, Nickie hurried out of the room, into the hall. Ethel and Fred scampered after her.

Alone in the kitchen, acutely aware that something unusual was happening but clueless as to what it meant, Amy said, "Kids?"

In the hallway, the overhead light came on.

When she crossed to the doorway, Amy found the hall deserted.

Toward the front of the house, somebody switched on a light in the living room. An intruder. Yet none of the dogs barked.

Chapter

9

Although Brian McCarthy had a talent for portraiture, he was not usually capable of swift execution.

The human head presents so many subtleties of form, structure, and proportion, so many complexities in the relationship of its features, that even Rembrandt, the greatest portrait painter of all time, struggled with his art and refined his craft until he died.

The head of a dog presented no less—and arguably a greater— challenge to an artist than did the human head. Many a master of their mediums, who could precisely render any man or woman, had been defeated in their attempts to portray dogs in full reality.

Remarkably, with this first effort at canine portraiture, sitting at his kitchen table, Brian found the speed that eluded him when he drew a human face. Decisions regarding form, structure, proportion, and tone did not require the ponderous consideration he usually brought to them. He worked with an assurance he had not known before, with a new grace in his hand.

The drawing appeared with such uncanny ease and swiftness that it almost seemed as if the whole image had been rendered earlier and stored magically in the pencil, from which it now flowed as smoothly as music from a recording.

During his courtship of Amy, his heart had been opened to many things, not least of all to the beauty and the joy of dogs, yet he still did not have one of his own. He didn't trust himself to be equal to the responsibility.

At first he didn't know that he was rendering not merely the ideal of a golden retriever but also a specific individual. As the face resolved in detail, he realized that from his pencils had come Nickie, so recently rescued.

He did not have more difficulty drawing eyes than he did any other detail of anatomy. This time, however, he achieved effects of line and tone and grading that continually surprised him.

To look real, the eyes must be full of light and marked by the mystery that light evokes in even the most forthright gaze. Brian focused with, for him, such unprecedented passion on the portrayal of this light, this mystery, that he might have been a medieval monk depicting the receiver of the Annunciation.

When he finished the drawing, he stared at it for a long time. Somehow the creation of the portrait had lifted his heart. Vanessa's hateful e-mails had left him under a pall of sorrow, which now weighed less heavily on him.

Hope and Nickie seemed inextricably entwined, and he felt that he could not have one without the other. He did not know exactly what he meant by this—or why it should be so.

In the study once more, he composed an e-mail to Vanessa, alias *pigkeeper*. He read the message half a dozen times before sending it.

I am at your mercy. I have no power over you, and you have every power over me. If one day you will let me have what I want, that will be because it serves you best to relent, not because I have earned it or deserve it.

In previous e-mail exchanges, he had either argued with Vanessa or had attempted to manipulate her, although never as obviously as she worked to sharpen his guilt and to put a point on his sorrow. This time he avoided all appeals to reason and all power games, and just acknowledged his helplessness.

He expected neither an immediate response nor any response at all; and even if his plea elicited only vitriol, he would not reply in kind. Over the years, she had humbled him, then further humbled him, until he harbored no more anger toward her than a wizened sailor of a thousand journeys harbored resentment toward the raging sea.

In the kitchen, at the table, he turned to a fresh page in the art-paper tablet. He sharpened his pencils.

An inexplicable exhilaration had overcome him, a perception that new possibilities lay before him. He felt as if he were on the brink of a revelation that would change his life.

He began to draw the dog's head, but this time not in a slight turn to the left with a moderate up view. Instead, he approached the subject straight on.

Furthermore, he intended to depict the face only from brow line to the part of the cheek called the cushion, thereby focusing on the eyes and the structures immediately surrounding them.

He marveled that his memory of the dog's appearance should be so exquisitely detailed. He'd seen her only on one occasion and not for long, yet in his mind's eye, she was as vivid as a fine photograph, a hologram.

From mind to hand to pencil to page, the golden's gaze took form in shades of gray. From this new perspective and proximity, the eyes were huge and deep, and full of light, of shadow.

Brian was seeking something, a unique quality that he had seen in this dog but that he had not at once consciously recognized. His subconscious wanted now to bring forth what had been glimpsed, to see it rendered and to understand it.

A tremulous expectation filled him, but his hand remained steady and swift.

Chapter

10

Veils and shimmery flourishes of eye-deceiving moonlight render the night subtly surreal, yet the pride with which the owners maintain this property is everywhere evident.

The rails and posts and pales of the picket fence are white geometric perfection in the gloom. The lawn lies as even underfoot as a croquet court, lush but precisely mown.

The single-story house is humble yet handsome, white with a dark trim of some color not discernible. A simply carved cornice enhances the eaves and is echoed by window surrounds, no doubt fashioned by the homeowner in his spare time.

From the bentwood rocking chairs on the front and back porches, the birdbaths, the miniature windmill, and the garden gnomes, Harrow infers that the residents are near or past retirement age. The place feels like a nest meant for a long and well-earned rest.

He doubts that a single porch step or floorboard creaks, but he doesn't risk treading on them. He pours the gasoline between the railings, first at the back porch, which looks out across fields and ancient oaks, and then at the front.

A thin drizzle of fuel across the grass connects the porches, and with the last contents of the can, he spills a fuse along the front walk toward the open gate in the picket fence.

While Moongirl waits for him at the safe end of the fuse, he returns to the house to set the empty utility can quietly on the porch. The still air hangs heavy with fumes.

He has dripped nothing on himself. As he walks away from the house, he cups his hands around his nose, and they smell fresh.

From a pocket of her leather jacket, Moongirl has extracted a box of matches. She uses only those with wooden stems.

She strikes a match, stoops, and ignites the wet trail on the walkway. Low blue-and-orange flames dance away from her, as if the magical night has brought forth a procession of capering faeries.

Together, she and Harrow walk to the west side of the house, where they have a view of both porches. The only doors are at the front and back. Along this wall are three windows.

Fire leaps high across the front of the house, seethes between the railings, and dispatches more dancing faeries along the drizzle that connects the porches.

As always, after an immediate *whoosh*, the flames initially churn in near silence, feeding on the gasoline, which needs no chewing. The crunch and crackle will come soon, when the fire takes wood in its teeth.

Chapter

11

Following the hallway to the living-room archway, Amy said, "Hello? Who's there?"

Golden retrievers are not bred to be guard dogs, and considering the size of their hearts and their irrepressible joy in life, they are less likely to bite than to bark, less likely to bark than to lick a hand in greeting. In spite of their size, they think they are lap dogs, and in spite of being dogs, they think they are also human, and nearly every human they meet is judged to have the potential to be a boon companion who might, at any moment, cry "Let's go!" and lead them on a great adventure.

Nevertheless, they have formidable teeth and are protective of family and home.

Amy assumed that any intruder who was able to induce three adult goldens to submit without one bark must be not foe but friend, or at least harmless. Yet she approached the living room with a curiosity that included a measure of wariness.

When Amy had answered Janet Brockman's plea to rescue Nickie, she had not left Fred and Ethel in a dark house. One lamp in her bedroom and a brass reading lamp in the living room provided comfort.

Now the hallway ceiling fixture blazed. Also, ahead and to her right, the front room loomed brighter than she had left it.

When she passed the open bedroom door on her left and stepped through the living-room archway, she found no intruder, only three delighted dogs.

As any golden would do in a new environment, Nickie had gone exploring, chasing down the most interesting of all the new smells, weaving among chairs and sofas, mapping the landscape, identifying the coziest corners.

Filled with pride of home, Fred and Ethel followed the newcomer, pausing to note everything that she had noted, as if sharing with her had made the bungalow new again to them.

Sniffing, grinning, chuffing with approval, tails lashing, the new girl and her welcoming committee rushed past Amy.

By the time that she turned to follow them, they had vanished across the hall, into her bedroom. A moment ago, only a nightstand lamp had illuminated that room, but now the ceiling fixture burned bright.

"Kids?"

Matching plump sheepskin-covered dog beds mushroomed in two corners of the bedroom.

As Amy crossed the threshold, Nickie bumped a tennis ball with her nose, and Fred snatched it on the roll. Nickie checked out but didn't want a plush blue bunny, so Ethel snared it.

The bedroom and the attached bath lacked an intruder, and by the time Amy followed the pack to the study, the fourth and last room in the bungalow, the ceiling light was on there, too.

Fred had dropped the ball, and Ethel had cast aside the bunny, and Nickie had decided not to stake a claim to a discarded pair of

Amy's socks that she had fished out of the knee space under the desk.

Paws thumping, nails clicking, tails knocking merrily against every crowding object, the dogs returned to the hall, then to the kitchen.

Puzzled, Amy went to the only window in the study and found it locked. Before leaving the room, she frowned at the wall switch and flipped it down, up, down, turning the ceiling fixture off, on, off.

She stood in the hall, listening to thirsty dogs lapping from the water bowls in the kitchen.

In the bedroom again, she checked both windows. The latches were engaged, as was the one in the bathroom.

She peered in the closet. No boogeyman.

The front-door deadbolt was locked. The security chain remained in place.

All three living-room windows were secure. With the dampers closed, no sinister Santa out of season could have come down the fireplace chimney to play games with the lights.

Behind her, she left on only the single nightstand lamp and the reading lamp in the living room. At the end of the hall, she stopped and looked back, but no gremlins had been at work.

In the kitchen, she found the three goldens lying on the floor, gathered around the refrigerator, heads raised and alert. They looked from her to the refrigerator, to her again.

Amy said, "What? You think it's snack time—or am I going to find a severed head in the lettuce drawer?"

Chapter

12

Fire spawns fitful drafts in the still night, brief twists of hot wind that stir Harrow's hair but dissipate behind him.

The people asleep in the house, if in fact anyone is at home, are strangers to Harrow. They have done nothing to him. They have done nothing *for* him, either.

They mean nothing to him.

He doesn't know what they mean to Moongirl. They are strangers to her, as well, but they have some meaning for her. They are more to her than a mere medicine for boredom. He wonders what that might be.

Although curious, he will not ask her. He believes that he is safer if she thinks his understanding of her is complete, if she believes they are alike.

Flames engulf the back porch, and the sounds of consumption begin to arise from the front.

Moongirl's hands are in the pockets of her black leather jacket. Her face remains expressionless. In her eyes is nothing more than a reflection of the fire.

Like her, Harrow has discipline of his intellect and of his body, but unlike her, he also has discipline of his emotions. Those are the three hallmarks of sanity.

Boredom is a state of mind akin to an emotion. Perhaps the emotion to which boredom most often leads is despair.

She seems too strong to be seriously discouraged by anything, yet she fights boredom with such reckless entertainments as this burning, which suggests that she dreads falling into an inescapable well of despair.

Laceworks of firelight flutter across the grass, and across Moongirl, dressing her as if she is an unholy bride.

A light appears in the middle window.

Someone has awakened.

Sheer curtains deny a clear view, but judging by the murkiness of the light and by the amorphous shadows, smoke already roils in the room.

The house is pier-supported. Evidently, the flames writhed at once into the crawl space, a thousand bright tongues flickering, hissing poisonous fumes up through the floor.

Harrow thinks he hears a muffled shout, perhaps a name, but he cannot be certain.

Instinct, imperfect in the human species, will harry the rudely awakened residents toward the front door, then toward the back. They will find a deep wall of flames at either exit.

The moon seems to recede as the night grows bright. Fire wraps the corners of the house.

"We could have driven in another direction," says Moongirl.

"Yes."

"We could have found a different house."

"Infinite choices," he agrees.

"It doesn't matter."

"No."

"It's all the same."

From inside, screaming arises, the shrill cry of a woman; and for sure, this time, a shout, the voice of a man.

"They thought they were different," she says.

"But now they know."

"They thought things mattered."

"The way they took care of the house."

"The carved cornice."

"The miniature windmill."

Now the character of the screaming changes from a cry of terror to shrieks of pain.

Sullen fire throbs inside, beyond the windows. The place has been tinder waiting to be lit.

Likewise, the people.

At the middle window, the sheer curtains vanish with a quick flare, like diaphanous sheets of flash paper between a magician's fingertips.

In front of the house, the lonely two-lane road dwindles into darkness that even the dawn might not relieve.

Glass shatters outward, and a tormented figure appears at the middle window, in silhouette against the backdrop of the burning room. A man. He is shouting again, but the shout is half a scream.

Already the woman's voice has been stifled.

The French panes do not allow an easy exit. The man struggles to twist open the lock, to raise the bottom sash.

Fire takes him. He falls back from the window, collapsing into the furnace that was once a bedroom, suffering into silence.

Moongirl asks, "What was he shouting?"

"I don't know."

"Shouting at us?"

"He couldn't see us."

"Then at who?"

"I don't know."

"He has no neighbors."

"No."

"No one to help."

"No one."

Heat bursts a window. Blisters of burning paint pop, pop, pop. Joints creak as nails grow soft.

"Are you hungry?" she asks.

"I could eat something."

"We've got that good ham."

"I'll make sandwiches."

"With the green-peppercorn mustard."

"Good mustard."

Spirals of flame conjure the illusion that the house is turning as it burns, like a carousel ablaze.

"So many colors in the fire," she says.

"I even see some green."

"Yes. There. At the corner. Green."

Smoke ladders up the night, but nothing climbs it except more smoke, fumes on fumes, soot ascending soot, higher and higher into the sky.

Chapter

13

With breakfast and the morning walk only a couple of hours away, Amy would not let the gang of three panhandle cookies from her. "No fat dogs," she admonished. In the refrigerator she kept a plastic bag of sliced carrots for such moments.

Sitting on the floor with the kids, she gave circles of crisp carrot first to Ethel, then to Fred, then to Nickie. They crunched the treats enthusiastically and licked their chops.

When she had given each of them six pieces, she said, "Enough. We don't want you to have bright orange poop, do we?"

She borrowed a dog bed from the study and put it in a third corner of her bedroom, and filled a second water dish to put beside the first.

By the time Amy changed into pajamas, the dogs appeared to have settled in their separate corners for what remained of the night.

She placed her slippers next to her bed, plumped her pillows, got under the covers—and discovered that Nickie had come to her. The golden had both slippers in her mouth.

This might have been a test of discipline or an invitation to play, although it did not feel like either. Even with a mouthful of footwear, Nickie managed a solemn look, and her gaze was intense.

"You want to bundle?" Amy asked.

At the word *bundle,* the other dogs raised their heads.

Most nights, Fred and Ethel slept contentedly in their corners. Occasionally, and not solely during thunderstorms, they preferred to snooze in a pile with Mom.

Even made anxious by thunder, they would not venture into Amy's queen-size bed without permission, which was given with the phrase *Let's bundle.*

Nickie did not know those words, but Fred and Ethel rose from their sheepskin berths in expectation of a formal invitation, ears raised, alert.

Wrung limp by recent events, Amy needed rest; and this would not be the first time that elusive sleep had come to her more easily when she nestled down in the security of the pack.

"Okay, kids," she said. "Let's bundle."

Ethel sprinted three steps, sprang, and Fred followed. On the bed, assessing the comfort of the mattress, the dogs turned, turned, turned, like cogs in a clockworks, then curled, dropped, and settled with sighs of satisfaction.

Remaining bedside with a mouthful of slippers, Nickie stared expectantly at her new master.

"Give," said Amy, and the golden obeyed, relinquishing her prize.

Amy put the slippers on the floor beside the bed.

Nickie picked them up and offered them again.

"You want me to go somewhere?" Amy asked.

The dog's large dark-brown eyes were as expressive as those of any human being. Amy liked many things about the appearance of this breed, but nothing more than their beautiful eyes.

"You don't need to go out. You pottied when we came home."

The beauty of a retriever's eyes is matched by the intelligence so evident in them. Sometimes, as now, dogs seemed intent upon conveying complex thoughts by an exertion of sheer will, striving to compensate for their lack of language with a directness of gaze and concentration.

"Give," she said, and again Nickie obeyed.

Confident that repetition would impress upon the pooch that the slippers belonged where she put them, Amy leaned over the edge of the bed and returned them to the floor.

At once, Nickie snatched them up and offered them again.

"If this is a fashion judgment," Amy said, "you're wrong. These are lovely slippers, and I'm not getting rid of them."

Chin on her paws, Ethel watched with interest. Chin on Ethel's head, Fred watched from a higher elevation.

Like children, dogs want discipline and are most secure when they have rules to live by. The happiest dogs are those with gentle masters who quietly but firmly demand respect.

Nevertheless, in dog training as in war, the better part of valor can be discretion.

This time, when Amy took possession of the slippers, she tucked them under her pillows.

Nickie regarded this development with surprise and then grinned, perhaps in triumph.

"Don't think for a second this means I'm going to be on the dog end of the leash." She patted the mattress beside her. "Nickie, up."

Either the retriever understood the command itself or the implication of the gesture. She sprang over Amy and onto the bed.

Fred took his chin off Ethel's head, and Ethel closed her eyes, and as the other kids had done, Nickie wound herself down into a cozy sleeping posture.

All the mounded fur and the sweet faces inspired a smile, and Amy sighed as the dogs had done when they had settled for the night.

To ensure that the bungalow remained a hair-free zone, she combed and brushed each dog for thirty minutes every morning, for another ten minutes every evening, and she vacuumed all the floors once a day. Nickie would add to the work load—and be worth every minute of it.

When Amy switched off the lamp, she felt weightless, afloat on a rising sea of sleep, into which she began dreamily to sink.

She was hooked and reeled back by a line cast from the shores of memory: *I have to wear slippers to bed so I won't be walking barefoot through the woods in my dream.*

Amy's eyes opened from darkness to darkness, and for a moment she could not breathe, as if the past were a drowning flood that filled her throat and lungs.

No. The game with the slippers could not have been for the purpose of reminding her of that long-ago conversation about dream-walking in the woods.

This new dog was just a dog, nothing more. In the storms of this world, a way forward can always be found, but there is no way back either to a time of peace or to a time of tempest.

To the observant, all dogs have an air of mystery, an inner life deeper than science will concede, but whatever the true nature of their minds or the condition of their souls, they are limited to the wisdom of their kind, and each is shaped by the experiences of its one life.

Nevertheless, the slippers now under her pillow reminded her of another pair of slippers, and the recollected words replayed in her mind: *I have to wear slippers to bed so I won't be walking barefoot through the woods in my dream.*

Ethel had begun to snore softly. Fred was a quiet sleeper except when he dreamed of chasing or of being chased.

The longer Amy lay listening for Nickie's rhythmic breathing, the more she began to suspect that the dog was awake, and not just awake but also watching her in the dark.

Although Amy's weariness did not abate, the possibility of sleep receded from her.

At last, unable to stifle her curiosity any longer, she reached out to where the dog was curled, expecting that her suspicion would not be confirmed, that Nickie would be fully settled.

Instead, in the gloom, her hand found the burly head, which was in fact raised and turned toward her, as if the dog were a sentinel on duty.

Holding its left ear, she gently massaged the tragus with her thumb, while her fingertips rubbed the back of the ear where it met the skull. If anything would cause a dog to purr like a cat, this was it, and Nickie submitted to the attention with palpable pleasure.

After a while, the golden lowered her head, resting her chin on Amy's abdomen.

I have to wear slippers to bed so I won't be walking barefoot through the woods in my dream.

In self-defense, Amy had long ago raised the drawbridge between these memories and her heart, but now they swam across the moat.

If it's just a dream woods, why wouldn't the ground be soft?

It's soft but it's cold.

It's a winter woods, is it?

Uh-huh. Lots of snow.

So dream yourself a summer woods.

I like the snow.

Then maybe you should wear boots to bed.

Maybe I should.

And thick woolen socks and long johns.

As Amy's heart began to race, she tried to shut out the voices in her mind. But her heart pounded like a fist on a door: memory demanding an audience.

She petted the furry head resting on her abdomen and, as defense against memories too terrible to revisit, she instead summoned into mind the many dogs that she had rescued, the abused and abandoned dogs, hundreds over the years. Victims of human indifference, of human cruelty, they had been physically and emotionally broken when they came to her, but so often they had been restored in body and mind, made jubilant again, brought back to golden glory.

She lived for the dogs.

In the dark she murmured lines from a poem by Robert Frost, which in grim times had sustained her: "'The woods are lovely, dark, and deep. But I have promises to keep. And miles to go before I sleep. And miles to go before I sleep.'"

Head resting on Amy's abdomen, Nickie dozed.

Now Amy Redwing, not this mysterious dog, was the sentinel on duty. Gradually her heart stopped pounding, stopped racing, and all was still and dark and as it should be.

Chapter

14

At the windows, dawn descended, pressing darkness down and westward, and away.

Traffic noise began to arise from the street, the wheels of commerce and occasionally a far voice.

On the kitchen table lay the drawing of Nickie and two studies, from memory, of her eyes. The second study included less surrounding facial structure than the first.

Brian had begun a third study. This one involved only the eyes in their deep sockets, the space between, the expressive eyebrows, and the lush lashes.

He continued to be enchanted by the task that he had set for himself. He also remained convinced that he had seen something in the dog's gaze that was of great importance, an ineffable quality that words could not describe but that his inexplicably enhanced talent, his seemingly *possessed* drawing hand, might be able to dredge from his subconscious and capture in an image, capture and define.

The irrationality of this conviction was not lost on him. An ineffable quality is, by its nature, one that can't be defined, only *felt*.

His determination to draw and redraw the dog's eyes, until he found what he sought, was nothing less than a compulsion. The extreme mental focus and the emotional intensity that he brought to the task perplexed him, even worried him—though not sufficiently to make him put down the pencil.

In Rembrandt's famous *Lady with a Pink,* the subject doesn't communicate directly with the viewer but is portrayed in a reverie that makes you want to enter her contemplation and understand the object of it. The artist gives her nearer eye a heightened color contrast, a clear iris, and a perfectly inserted highlight that suggests a mind, behind the eye, that is no stranger to profound feeling.

Brian had no illusions that his talent approached Rembrandt's. The subtlety of the translucent shadows and luminous refractions in this latest version of the dog's eyes was so far superior to the quality of anything he'd drawn before, both in concept and execution, that he wondered how he could have created it.

He half doubted that the drawing was his.

Although he was the only presence in the apartment, although he had watched the series of pencils in his hand produce the image, he became increasingly convinced that he did not possess the genius or the artistry required to lay down upon paper the startling dimension or the luminous mystery that now informed these finished eyes.

In his thirty-four years, he had no slightest experience of the supernatural, nor any interest in it. As an architect, he believed in line and light, in form and function, in the beauty of things built to last.

As he tore the most recent drawing from the tablet and put it aside, however, he could not dismiss the uncanny feeling that the talent on display here was not his own.

Perhaps this was what psychologists called a *flow state,* what professional athletes referred to as *being in the zone,* a moment of transcendence when the mind raises no barriers of self-doubt and therefore allows a talent to be expressed more fully than has ever been possible previously.

The problem with that explanation was, he didn't feel in full control, whereas in a flow state, you were supposed to experience absolute mastery of your gifts.

In front of him, the blank page in the tablet insisted on his attention.

Go even closer on the eyes this time, he thought. *Go all the way into the eyes.*

First, he needed a break. He put down the pencil—but at once picked it up, without even pausing to stretch and flex his fingers, as if his hand had a will of its own.

Almost as though observing from a distance, he watched himself use the X-acto knife to carve away the wood and point the pencil.

After he sharpened a variety of leads, to give them typical points, blunt points, and chisel points, and after he finished each on a block of sandpaper, he put the last pencil and the knife aside.

He pushed his chair back from the table, got up, and went to the kitchen sink to splash cold water in his face.

As he reached for the faucet handle, he realized that he had a pencil in his right hand.

He glanced at the table. The pencil that he thought he had left beside the art tablet was not there.

Before Amy had called him to assist on the rescue mission, he'd had only an hour's sleep. Weariness explained his current state of mind, these small confusions.

He put the pencil on the cutting board beside the sink and stared at it for a moment, as if expecting it to rise on point and doodle its way back to him.

After repeatedly immersing his face in double handfuls of cold water, he dried off with paper towels, yawned, rubbed his beard stubble with one hand, and then stretched luxuriously.

He needed caffeine. In the refrigerator were cans of Red Bull, which he kept on hand for those design deadlines that sometimes required him to pull an all-nighter.

The pencil was not clutched in his right hand when he opened the refrigerator door. It was in his left.

"Weariness, my ass."

He put the pencil on a glass shelf in the refrigerator, in front of a Tupperware container full of leftover pesto pasta.

After popping the tab on a Red Bull and taking a long swallow, he closed the fridge without retrieving the pencil. He clearly saw it on the shelf in front of the pesto pasta as the door swung shut.

When he returned to the table and put down the Red Bull, he realized that the pocket of his Hawaiian shirt contained a pencil.

This had to be a different pencil from the one in the fridge. It must have been in the pocket since he'd risen from the table to wash his face.

He counted the pencils on the table. Two should be missing: the one in his pocket, the one in the fridge. But he was short only one.

Disbelieving, he returned to the refrigerator. The pencil that he had left on the shelf in front of the Tupperware container was no longer there.

Now you see it. Now you don't.

Sitting at the table again, Brian took the pencil from his shirt pocket. With flourishes and a nimbleness akin to prestidigitation, his fingers manipulated the instrument into the proper drawing grip.

He had not consciously intended to play with the pencil in that fashion. His fingers appeared to be expressing a memory of diligent practice from a previous life when he had been a magician.

The point touched the paper, and graphite seemed to flow almost as swiftly as a liquid, pouring forth the enigmas of luminous flux and translucent veils in the dog's far-seeing eye.

He gave less thought to what he would draw, then less, then none at all. Independent of him, his inspired hand swiftly shaped shadows and suggested light.

On the nape of his neck, the fine hairs rose, but he was neither frightened nor even apprehensive. A quiet amazement had overtaken him.

As he had half suspected—and now knew beyond doubt—he could not claim to be the artist here. He was as much an instrument as was the pencil that he held. The artist remained unknown.

Chapter

15

After a few hours of sleep, Amy woke at 7:30, showered, dressed, served three bowls of kibble, and took the kids for a morning walk.

Three big dogs could have been a test of Amy's control and balance. Fortunately, Nickie seemed to have received good training. Each time Amy dropped the leashes to blue-bag the poop, Nickie respected a *sit-and-stay* command as reliably as did Fred and Ethel.

The pleasantly warm morning was freshened by a breeze as light as a caress, and the feathery fronds of queen palms cast shadows that resembled the plumed tails of the goldens.

Having overslept, Amy brushed all three dogs in just one hour. They lay as limp as citizens of leisure being pampered at a spa. She spent more time on Nickie than on the other two, but found no ticks.

By 9:40, the four of them were aboard the Expedition, outbound from Laguna Beach on an adventure.

They stopped first to see Dr. Sarkissian, one of a network of veterinarians who treated rescue dogs at a discount until they were placed in forever homes.

After an examination, Harry Sarkissian gave Nickie a full array of inoculations. He put her on medication to control fleas, ticks, and heartworm. Results of a blood workup would come back in two days.

"But there's nothing wrong with this girl," he predicted. "She's a beauty."

With Nickie, Amy returned to the Expedition, where Fred and Ethel sulked briefly. They knew a visit to the vet always included a cookie. Besides, they could smell it on their sister's breath.

Renata Hammersmith lived inland, where pockets of horse country still survived the relentless march of southern California suburbs.

She dressed so reliably in boots, jeans, and checkered shirts that it was easy for Amy to believe that the woman slept in a similar outfit, impossible to imagine her in pajamas or peignoir.

Surrounded by white ranch fencing, her three-acre property once featured horses grazing in a meadow that served as the front yard.

The horses became a luxury when Jerry, Renata's husband, was disabled. His beloved 1967 Ford Mustang was hit head-on by a pickup.

Paralyzed from the waist down, Jerry had also lost his spleen, a kidney, and a significant portion of his colon.

"But I'm still full of shit," he assured friends.

He had not lost his sense of humor.

Drunk, unemployed, and uninsured, the driver of the pickup had walked away from the collision with two broken teeth, an abrasion, and no remorse.

Six years ago, the Hammersmiths sold Jerry's construction business, banked the capital gains, cut expenses, and hoped to make the money stretch the rest of their lives. They were now fifty-two.

Because Renata could not look after Jerry and hold a job, she feared having to sell their land one day. She had lived always with elbow room. The thought of having neighbors a wall away chilled her.

Amy drove past the ranch house, where thriving red clematis festooned the veranda roof and the posts that supported it. With a cell-phone call en route, she had learned that Renata was working with the ghost dogs in the exercise yard.

The kennel, converted from a stable, adjoined a fenced green lawn. An immense California live oak shaded half the grass.

Six golden retrievers were sitting or lying at separate points in the big exercise yard, most of them in the shade. Renata sat on a blanket in the center of the space, a seventh golden at her side.

As Amy opened the tailgate and let her kids out of the SUV, she looked back the way she had come, past the house, to the county road.

On the farther side of the two-lane blacktop, opposite the entrance to the Hammersmith property, parked in the purple shadows cast by a small grove of jacarandas, stood the Land Rover that had been following her all morning.

When she opened the gate to the exercise yard, Fred and Ethel led Nickie directly to Renata, to receive the affection they knew she would bestow, and to greet Hugo, the golden at her side.

As Amy arrived amidst the slow swarm of four socializing dogs, Renata held up to her the binoculars that she had asked for on the phone.

With them, Amy looked back toward the distant jacarandas and adjusted the focus, pulling the Land Rover toward her.

The trees spilled a currency of shadows and a few coins of light across the windshield, conspiring to obscure the face of the man— if it was a man—who sat behind the wheel.

"Is it the wife-beater?" Renata asked.

"Can't tell. Probably not. I don't think he could have been sprung from jail this quick."

Amy sat on the blanket and put the binoculars aside.

The six ghost dogs watched with interest from their separate positions around the yard. None of them came forward to meet and greet.

"How're they doing?" Amy asked.

"Better. Slow but sure. If not the wife-beater, who?"

"Maybe I've got a secret admirer."

"Has someone been sending candy and flowers anonymously?"

"Secret admirers don't do that anymore, Renata. These days, they kidnap you, rape you, and kill you with power tools."

"What joys the revolution has brought."

Chapter

16

Vernon Lesley parked his rustbucket Chevy two blocks from Amy Redwing's bungalow.

The sedan was old and in need of body work. He had repaired the upholstery with duct tape. Because the car didn't clean up well, he never bothered to wash it.

For a long time, he had been embarrassed by the Chevy, but not once during the past year; because in his other life, he now owned a $150,000 sports car that made a Ferrari look like junkyard scrap.

He didn't bother locking the sedan. No one would want to steal it or anything in it.

Confident that he would attract no attention, he walked directly to Redwing's place and boldly around to the back porch.

He was thirty-nine years old, five feet eight, round-shouldered, and paunchy. Thinning beige hair. Brown eyes the shade of weak tea. His most distinctive facial feature was his receding chin.

People didn't merely look over him or past him; they looked *through* him.

In his line of work, invisibility gave him an advantage. He was a private detective.

Redwing had a respectable lock on her back door, not the crappy hardware so many people depended upon, but Vern finessed through it in less than a minute.

Her kitchen was a cheerful white-and-yellow space. Only a year ago, Vern would have envied her this cozy little home.

Now, in his other life, he owned a sleek modern house on a bluff overlooking the sea. He no longer envied anyone.

The Department of Motor Vehicles and the Internal Revenue Service believed that Vernon Lesley lived only in a one-bedroom apartment in a depressed neighborhood in Santa Ana. They had no clue that, under the name Von Longwood, he enjoyed a much larger life.

Von Longwood had never applied to the DMV for a driver's license and had never paid a dime in taxes. He left no footprints for the authorities to follow.

After pulling down all the blinds in the kitchen, Vern stood on a dinette chair to search the upper cabinets. Gradually he worked down to the lowest doors and drawers.

He took care to put everything back as he had found it. His client did not want Amy Redwing to know that her home had been searched.

Usually, when he conducted an illegal search, Vern liked to use a toilet, use it thoroughly, and leave it unflushed. He thought of it as his signature, the way Zorro slashed a **Z** in things with his sword.

With no other indication that the house had been violated, the owner would have to assume that he himself had left a full bowl.

In this instance, Vern intended to leave no calling card. Even if Redwing were disposed to think that she had forgotten to flush, the reaction of at least one of the dogs would probably make her suspicious.

Vern didn't like dogs, largely because he had never met one that liked him. People stared right through Vern, but dogs gave him long hard looks and invited him to examine their teeth.

In high school, he had been blessed with a rat named Cheesy. A good rat made an excellent pet, affectionate and cute. He and Cheesy had shared many good times, uncountable confidences. Such memories.

Off the kitchen lay a half bath. Vern resisted the temptation of the toilet.

He found nothing of interest in the bath except his reflection in the mirror. He paused to smile at himself.

For most of his life, he had not been charmed by mirrors. In fact he had avoided them.

These days, however, facing a mirror, he didn't see Vernon Lesley. He saw that lovable rogue Von Longwood, who had a thick head of hair and blue eyes.

In the kitchen again, he sorted through the pizzas, the packages of vegetables, and the containers of ice cream in the freezer. In the pantry, he checked the contents of every box that Redwing had opened, to be sure that it held what the exterior advertised.

When someone wished to hide mementos of another life, they often secreted the evidence in places that, to an inexperienced searcher, would seem to be unlikely repositories. Consequently, he made sure that the box of crackers actually contained crackers and that no tub of chocolate-caramel or strawberry-swirl ice cream contained instead a trove of old love letters.

He wasn't literally searching for love letters. In Amy Redwing's other life, she evidently had not been lucky in love or happy.

By contrast, as Von Longwood, Vern had enjoyed sex as often as four times in one day, and his fabulous sports car could *fly,* as could Von himself.

Renata referred to them as ghost dogs because they were as yet mere shades of the dogs they should have been.

They had been breeder dogs in a puppy mill, housed inhumanely, fed inadequately, and treated cruelly.

The females had been bred at their first heat—usually at six months—and then twice a year. After two or three years, if the stress of their situation prevented them from going into heat again, they would have been shot or abandoned at a county animal shelter.

In this case, the puppy mill had been raided and closed. Eleven female and four male breeder dogs were confiscated. Too sickly and fearful to be fit for adoption, these dogs faced imminent euthanasia.

Golden Heart had taken all fifteen and had brought them to the Hammersmith place, known in the organization as Last Chance Ranch.

Two males and three females had been in such grievous physical condition that they had died within the week, in spite of receiving the first veterinary care of their lives. Some of them had been so terrified of human beings that even a comforting touch would cause them to urinate or vomit in fear.

Their ashes were in urns in the Hammersmith house. A typed label with a name had been taped to each urn.

Renata and Jerry named them because, in puppy mills, breeder dogs have only numbers. No man *or* dog should die without a name.

Tick-infested, worm-plagued, flea-ridden, malnourished, they had to be shaved and medicated and, in some cases, patiently fed by hand.

The ad placed by the breeding operation to sell their puppies had said "farm-bred, raised by a loving family."

In the month that followed, though heroic efforts were made to heal the remaining dogs, four had conditions so intractable that, to end their suffering, they had to be put down.

So fearful were they of human beings that they remained wary of being touched even when they were desperate for comforting. In each dog's final hour, Golden Heart volunteers stroked it, murmured words of love, and held it as its life was, in mercy, given back to God.

Dog rescue is often joyful work, and often grim.

The six survivors were all females: the dogs now lying in the exercise yard, at various distances from Renata and Amy.

In the puppy mill, they had lived in cramped wire cages, without exercise or play. At Last Chance Ranch, this fenced yard had seemed to be a threatening vastness. They had first preferred the kennels.

Taken from the filthy cages at the mill, they had been fearful of every human being, of loud voices, of kindness because they had never encountered it, of cars because they had never ridden in one, of stairs because they had never climbed them, of soap and water because they had never been bathed, of hair dryers and of towels, of music and of the first toys given to them.

Four months later, these survivors had been to a large degree socialized; but they were not yet ready to be placed for adoption. They needed to be less shy to live with a forever family. They were still getting accustomed to lawn mowers and washing machines, still learning to trust slippery tile floors, hardwood floors, stairs.

Now, having said hello to Hugo, Renata's golden, Fred and Ethel gamboled into the yard, ready for fun, and Hugo went with them. They approached the former breeder dogs. Play bows were exchanged, chases undertaken. Renata had scattered tug toys in the grass, and these were snatched up with glee, dog challenging dog to take the prize.

Nickie did not at once join in their games, but watched with interest the only one of the six surviving girls that was reluctant to participate. Finally, Nickie plucked up a tug toy from beside Renata and trotted across the yard toward the wallflower.

"That's Honey," said Renata, naming the shyest of the group.

Honey had been maybe two and a half when she had been rescued. Her toenails had never been trimmed at the puppy mill, and she had not worn them away with exercise, so they had grown back and under her feet to the extent that she could barely stand. Her leg muscles had been somewhat atrophied, as well.

Her feet were healed now, her muscles stronger, but while the concept of play intrigued her, she was always the last into the game, if she joined at all.

Standing before Honey, Nickie tauntingly dangled the tug toy. When this didn't excite the shy dog, Nickie shook the toy vigorously.

"Your Nickie is a nightingale," Renata said.

Most dogs were sensitive to illness and depression in people and other dogs, but a few were especially determined to nurture those in need. Amy called them nightingales, after Florence Nightingale.

"She's something special," Amy said.

"You haven't had her a day yet."

"I hadn't had her an hour till I knew."

In but a minute, Nickie had teased Honey into a chase and then a happy tumble.

Amy stood with the binoculars again and scanned the shadows under the jacarandas on the farther side of the county road.

"He get out of the car where you can see him?" Renata asked.

"Nope. Still behind the wheel."

"Maybe he's a sonofabitch from one of the puppy mills you've put out of business."

"Maybe."

"He comes on this property, I'll put some bird shot in him."

"You used to say, one of those sonsofbitches ever came around here, you'd neuter him."

"The bird shot is just to make him cooperative. Then comes the neutering."

Chapter

18

The living room yielded nothing of interest to Vernon Lesley, but in the back of the bedroom closet, he found two shoe boxes full of photographs.

His client had provided a list of items related to Amy Redwing's other life that she might not have destroyed when she shed her past, changed her name, and relocated to southern California. Photographs were at the top of that list.

The box contained primarily snapshots and the digital-camera memory cards from which some of them had been printed. The most recent were almost nine years old.

Vern sat on the edge of Redwing's bed and patiently pored through numerous envelopes of photos to see if they contained any pornographic material. His client hadn't asked him to conduct such a meticulous inspection; but Amy Redwing happened to be an attractive woman, and Vern happened to be curious.

Unfortunately, not one picture proved to be erotic or even exotic. He had never seen a more mundane collection of snapshots.

Although he didn't know Redwing's story, to Vern it seemed that her current life and her former one had been equally boring.

In Vern's other life, as Von Longwood, he tooled around on a radically customized motorcycle, a real *hog,* and he was a master of tae kwon do with the costumes to prove it, and in general he lived large. He didn't understand why anyone would want another life that was as drab as the first.

In this life, Redwing even looked similar to how she had looked in her prior life. Her hair was long now, short then; she had done some things with makeup then that she didn't do now; she had dressed more stylishly in those days. That was the extent of her makeover.

She had remained a brunette even though she might have looked hotter as a blonde. And judging by what evidence Vern possessed, she hadn't undergone breast enlargement, which maybe she should have.

Whereas Vernon Lesley stood five eight, Von Longwood towered an awesome six feet six. Vern slouched through life with round shoulders and a potbelly, but Von had biceps to rival those of Schwarzenegger when he had been a great action-movie star instead of a governor.

Von had tattoos, an earring with a tiny skull dangling from it, a muscular chest instead of man boobs, and *wings*. They were huge, soft, feathery wings, but so strong, and when Von wanted to fly, *no one* could keep him grounded.

Vernon Lesley's other life unfolded in Second Life, the Internet site that offered a vivid virtual world populated by avatars like Von Longwood.

Some people mocked this kind of role-playing, but they were ignorant. Virtual worlds were more *imaginative* than the real world, more exotic, more colorful, yet they were becoming more convincingly detailed by the week. They were the future.

Vern had more fun in his other life than in this one, more and better friends, and more memorable experiences. He was freer as Von Longwood than he could ever be as Vernon Lesley. He had never been creative in his first life, but in his second, he had designed and built a nightclub, and he had even bought an island that he intended to populate with fantastic creatures of his own invention.

Any of that, any moment of it, beat sitting in a stranger's bedroom, poring through boxes of boring photographs, hoping to find a nude shot.

From an inner pocket of his sport coat, he withdrew a white plastic trash bag and unfolded it. He put all the photos in the bag, and then he returned the empty shoe boxes to the back of the closet, leaving them exactly where he had discovered them.

As far as he could tell, the only significant difference between Redwing's two lives was the addition of dogs to this one. He saw no mutts in the photographs.

In one of her nightstands, he found a SIG P245 pistol loaded with +P .45 ACPs. This struck him as a perfectly manageable weapon for a woman who did not have the balance benefit of surgically enlarged breasts. He returned the gun to the drawer.

He was not surprised to find a loaded pistol. These days, if Vern had been a woman living alone, he would have slept with a shotgun.

From the bedroom, he proceeded to her study. Eventually he discovered a manila envelope taped to the underside of a desk drawer.

Carefully, he peeled off the Scotch tape with which the envelope had been sealed, pried up the clasp. His expired hope of discovering some homemade pornography had been resuscitated.

Instead, he found documents related to the woman's name change. Well, this was the real world, so you shouldn't expect many thrills.

She had also been *Amy* in her previous life, but she had swapped the surname *Cogland* for *Redwing*. Of this, Vern approved. *Redwing* was a cool name, even good enough for a Second Life avatar.

She had received a new Social Security card under this name, a passport, and a Connecticut driver's license, which she had no doubt used to obtain a California license after moving across country.

Accompanying the documents was a copy of a judge's order sealing the court's actions and removing them from public record.

Intrigued, Vern read the legal documents more closely than he had the first time. He suspected that the name *Cogland* ought to ring a whole tabernacle's worth of bells, but it didn't.

If Redwing had been in the news during her Cogland life, Vern might not have read or heard about her. He had never been interested in the news.

Before Second Life, he'd spent most of his leisure time playing in on-line game groups of the Dungeons and Dragons variety. He had slain a vast menagerie of monsters, and no dungeon had held him long.

Vern put all of these papers in the white trash bag with the photographs and the digital-camera memory cards.

Occasionally, Redwing might reach under the desk drawer and feel the envelope to confirm that the hidden material remained where she had put it.

Vern took several sheets of paper from her computer printer. He folded them and inserted them in the envelope to approximate the feel of the original documents.

With the brass clasp, he secured the flap. From the dispenser on her desk, he pulled a length of tape and sealed the flap just as it had been, and then he taped the envelope under the drawer, where he had found it.

He was left with only the lengths of old tape. He wadded them in a ball and dropped them in the white trash bag.

Although Vernon had searched the half bath off the kitchen, he had not yet explored the full bath that adjoined her bedroom. He had been concerned that, in a moment of reckless bravado, he would be tempted to leave his traditional signature.

He was a professional, he had a job to finish, and he needed the money for his island of fantastic creatures.

In her bathroom, the lid of the toilet stood open, exposing the seat and the bowl. At once he put it down.

He took the lid off the tank. Sometimes people sealed things in a plastic bag and submerged it in the toilet tank. Not Redwing.

If he squinted when he looked in the mirror above the sink, he could see Von Longwood. Vern smiled and said, "Lookin' good, dude."

Chapter

19

Shortly before nine o'clock, Thursday morning, Brian heard his three employees coming to work in the offices below his apartment.

Earlier he had left a voice mail for Gretchen, his assistant, asking her to reschedule his Thursday appointments to the following week. He told her that inspiration had seized him, that he would be drawing in his apartment, and that he should not be interrupted.

Inspiration had more than seized him. A singularly persistent muse—insistent, incandescent—had overwhelmed him, filled him with a quiet excitement, and he labored in a state of enchantment.

Supposedly true tales of the supernatural had never struck him as credible; yet Brian now sensed that he was channeling a talent greater than his own. If what he felt was true, then the presence working through him must be benign, for he had seldom in his life felt this happy.

Although he had put a slantboard under the art-paper tablet, his fingers should have ached, and his hand should have cramped. He had been at this for at least five hours, with intense focus.

As if the laws of physics and physiology had been suspended, he suffered no stiffness in his hand, no slightest pain. The longer he drew, the more fluidly the images appeared upon the paper.

The eyes of the dog . . . Brian stopped drawing the surrounding facial structures, yielding to a fascination with just the glistening curves from lid to lid, from inner to outer canthus, the mysterious play of light upon and within the cornea, iris, lens, and pupil.

In each new drawing, the quality of the incoming light was different from that in previous renditions, was received by the eyes at different angles, obliquely and directly.

Out of his pencil flowed larger and still larger eyes, in pairs, filling the entire page.

Then he began rendering one eye per page, enlarging the scale for a more detailed study of the patterns of intraocular radiance.

When next he glanced at the clock, he was unnerved to discover that an hour and a half had passed since he had heard his small staff coming to work downstairs. Yet he did not put down the pencil.

Although the elliptical perimeter of an eye still framed the subject, though the iris and the pupil could still be discerned, enigmas of light and shadow began to dominate each composition to such an extent that the drawings became almost abstract.

Soon Brian began to see hieroglyphics in these soft yet complex patterns, strange symbols that blazed with meaning when glimpsed from the corner of an eye. They faded into gray haze or diffused into luminous mists when he attempted to look at them directly.

Even as meaning eluded him, he grew convinced that whatever the source of these images, whether they came from his intuition or were the work of a phantom presence that guided his hand, they contained a hidden truth and were leading him toward a shattering revelation.

He tore off another page, put it aside. He had used at least a third of the tablet. Drawings layered the table.

Only after his hand had worked for a while on the clean page did he realize that he was being led into a still deeper exploration of the dog's mesmerizing gaze. Instead of merely portraying the beauty of the dusky yet luminous canine eyes as they appeared from without, Brian's busy pencil took him *within* that architecture of shade and sheen, not into the substance of the eyeball itself, but inside the warp and woof of shadow and light within cornea, iris, pupil, lens.

This was a vision of which he, as an artist, could never have conceived. The eye as a recognizable subject disappeared from the page, leaving only the incoming luminous rays and the companion shadows as they traveled through the processing layers of the eye. The drawing became entirely abstract, yet achingly more beautiful, numinous. Here was genius at work, and Brian knew he was no genius.

He had passed into an altered state of consciousness, into a trance of delight.

At times he swore that he saw the point of the working pencil pass through the paper without puncturing it, laying down its graphite *beyond* the page, as if constructing an image down, down, down through an infinite number of surfaces.

Any good artist can create the illusion of three dimensions; but as these many-petaled patterns were refined, they blossomed toward him and simultaneously invited him to fall away within them. His pencil seemed to be a key to dimensions beyond a third.

The meaningful hieroglyphics that earlier he'd glimpsed embedded in the drawing began to glow again in his imagination if not in fact, brighter than they had been previously. Then, as the drawing appeared to flower toward him, he became aware of some secret at its center, a shimmering amazement that might ultimately be beyond understanding, that could never be adequately drawn, yet his pencil worked, worked—

Through the room swept a sound so terrible that Brian flung down the pencil and thrust to his feet, knocking over the chair.

Not a simple sound but many noises simultaneously: hiss, whizz, soft clicking, rustle and flump, deep throb and ruffle, *crumpcrump-crumpcrump*. Loud, but not a blast. Not heavy like the hard crash of thunder, but heavy like the subsequent roll.

He felt as if he had been folded into the sound—as if it were a great blanket—folded into it and shaken out, folded in, shaken out.

Concussion waves thrummed in his ear drums, quivered through his teeth, traveled the hollows of his bones.

Sudden silence surprised him. The alarming resonance had seemed as if it would escalate and endure until everything in sight had been shaken apart, like the voice of an earthquake speaking deep within the breaking earth, but it lasted only three or four seconds.

For a moment he was paralyzed, throat tight, waiting for the phenomenon to repeat.

After a hush had held the kitchen for half a minute, Brian went to the window and peered out, half expecting to see a column of smoke rising in the distance, evidence of an explosion. The sky was clear.

The attraction of the unfinished image on the art paper remained powerful. His perception of a pending revelation returned.

He set the fallen chair upright and settled at the table once more. He picked up the pencil.

As his hand moved and the pencil point whispered against paper, further detailing the abstract image, the sound came again, but not loud this time. With rustle and flutter, something approached in the kitchen behind him.

Chapter

20

After play, the dogs happily lapped at the large water bowls lined up just outside the kennel, in the shade of the enormous oak.

A *come* command brought Fred, Ethel, Nickie, and Hugo back to the blanket on which Amy sat with Renata.

The six breeder dogs settled on the lawn at a distance, as they had been before the games. They trusted other dogs implicitly, but they were still wary of people, even of those who had rescued them.

After a while, Renata opened a bag of wheat-free cookies. She gave treats to Ethel and Hugo, while Amy rewarded Nickie and Fred.

The prospect of cookies brought the six ghost dogs to their feet. They approached hesitantly, tails swishing.

Amy's kids made her proud as they eased away—albeit somewhat reluctantly—to allow the newcomers to receive treats.

Gently, with lips and tongue, the breeder dogs finessed the cookies from Amy's fingers. She felt not the slightest contact with a tooth, and none of the six tried to snatch away the bag of goodies.

"Ever been bitten by a puppy-mill breeder?" Amy asked Renata.

"Nope. They come here covered in sores, some half-blind from untreated eye infections, spent their lives in cages hardly bigger than them, never knew a human being wasn't a greedy hateful bastard, never knew a gentle touch or any kindness. They ought to savage us. But they have the softest mouths, don't they? The gentlest hearts."

Some nights, Amy lay sleepless, unable to stop thinking about the hell of some dogs' lives, feeling angry and helpless.

Most puppy farms had ten or twenty breeder dogs, but some big operators kept a thousand or more in cruel conditions. These animals did not truly live, merely existed, and in perpetual black despair.

Their litters had a hope of a real life, but not the breeders. And because mill owners had no interest in maintaining the quality and improving the genetics of the breed, many of the puppies would suffer diseases and joint conditions that would shorten their lives.

Responsible pet stores like Petco and PetSmart had adoption programs for homeless dogs, but didn't sell puppies.

Other stores, Internet merchants, and newspaper advertisers who claimed to have puppies from small breeders and loving farm families were usually selling animals produced by brutalized breeder dogs.

An American Kennel Club registration specified that the dog was a purebred, not that it had been bred humanely. Every year, hundreds of thousands of puppy-mill products, sired and whelped by dogs living in desperate conditions, came with the "proper papers."

Amy gave talks at schools, at senior centers, to any audience that would listen: *Accept a rescue dog. Or buy from a reputable breeder rec-*

ommended by the parent club for each breed, such as the Golden Retriever
Club of America. Go to animal shelters. Each year, four million shelter dogs
die for lack of a home. Four million. Give love to a homeless dog, and
you'll be repaid tenfold. Give money to the puppy-mill barons, and you'll
be perpetuating a great horror.

Her audiences were always attentive. They applauded. Maybe she reached some of them.

She never imagined that she was changing the world. It couldn't be changed. So many people's indifference to the suffering of dogs was proof, to her, that the world was fallen and that one day there would be—must be—judgment. All she could do was try to rescue a few hundred dogs a year from misery and premature death.

When she and Renata finished dispensing treats, three breeder dogs shied away after a few minutes of cuddling. Two lingered longer before retreating, but one—Cinnamon—settled beside Renata as if to say *Okay, I'm going to take a chance, I'm going to trust this.*

Renata said, "Cinnamon's gonna be one of your soul-savers."

Amy believed that dogs had a spiritual purpose. The opportunity to love a dog and to treat it with kindness was an opportunity for a lost and selfish human heart to be redeemed. They are powerless and innocent, and it is how we treat the humblest among us that surely determines the fate of our souls.

Cinnamon turned to look at Amy. She had the eyes of a redeemer.

The geometry of judgment is a circle. Hate is a snake that turns to consume itself from the tail, a circle that diminishes to a point, then to nothing. Pride is such a snake, and envy, and greed. Love, however, is a hoop, a wheel, that rolls on forever. We are rescued by those whom we have rescued. The saved become the saviors of their saviors.

When Amy left the Last Chance Ranch with her three kids, she turned slowly onto the county road, hesitating long enough to read the license plate on the Land Rover.

As she headed west, the other vehicle shed the shade of the jacarandas and followed. Maybe the driver thought she was too naive to recognize the existence of a tail. Or maybe he didn't care that she knew she was being followed.

Chapter
21

The rustle and hiss and *crumpcrump-crumpcrump* rose behind Brian, quieter than the first time, almost stealthy. He turned in his chair to look, but he remained alone in the kitchen.

When the sound repeated, he glanced at the ceiling, wondering if wind might be troubling something on the roof. But the window revealed a morning as still as that on an airless world.

As he worked obsessively on the center of the current drawing of the dog's eye, he broke a lead point. A second. A third.

While he sharpened the pencils, only the crisp scraping of the X-acto blade punctuated the expectant hush.

At its loudest, the unidentified sound had seemed terrible not because it struck fear in him—which it did, a little—but because it suggested an immense and humbling power.

Born in a tornado, Brian had considerable respect for the chaos that nature could spawn and for the sudden order—call it fate—that was often revealed when the apparent chaos clarified. This strange sound of many parts had a chaotic quality; but he sensed in it his fate.

Pencils sharpened, he returned to the drawing.

Moments later, when the sound occurred yet again, he was pretty sure that it had come from overhead. Perhaps from the attic.

The drawing had reestablished its hypnotic hold on him, however, and again he felt an impending revelation. Discovering the source of the sound was a less urgent task than completing the petal-over-petal pattern of light and shadow at the center of the image.

He bent forward. The drawing seemed to fold open to fill his field of vision.

After he'd been working for a few minutes, a shadow swept across the page. Although shapeless and swift, it inspired in him an alarm akin to what he'd felt at the first—and loudest—of the sounds, and he startled up from the chair.

Because it had one curtained window, the kitchen would have been gloomy without the overhead light.

A moth might have arced around the ceiling fixture, casting down an exaggerated silhouette. Nothing but a moth could have swooped so silently.

Brian turned in a circle, searching the room. If the insect had come to rest anywhere, he could not spot it.

To his right, at the periphery of vision, he glimpsed another shadow shiver up the wall. Or thought he did. He turned his head, raised his eyes, saw nothing—

—and then fleetingly caught sight of a sharkish shadow darting across the floor. Or thought he did.

His gaze descended to the unfinished drawing. His hands were trembling too badly to make good use of a pencil.

Alert, Brian stood in the center of the room. No more shadows took flight, but the strange sound issued faintly from elsewhere in the apartment.

He hesitated, then stepped out of the kitchen.

His reflection in a hallway mirror dismayed him. His face was pale except for the ashy look of the skin under his bloodshot eyes.

At the end of the hall, he stood under a trapdoor to the attic. To reach the recessed handle, he would need a stepladder.

The longer he stared at the trap, the more he became convinced that something crouched in the higher chamber, or hung upside down from a rafter, listening.

Exhaustion whetted his imagination even as it dulled his mind. Reason had deserted him. Nothing but dust waited in the attic, dust and spiders.

He'd had only one hour of sleep in the past thirty-six. Hour after hour of compulsive drawing had further drained him.

In the bedroom, without undressing, he stretched out on his disheveled bed, from which Amy's phone call had roused him nearly twelve hours previously.

The blinds were closed. A fan of gray light spread through the open doorway, from the hall.

His eyes were hot and grainy, but he did not close them. On the ceiling, none of the mottled shadows moved.

From memory rose the crystalline voice of the child singing in Celtic.

Her eyes, a purple shade of blue.

Carl Brockman's eyes like shotgun barrels.

The word *pigkeeper* on his computer screen.

Desperate for rest, Brian dreaded closing his eyes. He had the crazy idea that Death waited to take him in his sleep. In dreams, a winged presence would descend on him, cover his mouth with hers, and suck the breath of life from him.

Chapter
22

After more than five hours of sleep, Harrow wakes past noon, not in the windowless room where they have sex, but in the main bedroom of the yellow-brick house.

The draperies are shut, but he can tell that Moongirl is already gone. Her presence would have imparted an unmistakable quality to the darkness because her mood, that of a perpetually pending storm, adds significant millibars to the natural atmospheric pressure.

In the kitchen, he brews strong coffee. Through a window, he sees her in the pocket yard, that small pool of grass so green in a sea of rock.

Carrying his mug of steaming brew, he steps outside. The day is warm for late September.

The yellow-brick house is anchored in a landscape of beige granite. Rounded forms of stone, like the knuckles of giant fists, press up against the perimeter of the sun-washed brick patio.

Harrow crosses fissured slabs of weather-smoothed rock to the yard. Over the ages, wind had blown soil into a deep oval declivity in the granite, and later had seeded it.

From the center of the grassy oval rises an eighty-foot Montezuma pine, its great spreading branches filtering the midday sun through tufts of gracefully drooping, ten-inch-long needles.

In feathery shadows and plumes of sunshine, Moongirl sits upon a blanket, aware that she is a vision. Even in this dramatic landscape, she is the focus and lodestar. She draws his gaze as irresistibly as gravity pulls a dropped stone down a well, into the drowning dark.

She is wearing only black panties and a simple but expensive diamond necklace that Harrow gave her. She is ripe but lithe, with sun-bronzed skin and the self-possessed air of a cat. Dappled with shadows and golden light, she reminds him of a leopard at leisure, fresh from a killing, fed and content.

Men have given her so much for so long that she expects gifts in the same way she expects to receive air every time she inhales: as a natural right. She accepts every offering, no matter how extravagant, with no more thanks than she expresses when she turns a spigot and receives water from a tap.

Beside her is a black-lacquered box lined with red velvet, in which she keeps an array of polishes, scissors, files, emery boards, and other instruments for the care of her nails.

Although she never visits a manicurist, her fingernails are exquisitely shaped, though shorter and more pointed than is the fashion these days. She is content to spend hours at this task.

Her fear of boredom turns her inward. To Moongirl, other people seem as flat as actors on a TV screen, and she is unable to imagine that they possess her dimension. The outer world is gray and empty, but her inner world is rich.

Harrow sits on the grass, a few feet from her blanket, as she does not encourage closeness in moments like this. He drinks coffee, watches her as she paints her toenails, and wonders what occupies her mind when she is in such a reverie.

He would not be surprised to learn that no conscious thoughts whatsoever trouble her right now, that she is in a trance.

In an effort to understand her, he discovered a condition called automatism. This is a state during which behavior is not controlled by the conscious mind, and it may or may not apply to her.

Usually, automatisms last a few minutes. But as with all things, there are atypical events, and Moongirl is nothing if not atypical.

In the grip of automatism, perhaps she can spend hours on her toenails without being aware that she is grooming herself. Later, she would have no recollection of trimming, filing, and polishing.

Conceivably, she could kill a man during such a spell, never be conscious of committing violence, and have no memory of murder.

He would like to watch her in an act of automatismic homicide. How breathtakingly terrible her beauty would be then: her eyes blank and her features without expression as she wielded a flensing knife.

He doubts that she has killed in such a condition or ever will, because murder—especially by fire—is the one thing the outer world can offer her that dependably staves off boredom. She does not need to kill in a trance when she can, without compunction and with deep satisfaction, kill while fully conscious.

Frequently she passes the better part of the day in grooming activities. She is eternally fascinated by herself, and her body is her best defense against boredom.

Sometimes she spends an entire afternoon washing her golden hair, applying to it a series of natural-substance rinses, slowly brushing it dry in the sun, and giving herself a long scalp and neck massage.

A restless man by nature, Harrow is nevertheless able to watch her for hours as she grooms herself. He is soothed by her flawless beauty, by her bottomless calm, and by her perfect self-absorption, and she inspires in him a curious hopeful feeling, though he has not yet been able to identify what it is that he hopes *for.*

Usually Moongirl grooms herself in silence, and Harrow is not sure that she is aware of his presence. This time, after a while, she speaks: "Have you heard from him?"

"No."

"I'm tired of this place."

"We won't stay much longer."

"He better call soon."

"He will."

"I'm tired of the noise."

"What noise?" he asks.

"The sea breaking on the shore."

"Most people like it."

"It makes me think," she says.

"Think about what?"

"Everything."

He does not reply.

"I don't want to think," she says.

"About what?"

"About anything."

"When this is done, we'll go to the desert."

"It better be done soon."

"All sand and sun, no surf."

With slow deliberate strokes of the brush, she paints a toenail purple.

As the earth turns slowly away from the sun, the feathery pine shadows stretch their wings toward the house.

Beyond the pocket yard, out of sight below the shelving slabs of granite, waves pound the beach.

To the west, a gunmetal-blue sea looks hard, cold. It alchemizes the molten-gold sunshine into shiny steel scales, which churn forward like the metal treads of war machines.

After a while she says, "I had a dream."

Harrow waits.

"There was a dog."

"What dog?"

"A golden retriever."

"It would be, wouldn't it?"

"I didn't like its eyes."

"What about them?"

She says nothing.

Then later: "If you see it, kill it."

"What—the dog?"

"Yes."

"It was in a dream."

"But it's real, too."

"Not a dangerous breed."

"This one is."

"If you say so."

"Kill it on sight."

"All right."

"Kill it good."

"All right."

"Kill it hard."

Chapter

23

A faint onshore breeze washed waves of golden grass up the meadow toward the hilltop, and the elongated oak-tree shadows rippled in the flow.

The sweet grassy scent, the brightness that fell from the air, and the majesty of the oaks was as close as Amy expected to get to Heaven this side of death.

Golden Heart had received these twelve acres from the estate of Julia Papadakis, who had fostered many a golden retriever between its rescue and its forever home.

Julia's only living relative, a niece named Linnea, unhappy with a thirty-million-dollar inheritance, had challenged the will, seeking to add this valuable land to her portfolio. Linnea had millions for attorney fees. Amy's counterattack was mounted on a budget.

Currently, even after years of operation, Golden Heart had no office other than Amy's study, no care facilities for the dogs other than the volunteers' homes. When she brought in more dogs than could be fostered by their members, she had to board them in the kennels of the animal hospitals that offered her a discount.

She was loath to board a single rescue. Even if they didn't arrive beaten or tick-infested, even if they were healthy dogs, they were nevertheless anxious and in need of affection in excess of what any ordinary kennel staff could offer.

Here on this hill, in this meadow, with determination and the grace of God, she would oversee the construction of a facility where Golden Heart could receive new rescues, evaluate them, bathe them, and prepare them for their new homes. For those who couldn't quickly be placed in a forever home or in a foster situation, heated and air-conditioned kennels of generous size, with clean bedding, would be staffed around the clock. There would be a simple clinic, a well-equipped grooming salon, a fenced playground, a training room, a playroom for use in rainy weather. . . .

Until the bequest was successfully defended in court, however, only Amy's kids could enjoy this sunny meadow and the oak shade. Fred and Ethel bounded now through the tall grass, chasing each other, tempted this way and that by rabbit scent, squirrel scent.

Nickie remained at her master's side.

Amy had departed from the blacktop and had driven the Expedition overland, parking on the hilltop, while the Land Rover had pulled to the shoulder of the highway.

Evidently not tempted by the wild scents or by the prospect of play, Nickie remained focused on the vehicle far below.

Although Amy had brought Renata's binoculars, she didn't bother to use them. The driver remained in the Rover, and at this distance, even with the powerful field glasses, she would not be able to see his face.

She wondered if Linnea Papadakis had put her under surveillance.

Although an injunction prevented Golden Heart from develop-
ing this land until Linnea's challenge to her aunt's last will and
testament had been adjudicated, Amy was not enjoined from visiting the property. She couldn't imagine what Linnea hoped to gain
by having her watched.

Low in her throat, Nickie growled.

Chapter

24

When he had finished searching every corner of Redwing's house, Vernon Lesley stood in her kitchen and placed a cell-phone call to Bobby Onions.

"You still on her?"

"I'd like to be on her," said Onions.

"Don't be tiresome."

"She's out in this field."

"What field?"

Onions had a state-of-the-art satellite navigation system that displayed the precise latitude and longitude of his Land Rover, in degrees and minutes, on the vehicle's computer screen. He read these coordinates to Vern.

"For all I know," Vern said wearily, "that could be someplace in Cambodia."

"It couldn't possibly be in Cambodia. You don't know jack about latitude and longitude. How do you expect to do your job, you don't know the essentials?"

"I don't need to know latitude and longitude to be a gumshoe."

"Gumshoe," Onions said disdainfully. "So do you still call the refrigerator an icebox? It's a new century, Vern. These days, we're in a paramilitary profession."

"Private investigation isn't a paramilitary profession."

"The world gets more dangerous by the week. People need private detectives, private bodyguards, private security, private *police*, and we're all those things. Police are paramilitary."

"We're not police," Vern said.

"You've got your philosophy of the profession, and I've got mine," said Bobby Onions. "The point is, I'm still on her, and I know the *precise* cartographic coordinates. If I had to call down a missile strike on her, she'd be toast."

"Missile strike? She's one woman."

"Osama bin Laden is one man. They ever got precise coordinates on him, they'd call down a missile strike."

"You're just a private dick. You don't have any authority to order a missile strike."

"I'm only saying if I did, then I could because I've got the precise coordinates."

Silently vowing to find another gumshoe for any future team jobs, Vern said, "Good for you."

"Anyway, she's on this hilltop, out in the sun, not in the tree shadows, nice silhouette against the sky. Easiest thing in the world to pick her off with a SIG 550 Sniper."

Vern winced. "Tell me you're not watching her through the scope of a rifle."

"I'm not. Of course I'm not. I'm just saying."

"Do you have a SIG 550 Sniper?" Vern asked.

"Minimum basic ordnance, Vern. Never know when you'll need it."

"Where is your rifle right now, Bobby?"

"Relax. It's wrapped in a blanket in the back of the Rover."

"We're not hit men, Bobby."

"I know we're not. I know, Vern. I know better than you what we are. Relax."

"Anyway, nobody wants her dead."

"There isn't nobody that somebody doesn't want dead, Vern. Bet a hundred people wouldn't mind you dead."

"How many you think wouldn't mind you dead, Bobby?"

"Probably a thousand," Bobby Onions said with what sounded like a note of pride.

"All you were supposed to do was watch her while I searched her house, and warn me if she started to come home."

"That's all I've done, Vern. She's up there on the hill with her dogs, silhouetted against the sky."

Vern said, "I'm done here. I'm leaving as soon as I hang up. So you don't need to watch her anymore."

"I don't mind watching her. I'm on the clock for you anyway until after the meeting with the wallet."

"Wallet? What wallet?"

"That's what I call the client. I call a client the wallet."

"I call him the client."

"Doesn't surprise me, Vern. What do you call the subject of a surveillance, like this woman?"

"I call her the subject," said Vern, "the mark, the bird."

"That's all so old," Bobby said disdainfully. "These days, the mark is called the monkey."

"Why?" Vern wondered.

"Because it's not the Jurassic Period anymore, Vern."

"You're twenty-four. I'm only thirty-nine."

"Fifteen years, Vern. These days, that's an Ice Age. Times change fast. You still want to meet at two-thirty before we go see the wallet?"

"Yeah. Two-thirty."

"Same rally you said before?"

"Rally?"

"Rallying point, Vern, meeting place. Get it?"

"Yeah. Same rally as before. Two-thirty. Hey, Bobby."

"Yeah?"

"If some guy's an asshole, what do people call him these days?"

"Far as I know, that's what they call him."

"I guess *asshole* is a kind of timeless word. See you at two-thirty."

Vern terminated the call and looked around the cheerful yellow-and-white kitchen. He wished he didn't have to leave. Amy Cogland, alias Amy Redwing, had a sweet life here.

After locking the bungalow behind him, Vern walked back to his rustbucket Chevy, carrying the white trash bag of items that he had confiscated during the search. He felt old and dumpy, and melancholy.

As he drove away from Redwing's neighborhood, he thought about Von Longwood and the flying sports car in Second Life, and his mood began to improve.

Chapter

25

A half dozen sea gulls drop out of the sky, shriek to perches on the higher branches of the Montezuma pine, fall silent in the same instant, seem simultaneously to detect a danger, and as one burst into flight, with a violent drumming of wings.

Either disturbed by the gulls or coming loose by coincidence, a ten-inch pine cone rattles down through the branches and lands on the blanket beside Moongirl.

She does not react to the sudden shrill cries of the gulls or to the thunder of their wings, or to the fall of the heavy cone. With the manicurist's brush, she smoothly spreads purple polish across a toenail.

After a while, she says, "I hate the gulls."

"We'll go to the desert soon," Harrow promises.

"Someplace very hot."

"Palm Desert or Rancho Mirage."

"No waves breaking."

"No gulls," he says.

"Just hot silent sun."

"And moonlit sand at night," he says.

"I hope the sky is white."

"You mean the desert sky."

"Sometimes it's almost white."

"That's more like August," he says.

"Bone-white around the sun. I've seen it."

"At high altitudes like Santa Fe."

"Bone-white."

"If you want it, then it will be."

"We'll go from fire to fire."

He doesn't understand, so he waits.

She finishes painting the last toenail. She returns the brush to the bottle of purple polish.

She tosses her head to cast her long hair behind her shoulders, and her bare breasts sway.

Far out on the scaly sea, a ship is northbound. Another sails south.

When one profile passes behind the other, perhaps the ships will cancel each other, and cease to exist.

This is not a thought he would have had before hooking up with Moongirl.

Eventually all ships sink or they are disassembled for scrap. In time, anything that was something becomes nothing. Existence has no ultimate purpose except cessation.

So why shouldn't the existence of any one thing—ship or person—terminate at any moment, without cause or reason?

"We'll burn them all," she says.

"If that's what you want."

"Tomorrow night."

"If they get here by then."

"They will. Burn them down to bones."

"All right."

"Burn them, then to the desert. From fire to fire."

Harrow says, "When you say burn them *all* . . ."

"Yeah. Her, too."

"I thought it might be time."

"It's ten years overdue."

He says, "When the burning's done . . ."

Moongirl meets his eyes.

". . . who leaves here and how?" he finishes.

"Me," she says. "And you. Together."

He thinks she means it. He will be wary nonetheless.

"White sky pressing down on flat white sand," she says. "All that heat."

He watches her for a while as she blows on her wet nails. Then he asks, "Have you fed her?"

"It's a waste of food now."

"We may need her in good shape."

"Why?"

"Show and tell. He'll want to see her."

"To lure him in."

"Yes."

"So we'll feed her."

He starts to get up.

She says, "When my nails are dry."

Harrow settles to the grass once more, to watch her blow.

After a while, he gazes at the sea, which is now so sun-silvered that it appears to be almost white.

He can't locate either the northbound or the southbound ship. Perhaps they are hidden in the solar glare.

Chapter

26

The Land Rover left while Amy and the kids were enjoying the meadow. Later, when she drove to the south-county animal shelter to keep an appointment, no one followed her.

"What was that about?" she asked the dogs, but they had no idea.

At the shelter, she locked her kids in the Expedition, leaving four windows down a couple of inches for air circulation.

Neither Fred nor Ethel, nor Nickie, expressed any desire to accompany her. They knew what kind of place this was. All three were subdued.

Her accountant, Danielle Chiboku, also a Golden Heart volunteer, waited for her in the dreary reception area.

"You bought that rescue last night for two thousand bucks?" Dani asked first thing.

"Kind of, sort of, if you want to see it that way, I guess you could say maybe I did, in a manner of speaking."

"What am I going to do with you?" Dani asked.

"Gee, Mom, I guess you'll have to send me to a military school to straighten me out."

"If I were your mother, you'd know the value of a dollar."

"You're only five years older than I am. You couldn't be my mom. You could be my *stepmother* if you married my father."

"Amy—"

"But since I've never known who my father was, I'm not able to introduce you. Anyway, the two thousand bucks wasn't Golden Heart's money. It was mine."

"Yes, and every year when the organization doesn't quite raise enough donations to cover its work, you make up the difference."

"I always expect Batman, in his Bruce Wayne identity, to write me a check, but he never comes through."

"If you keep this up, you'll be broke in five years."

"You're my accountant. You can't let that happen. Put me in some investment with a two-hundred-percent return."

"I'm dead serious, Amy. Five years."

"Five years is an eternity. Anything could happen in five years. The dogs need me now. Did I ever tell you how much you look like Audrey Hepburn?"

"Don't try to change the subject. Audrey Hepburn wasn't half Japanese and half Norwegian."

"How *did* your parents meet, anyway? Working on a whaling ship? Blubber and ambergris and love at first sight? Hey, did Mookie meet with Janet Brockman yet?"

Mukai Chiboku—Mookie to his friends—was Dani's husband and Golden Heart's attorney.

"He's going to handle her divorce pro bono," Dani said. "The little boy and girl half broke his heart."

Mookie, specializing in real-estate law, had offices in a plain two-story building in Corona del Mar. Few passersby would imagine he had six clients whose combined holdings exceeded a billion dollars.

Dogs were welcome in his office. He went to work every day

with his golden, Baiko, who had been named after a master of haiku, and he always greeted Fred and Ethel by exclaiming "Sweet babies!"

"You ready for this?" Amy asked.

"No."

"Me neither."

The shelter workers knew them well. She and Dani walked this facility at least once a week.

An animal-control officer named Luther Osteen led them out of reception, past the shelter offices, into the kennels at the back of the building.

Small but clean cages flanked a concrete run, and all of them contained dogs. Larger animals were housed one to a space. Sometimes the smaller individuals shared a cage.

A few were so depressed, they lay staring at nothing, and did not raise their heads.

Most came to the doors of their cages. Some appeared forlorn, but others wagged their tails and seemed tentatively hopeful.

Occasionally one of the smaller dogs barked, but most of the inmates were quiet, as if aware that their fate—adoption or death—depended in part on their demeanor.

The majority were mutts. About a quarter looked like purebreds. Every dog here was beautiful, each in its own way, and the clock was running out for all of them.

Because the volume of abandoned and abused dogs far exceeded the resources of all the rescue groups combined, each organization had to limit itself to a single breed.

The shelter worked hard to place the mixed breeds, the mutts. Yet thousands every year would have to be euthanized.

Amy wanted to stop at every cage, scratch and cuddle each dog, but raising their hopes would have been cruel, and leaving them behind after making their acquaintance would have devastated her.

Luther Osteen had two dogs for their consideration, the first a pure golden named Mandy. She was a sweet girl, nine years old, her face mostly white with age.

Mandy's owners had retired. They wanted to spend a few years traveling through Europe. Mandy no longer fit their lifestyle.

"She's got some arthritis," Luther said, "and her teeth haven't been so well cared for, but she has a few good years in her yet. Hard for us to place an older dog like her. She's probably given back ten times the love she's gotten over the years, so it'd be right if she had a chance to be with someone who'd give her a better deal."

"We'll take her," Dani said.

The second orphan was a male, part golden, part something else not easily identified, perhaps Australian shepherd. He'd been running loose in an industrial park, wearing a collar with no license.

"Looks like he was abandoned there," Luther said, "must've been fending for himself a couple weeks, he's so thin."

The nameless dog stood at the cage door, pressing its black nose through a gap in the wire grid.

"How old, you think?" Dani asked.

"Figure he's maybe three or four years. No obvious disease."

"Fixed?" Amy asked.

"No. But you take him, we'll pay for that. He's got some ticks, but not a lot."

Finding forever homes for hundreds of purebreds a year was hard enough. The mixed breeds were more difficult to place.

The tail moved continuously. The ears were raised. The brown eyes pleaded.

"The boy's housebroken," Luther said, "and he knows some basic commands like *sit* and *down*."

That the dog had some training made him easier to place, so with relief, Amy said, "We'll take him."

"You go deal with the paperwork," Luther said. "I'll bring them both out to you."

Returning along the kennel run, between the rows of cages, Dani took Amy's hand. She always did. Her eyes were full of unshed tears, which Amy saw before her own vision blurred.

Coming in past all these dogs, most of whom would be euthanized, always proved to be a tough walk, but the return trip, leaving them to their fate, was brutal.

Sometimes, Amy despaired for the human race, and never more so than on those days when she visited the county shelter.

Some repay loyalty with faithlessness and give no thought to their own final hours, when they might have to ask another to grant them the mercy that they withheld from those who trusted them.

Chapter

27

Harrow makes a ham-and-cheese sandwich, adds two sweet pickles to the plate, and puts the plate on a tray with a container of deli potato salad. He adds two lunchbox bags of potato chips and a small bag of Pepperidge Farm cookies. She likes root beer, so he puts two cold cans on the tray.

Just as he finishes, Moongirl enters the kitchen. She has dressed in black slacks and a black sweater. She still wears the diamond necklace that he gave her, but the diamond bracelet is a gift from some man before him.

Regarding the laden tray, she says, "I would've done this."

"Saved you the trouble."

Her green gaze is as sharp as a broken bottle. "Always doing things for me."

He knows this wire well. He has walked it with her many times before.

"I enjoy it," he says.

"Doing things for me."

"Yes."

"What about her?"

"What about her?" he asks.

"You give her what she likes."

He shrugged. "It's what we have."

"Which you bought."

"Next time give me a list."

"Then you'll buy what I want her to have."

"Of course."

She takes the lid off the container of potato salad and smells it. "You pity her, don't you?"

"No."

"Don't you?"

"Why should I?"

She spits in the potato salad. "You shouldn't."

He says nothing.

Again she spits in the potato salad.

She stares at him, reading his reaction.

Unlike her, he is in control not just of his body and intellect but also of his emotions. He meets her stare unwaveringly.

"Save your sympathy for me," she says.

"I feel nothing for her."

"Not even disgust?"

"She's just a thing," he says.

Moongirl can maintain a stare halfway to forever. Finally she holds out the container of potato salad and says, "You too."

Without hesitation, he spits in it.

She smiles at him.

He dares not return the smile. She will take it as mockery.

A third time, she spits in the potato salad, then returns the lid to the container and places the container on the tray.

She says, "Maybe I'll let you strike the match."

He is not sure of the safe reply, so he says nothing.

"Tomorrow night," she says.

"You'll want to do it."

"You won't?"

"I will if it's what you want."

"What do *you* want?" she asks.

"You."

"Why?"

"What else is there."

"Boredom," she says.

"Yes."

She picks up the tray.

"I'll carry that for you," he says.

"No. You go ahead, unlock the door."

He precedes her through the house.

Behind him, she says, "We'll have a little fun now."

Chapter

28

From the back of Amy's Expedition, Fred and Ethel and Nickie watched solemnly as Mandy and the nameless dog were loaded into Dani Chiboku's SUV.

A few clouds had materialized. Although at ground level the air hung as still as old clothes in the back of a closet, at the higher altitude white cloaks were flung across the sky, billowing eastward, tattering to the west.

With the dogs safely aboard, Dani closed the tailgate and said, "Seriously, Amy, five years."

"Something will happen. We'll have more and better fundraisers. I'm applying everywhere for grants."

"But the number of dogs that need to be rescued keeps rising in direct proportion to the amount of money you generate."

"So far, yeah, but it's not an economic *law*. Eventually the need and the resources are gonna come into balance. People just can't keep throwing so many dogs away."

"Look around, girl. The world's never been meaner. It's going to get worse."

"No. I've known it worse than this."

Amy seldom spoke of her past and always with circumspection. She sometimes wondered if friends accepted her as merely a private person or if instead they suspected her of having secrets.

The sharp interest in Dani's eyes and the curiosity that pinched and dimpled every feature of her face answered that question.

When Amy offered nothing more, Dani said, "You should start to think about getting a job."

"This is my job. The dogs."

"It may be a passion. It may even be a calling. But, girl, it isn't a job. *A job pays you.*"

"There's nothing else I can do, Dani. I've been doing just this for like ten years. I'm unemployable."

"I don't believe that. You're smart, you've got drive—"

"I'm a spoiled little rich girl living off an inheritance."

"You're not rich anymore, if you ever were, and you don't know what spoiled is." Dani shook her head. "Love you like a sister, Amy."

Amy nodded. "Me too."

"Maybe someday you'll open up to me like a sister would."

"I'm afraid what you see is what you get. Nothing to open up." She kissed Dani on the cheek. "I'm not a book, I'm a pamphlet."

Buttering her words with sarcasm, Dani said, "Yeah, right."

"Tell Mookie I'm grateful for him taking Janet Brockman's case."

Opening the driver's door of her SUV, Dani said, "What's the story with the little girl?"

"Theresa? I don't know. She may be some kind of autistic or just traumatized from . . . the way it was in that house."

"Mookie says a strange thing happened at the office."

Amy raised one hand to the locket at her throat. The pendant featured a cameo carved from soapstone, but instead of the classic profile of a woman, the subject was a golden retriever. She never wore other jewelry, nor owned any.

"The girl goes straight to Baiko," Dani said, "sits on the floor with him, pets him."

The previous night, as Amy had carried the sleepy child into Lottie Augustine's house, Theresa had reached up and touched the locket.

"Later, when they're leaving the office, she says to Mookie, 'No more cancer.'"

The wind, Theresa had said so softly, fingering the locket. *The wind . . . the chimes.*

"Mookie hadn't mentioned that Baiko had just gone through chemo. Didn't say a word about the cancer."

"Maybe Lottie told them," Amy suggested.

"Not very likely, is it?"

Twenty years ago, Lottie had lost her only child to cancer. Five years later, her husband died of the same malignancy. As if *cancer* were the secret and the truest name of the devil, which would conjure him in a sulfurous cloud even if whispered, Lottie never spoke of the disease.

"The girl says to Mookie, 'No more cancer,' and then she says, 'It won't come back.'"

The wind . . . the chimes.

"Amy?"

"She's a strange child," Amy said.

"Mookie says she's got troubling eyes."

"I thought beautiful."

"I haven't seen her myself."

"Beautiful but bruised," Amy said.

"Let's hope she's right."

"What?"

"About Baiko's cancer."

"I suspect she is," Amy said. "I'm sure she is."

She stood by the driver's door of her Expedition and watched Dani Chiboku drive away with the two latest rescues.

The day remained sunny, but she could no longer feel its warmth.

A moving shadow wiped the sun glare off the Expedition.

When Amy looked up, the covey of eastward-racing clouds seemed to be too high to cast such a shadow.

A change was coming. She didn't know what it would be, but she knew it would not be a change for the better.

She did not like change. She wanted continuity and the peace that came with it: day folding into night, night into day, dogs saved and passed to loving homes, and more dogs saved.

A change was coming, and she was afraid.

Chapter

29

The client was waiting for them east of Lake Elsinor, out where the merciless desert had met its match in the relentless tract-house builders.

Bobby Onions drove them to the rendezvous in his cool Land Rover because no way in hell would he ride in Vernon Lesley's Chevy, which Bobby called "wimp wheels, a losermobile."

Vern refrained from mentioning that every time he needed an extra hand, Bobby was available for hire, which suggested that clients were not standing in line outside Onions Investigations.

Inexplicably, the freeway traffic was light. Whatever the reason, Vern knew the explanation wasn't that the Rapture had occurred, that the saved had been taken straight to Heaven.

Mrs. Bonnaventura, who lived in the crappy apartment next to Vern's crappy apartment, believed in the imminence of the Rapture. Housebound by emphysema, she kept two things close to her: a wheeled tank of oxygen, which she received through nasal cannula, and a small bag that she had packed for the miraculous ascent.

In the bag were a Bible, a change of underwear, photos of dead

loved ones—family and friends—whom Mrs. Bonnaventura intended to track down without delay upon reaching Paradise, and
breath mints.

She knew she wouldn't need the oxygen tank in Heaven, where
she would be restored to her youth, and she couldn't explain to Vern
why she packed the underwear or the breath mints. She'd said, "I
just don't want to take any chances, it would be so embarrassing."

When she talked about meeting God, Mrs. Bonnaventura
glowed. The prospect of a divine howdy-do delighted her.

Vern didn't believe in the Rapture, and he was neutral on the
existence of God. But one thing he knew for sure: If God existed,
meeting Him after death would be so terrifying that you'd probably
die a second time from sheer fright.

Even someone like Mrs. Bonnaventura, who had lived a mostly
blameless life, when ushered into the awesome presence of the
Creator of the infinite universe and also of the butterfly, would discover ten thousand fearsome new layers of meaning in the word
humility.

Mrs. Bonnaventura said God was pure love, as if this quality of
the Lord made meeting him a less weighty event, as if it would be
like—but even nicer than—meeting Oprah Winfrey.

Vern figured that if God existed, a God of pure love, then for sure
there had to be a Purgatory, because you would need a place of puri-
fication before you dared go upstairs for the Ultimate Hug. Even a
sweet woman like Mrs. Bonnaventura, rapturing directly from this
life to God's presence, would detonate as violently as antimatter
meeting matter, like in that old episode of *Star Trek.*

Interrupting Vern's theological musings, piloting the Rover with
one hand, rubbing the back of his neck with the other, Bobby Onions
said, "So what's the story with the bounce?"

"Bounce?"

"The woman."

"What woman?" Vern wondered.

"What woman could it be?" Bobby said impatiently. "Redwing."

"You said someone you're investigating, you call a monkey."

"That's a man *or* a woman. Besides, I'm not investigating her anymore."

"So why do you call her the bounce?"

"When a woman has the right stuff in the right places to bounce in the right way, she's hot. A bounce is a sexy lady."

"What do you call a sexy guy?" Vern asked.

"I don't find guys sexy." Bobby frowned. He put both hands on the wheel and sat up straighter. "You don't find guys sexy, do you?"

"No. Hell, no. Don't talk crazy."

"So what is this Von Longwood business?" Bobby asked.

"What do you mean? He's my avatar. In Second Life."

"I don't know about that."

"I told you. Don't you listen?"

"You're always talking about him."

"And you're never listening. He's an avatar, like a cartoon version of me, just another identity. He's me, I'm him."

Scowling into the desert glare as they turned onto an exit ramp, Bobby said, "It sounds kinky to me."

"It's not kinky. Mostly it's a role-playing game."

"I heard about these two gay guys—one dressed up like a nurse, the other like a Nazi, then they'd go at each other."

"Not that kind of role-playing. It's cool. Go on-line, look up Second Life, educate yourself."

"I don't need the Internet. I've already got me a life, and it's packed full. I don't need a *play* life."

Simmering, Vern said, "The next road, go left."

Cottonwoods and clusters of wild oleander thrived along a dry streambed, but on the hills of rock and sand, nothing grew other than withered mesquite and sage and bunch-grass.

"How much you pay for your fabulous flying car?" Bobby asked, punctuating the question with a smirk.

Although he knew he was being mocked, Vern could not resist saying with some pride, "A hundred fifty thousand Linden dollars."

"What's a Linden dollar?"

"That's the money you buy to spend in Second Life. Linden Labs, they started Second Life."

"How much is that in real money?"

"Six hundred bucks."

"You paid six hundred bucks for a cartoon car? No wonder you drive a losermobile in your real life."

Vern almost said *My second life is my real life,* but he knew a Philistine like Bobby would never understand.

Instead, he said, "So which is the real you—Bobby Onions or Barney Smallburg?"

The starboard wheels stuttered on the graveled shoulder of the road, but then found the pavement again.

"You sonofabitch," said Barney-Bobby. "You *investigated* me."

"Anybody I'm gonna hire to back me up on a job—I find out who he is first. You changed your name two years before you got your PI license. I've known it since the first case you worked with me."

"In a paramilitary profession," said Barney-Bobby, "image is important."

"Maybe you're right. *Barney Smallburg* doesn't sound like a guy with gonads."

"Compared to *Vernon Lesley,* it sounds totally kick-ass."

"You'll be making a right turn in about half a mile."

Runty cactuses clawed out a life on a sand-and-shale hillside, their spiky shadows creeping eastward as the westering sun sought the distant sea.

"Tell you what," said Barney-Bobby. "You never tell anyone I changed my name, I'll stop riding you about Von Longwood."

"Fair enough."

"You're of the old school, I'm of the new," Bobby said, "but I've got a lot of respect for you, Vern."

That was bullshit, but Vern didn't care. What people thought of him in his first life was of no concern to him anymore. He had his refuge now, and his wings.

"So what's the story with the bounce?" Bobby asked.

"She had her own other life before the current one. She's hiding under the name *Redwing*."

"Hiding from who?"

"I don't know. But they found her. And they hired me to search for every proof she kept of that life and take it from her."

"What proof?"

"Documents, snapshots."

"Why take it from her?"

"You ask too many questions," Vern said.

"You, me, every good procto has to have curiosity."

Procto. Vern decided not to ask for a definition. He said, "All I care is, it's a good payday."

As Vern had instructed, Bobby turned right on a badly fissured blacktop road so long neglected that weeds sprouted from the cracks in the pavement.

"Are you ironed?" Bobby Onions asked. "You don't look ironed."

Squinting down at his shirt and pants, Vern said, "I always buy this wrinkleproof polyester-blend crap. I just let the wrinkles hang out. What the hell do you care anyway?"

Bobby sighed. "'Are you ironed' means are you carrying iron, are you packing a gun?"

"You aren't living in a movie, Bobby. When did you ever hear of a PI getting shot by a client in real life?"

"It could always happen."

"To the best of your knowledge, has it *ever* happened?"

"All it takes is once to get yourself dead." Bobby patted the left side of his sport coat. "I'm packing a real door-buster."

"I didn't want to ask," Vern said, "'cause I thought maybe you had a huge tumor or something."

"Bullshit. It doesn't show. It's in a custom holster, and I had the tailor do some work on the jacket."

The road topped a rise. A great flat plain opened before them.

In the foreground, still a quarter of a mile distant, stood a series of Quonset huts of different sizes, a few quite large, their ribbed-steel curves so abraded by sand and by time that the sun could not tease a true shine from them, only a soft gray luster.

"What's this place?" Bobby asked, letting up on the accelerator.

"Something military from a long time ago. Abandoned now. Weapons bunkers off to the left there. Offices, maintenance buildings. This land's so flat and hard, there's a natural runway, they didn't have to pave it."

Beyond the buildings stood a twin-engine Cessna.

The dry weeds in the fractured roadway whispered against the undercarriage as the Land Rover lost speed, ticked . . . ticked . . . ticked like the rubber pointer on a slowing wheel of fortune.

A man stepped out of the open door of one of the Quonset huts.

"That'll be him," said Vernon Lesley.

Chapter

30

H arrow disengages the deadbolt, steps back to let Moongirl carry the tray through the doorway, and follows her across the threshold.

The exterior storm shutters have been bolted over the three windows. Because they are poorly fitted and cracked with age, some sunshine finds its way around them, between them, and into the room. A blade of golden light cleaves one shadow into two. Another stiletto pricks a clear cut-glass vase, and the beveled edges conduct only the red portion of the spectrum, so it appears almost as if the vase is decorated with a motif of bloody thorns.

Most of the light issues from a brass lamp on the large desk, at which the child sits.

She is in one of her two uniforms: sneakers, gray sweat pants, and a sweatshirt. In very hot weather, she is permitted to exchange the sweatshirt for a T-shirt.

Intent upon her sewing, she does not at once look up.

Moongirl puts the tray on the desk.

Although just ten years old, the child has about her an aura of age, and she possesses a kind of patience that most children do not.

She has enhanced the hem of a small white dress with embroidery, a simple elegant pattern of leaves and roses. Now she is tailoring the garment to the doll for which it has been made.

Her thick tongue is captured between her teeth, not merely an indication of the intensity of her concentration but also evidence of her difference.

In the chair beside the desk sits another doll in a costume of the child's design. Moongirl puts this doll on the floor and sits in the chair, watching her daughter.

The young seamstress has stubby fingers, and her hands are not nimble with the needle. Yet she creates beautiful embroidery and, with the doll's dress, accomplishes all that she intends.

Having learned the protocols of these encounters, Harrow sits on the arm of an upholstered chair, near enough to observe the subtlest of details, but at a respectful distance.

"How're you doing?" Moongirl asks.

"Okay," says the seamstress.

"Aren't you going to ask me how I'm doing?"

Still concentrating on the doll's dress, the child says, "Sure. How you doin'?"

Her voice is thick but not at all difficult to understand, for although her tongue is enlarged, it is not also fissured, as are the tongues of many others with her condition.

"That's a beautiful doll," says Moongirl.

"I like her."

"She has such a pretty mouth."

"I like her eyes."

"If she could talk, she'd have a pretty voice."

"I call her Monique."

"Where did you hear that name?"

"On TV."

"Can you spell Monique?"

"Not much."

"Not at all, huh?"

"No," the child admits.

"Well, that's all right."

In the lamplight, as in any light, the child's features have the soft, heavy contours associated with mental retardation.

"If her name were Jane," says Moongirl, "you couldn't spell that either, could you?"

"Maybe I could learn."

The sloped brow, the inner epicanthic folds of the eyes, the ears set low on a head too small to be in correct proportion to the body are all signifiers of Down's syndrome.

"You think you could learn?" Moongirl asks.

"Some, I think."

"To read and write?"

"Maybe."

After a few weeks, Harrow had learned to see a gentleness in the daughter's face, a sweetness that made her seem less alien than she had been to him at first.

"How would you learn?"

"School."

"Oh, baby," Moongirl says with feigned sadness.

"I'd try hard."

"But they don't want you."

"I'd be good."

"Good but dumb, baby."

The child says nothing.

"They don't want dumb."

By the time she came into Harrow's life with her mother, the child seemed to be past genuine tears. Her eyes are clear now.

"It's unfair, isn't it?" says Moongirl.

"Yeah."

"You didn't ask to be dumb."

Sometimes, lately, Harrow sees in the child's unfortunate face a quality that is not beauty but that is akin to it. The word that best defines this quality eludes him, so he thinks of it only as the Look.

"Nobody asks to be dumb and ugly."

Ceaselessly, the child hems the doll's dress, drawing white thread through white fabric, making a series of precise and identical stitches that brings into Harrow's mind the word *purity*, though he doesn't know why.

He returns his attention to the girl's face, but the word that would capture the essence of the Look is not *purity*.

"Time to eat," says Moongirl.

"In a little while," the child replies.

"No, baby. Now."

Harrow is intrigued by this mother-daughter relationship because in it lie the answers with which he might unravel the tightest knots of Moongirl's madness.

In a tone suggesting the steel sheathed in her soft voice, she calls her daughter by the only name she has ever given her: "Piggy, it's time to eat."

Reluctantly the child sets the doll aside, puts down the needle and thread, and pulls the tray in front of her.

For the first time since they entered the room, Moongirl looks at Harrow. In her green gaze is something more intensely felt than mere triumph, something sharper than savage glee, and a far colder satisfaction than Harrow has ever seen in other eyes.

When she is naked and riding him in the windowless room, this is perhaps the very gaze with which she favors him in absolute darkness.

He meets her stare, confident that she will not read in him any attitude that will annoy or offend her.

Virtue and *vice* are empty words. His well-considered philosophy has led him to deny such words authority over him; her insanity has brought her to the same rejection of all values, for in the chaos of existence, madness is a legitimate path to enlightenment.

Actions are either taken or not taken, consequences incurred or not incurred, and no meaning can be found in any of it.

Moongirl had accused him of pity.

But he does not pity the child. He is merely intrigued by her perseverance, by the devices with which she endures her suffering.

Piggy lifts the top slice of bread off her sandwich and lays it aside. She examines both sides of the lettuce leaf and places it on the bread.

Smiling, Moongirl retrieves from the floor the doll that she displaced when she first sat in the chair beside the desk.

Solemnly, Piggy examines the tomato, the ham, the cheese, and the bottom slice of bread, disassembling her sandwich and rebuilding it upside down.

Sandwiches sometimes contain the unexpected. A rusty nail that gouges the gums. A live worm. A dead cockroach.

The child does not know that Harrow made this ham-and-cheese delight. She must assume that her mother put it together.

Finding nothing unwholesome, Piggy picks up her sandwich in both hands and takes a bite.

Pretending to have no interest in her daughter's meal, Moongirl examines the beautifully dressed doll that she retrieved from the floor.

In spite of her intellectual limitations, Piggy is, at a modest level, an effective autodidact. She has some talent for art and has taught herself both to draw and to compose visually striking collages from pictures that she clips out of magazines.

Among the crafts she's taught herself are sewing and embroidery. When they moved into this place, Piggy found an elaborate sewing kit and hundreds of spools of thread left behind by the former owners. By painstaking trial and error, by what Harrow supposes might be called a simpleton's intuition, she has developed this skill with which she fills the lonely hours.

Now, from the clutter of seamstress tools on the desk, Moongirl selects a small pair of scissors with thin, sharply pointed blades. She uses them to snip at the finished embroidery on the doll's dress. She works both sides of the cloth, and soon she has a small colorful pile of cut threads that she has pulled loose from the garment.

Piggy wisely makes no comment about this destruction of her work. She gives no indication that she even sees what her mother is doing.

"Sandwich good?" Moongirl asks.

"Good," says Piggy.

If Moongirl really intends to set her daughter afire tomorrow night, this is one of the last opportunities she will have to torment the child. She will not waste it.

"Have some potato salad," she says.

Piggy makes a wordless sound of agreement, but instead of prying the lid off the container, she takes another bite of the sandwich.

Considering all the places Harrow might have been if he had made different choices, he is fortunate to be here, now, for this. He had once thought that only money mattered. But he has since discovered that money matters only because it can buy power, and power matters only if it is exercised with imagination and without conscience.

More than anyone he has ever met, Moongirl understands power, the possibilities of it, the beauty of it, and the art with which it must be employed in order to achieve the most satisfying effects.

She says, "It's really good potato salad, Piggy."

Because the world turns and the world changes, the shutter-piercing blade of sunlight should have moved off the cut-glass vase by now, but still it inspires within the bevels a pattern of crimson thorns.

"Piggy?"

For the first time, Harrow notices that the prisms in the vase separate the blue and yellow wavelengths out of the sunshine and translate them to the ceiling. Above the girl, an auroral luminosity shimmers on the plaster.

Moongirl is staring at her daughter with feral intensity. The veins are swollen in her temples.

Tomorrow night, the fire, but now the fireworks.

Chapter

31

When he saw the man step out of the Quonset hut, a tiny figure nearly a quarter-mile away, Bobby Onions eased up on the accelerator and coasted forward.

"Who is the guy?" he asked.

Vern said, "He calls himself Eliot Rosewater."

"You don't think that's his name?"

"No."

"What's it say on the check?"

"He pays cash."

Slowly the Land Rover rocked across a series of potholes.

When Bobby consulted the rearview mirror, Vern knew what he would see. They had traveled little more than a quarter of a mile from the county road, but it looked like a long way back.

Directly ahead, the board-flat plain began to rise to foothills about a thousand yards beyond the buildings. To the east, the land dwindled into a haze of dust, and far away to the west, it melted into the declining sun.

Bobby asked, "Why's the meet have to be in such a godforsaken place?"

"The desert has its own stark beauty," Vern said.

"What're you—pimping for the Mojave Chamber of Commerce?"

"Come on, Bobby, pick up some speed. He's waiting."

The land was as colorless as concrete, and most of the sun-parched vegetation bristled gray, except for swaths of struggling purple sage.

"Too lonely," Bobby said.

"Will you relax? He doesn't want to risk being seen with me. I committed a couple felonies for him today—remember? And since I'd rather not lose my PI license, discretion is fine with me, too."

In these last hours of the day, the desert light hammered down through the parched air as hard as it had done at noon. The gnarled and stunted mesquite resembled wrought-iron sculpture, and the curved profiles of the Quonsets had edges sharp enough to cut the sky.

"Besides," Vern said, "he's not gonna leave his plane untended out here just so we can all meet in a cozy doughnut shop. I've dealt with him before. It's all right."

"When before?"

"Eight months ago. I searched this architect's place for him."

"What architect?"

"That's already more than you need to know."

"Back then, the rally was here?"

"The meet was here, yeah."

"You didn't use me. Who'd you use for backup?"

Vern sighed. "If you have to know, it was Dirk Cutter."

"For God's sake, Vern, he's brain-dead. You'd use Dirk Cutter before you'd call me?"

"At least that's his real name, he didn't change it. I used him be-cause he had a four-wheel drive. You didn't have the Rover then."

"Yeah. All right. I was still driving that crappy Honda."

"And my Chevy couldn't handle this terrain. How do you afford a Rover, anyway?"

Bobby grinned and winked. "A grateful lady."

Wincing, Vern said, "I don't want to hear about it."

"I'll tell you on the way home," Bobby promised, and pressed gently on the accelerator. "So why the architect?"

"You never shut up, do you? You never stop."

"I'm a procto. I bore right in. I'm all curiosity."

Because he didn't want to give Bobby the satisfaction of asking him what *procto* meant, and because he worried that he *would* ask him if he didn't say something else, Vern relented: "The architect has a thing with the bounce. This guy wanted to know all about him because he was dating the bounce."

"The bounce from today?" Bobby asked.

"What other bounce do I know?"

Letting their speed fall, Bobby said, "He wants to know about the architect because the architect's bouncing the bounce, then eight months later he has you do a job on the bounce. What's that about?"

"I don't know."

"It's real interesting, isn't it?"

"Not that interesting," Vern said.

"You could ask him."

"If he didn't tell me up front, it's none of my business. You don't ask the client why."

"Get out of the Stone Age, Vern. He's *the wallet*."

"The client, the wallet—it doesn't matter. I don't ask if he doesn't volunteer."

"Where's he fly in from?"

"I don't know. I don't care."

"It's really mysterious, isn't it?"

"Not that mysterious," Vern said. "And don't *you* ask him any-thing, either. You do, he won't throw more business my way."

"He must pay well."

"Brilliant deduction. I don't agree to burglarize a place for chump change."

"The plane's too far away to read the registration number."

"Forget about the plane. You're making me crazy."

As Bobby braked to a stop near the Quonset hut, he said, "Hey, he's a nobody."

"He pays like a somebody."

"I mean, he's harmless. He's a fat-faced bald guy like you."

"The lady is an idiot."

"What lady?"

"The grateful one behind the Rover."

Bobby actually glanced at the rearview mirror, as if expecting to see a woman standing behind them, and then said, "Oh. Yeah. Well, she's not an idiot, but she's not that smart, either."

Carrying the white trash bag that contained everything he had confiscated at Redwing's house, Vernon Lesley walked forward from the Land Rover. "Mr. Rosewater, I hope we didn't keep you waiting."

"No, no, Mr. Lesley. I like the desert. The air's invigorating."

The air was hot, dry enough to chap lips in thirty seconds, and tainted by both an alkaline trace odor and exotic desert pollen that made Vern's eyes burn.

He had not been born for the outdoors. He didn't much like the indoors, either. He just wanted to get this finished, go home, and step into Second Life, where there were no tarantulas or scorpions.

He had forgotten to tell Bobby Onions to stay in the Rover, and now the procto swaggered forward to join them.

Eliot Rosewater had the good sense to pretend that Bobby wasn't there. "Did you find what I hoped, Mr. Lesley?"

Tendering the trash bag, Vern said, "Yes, sir, and maybe a bit more than you hoped for."

"Splendid," Rosewater said, accepting the bag. "She would have taken pains to hide evidence of her past."

"Nobody could've used a finer comb in that bungalow than I did, Mr. Rosewater. I didn't miss anything."

"You're quite sure."

"I value your business, sir. I'm dead sure."

Bobby started to say something that would no doubt have been inane, and then his head exploded.

Maybe Vern heard a sound issue from within the nearest Quonset hut or saw a glimmer of movement in the darkness beyond the open door, because a split second before Bobby's skull came apart, Vern was reaching under his shirt for the holstered revolver in the small of his back.

While the blood spray still hung in the air, he squatted and squeezed off three rounds through the open door.

Rosewater flung himself down, and rolled, as though he'd had some experience at this kind of thing.

Vern wanted to run to him and stand over him and pop him, but he couldn't be sure that he had hit the shooter in the hut, and if he lingered, he would be making an easy target of himself.

The engine of the Land Rover had been switched off. Bobby probably had not left the keys in the ignition.

For a quarter of an instant, Vern considered running away among the buildings, but these guys knew the layout better than he did, and any cat-and-mouse game wasn't likely to turn out well for him.

Instead, he sprinted west, directly into the low sun, because the glare would make him a harder target.

The plain offered no hiding place, but Vern was faster than he looked. Maybe fifteen years younger and thirty pounds lighter than Rosewater, he was confident of being able to outrun him.

If the shooter in the hut had not been wounded by the return fire, if he gave pursuit, Vern might be in trouble, but he didn't glance back because he wanted to have hope.

He ran as fast as he had ever run, heart slamming, and then he demanded more of himself. In the still air, he created a wind of his own. Without realizing what he was doing, he had raised his arms, trying to get some lift.

But Vern Lesley didn't have wings. Von Longwood had the wings, over there in Second Life, where he owned a car that could fly, too, and where he sometimes enjoyed sex four times a day.

Hope shaken, he glanced back and saw a guy closing on him. His pursuer looked as young as Bobby Onions but bigger and smarter.

Von Longwood didn't take crap from anyone, and if Vern had to go down, he preferred to do it with Von's style. He stopped, swiveled, and squeezed off all of the remaining rounds in his revolver.

The pursuer didn't weave or dodge but came boldly through the deadly horizontal hail, as if *he* were the real Von Longwood.

Now Vern's only hope was the Rapture, float straight up to Heaven without a change of underwear or breath mints, but that didn't work out, either. A bullet burst his gut, another knocked the air out of him, and he rode a third round into oblivion.

Chapter

32

After coming up the stairs and through the door, the dogs did what dogs do: immediately went on a tour of the apartment, scouting the territory, by the nose alone taking in more information than did human beings with all five senses.

Brian was not surprised to see that Nickie, although the newest member of the pack, had already assumed its leadership.

Following the dogs through the door, Amy said, "What's wrong?"

When he called her, he had not been entirely coherent. Now he said, "Come with me. The kitchen. I want to show you."

Hurrying after him, she said, "Now you've *really* got bed hair. You look like you slept in a hurricane."

"I was drawing. Hours and hours, drawing. I was exhausted. Laid down. Fell asleep. Had a dream."

In the kitchen, he took her by the shoulders and met her eyes. "You know me. You know who I am."

"You're Brian McCarthy. You're an architect."

"Exactly."

"Is this a test to see if I have Alzheimer's?"

"Okay. Listen. Am I practical? Am I prudent? Am I levelheaded? Am I gullible?"

"Yes. Yes. Yes. No."

"Am I smart? Am I a bright guy?"

"Smart. Bright. Guy. Three for three."

"I'm sober, right? I'm rational, right? I'm not given to wild superstition, am I?"

"Right. Right. No."

"I never believe in stuff like Antoine."

Clearly puzzled, she asked, "Antoine who?"

"Antoine," he said impatiently, "Antoine, the blind driving dog in the Philippines."

"Antoine isn't blind."

"You said he was blind."

"*Marco* is blind, not the dog."

"Whatever. It doesn't matter."

"It matters to Antoine and Marco."

"The point is, I'm a skeptic."

"Marco drives. Antoine directs him."

"See? That's nuts. Dogs can't talk."

"It's a psychic thing."

He took a deep breath. "Are you like this with everyone?"

"Like what?"

"Crazy-making."

"Not with everyone. Mostly with you."

He frowned. "Did you just tell me something important?"

"What do you think?"

"I think you did. What was it?"

"You're a smart, bright, sober, rational, levelheaded, kinda cute architect. You figure it out."

His head was spinning too much to crunch the meaning out of her words. He just kissed her.

"Too much is happening," he said. "Let's stay focused. Come here. Look at these."

He led her to the kitchen table on which were stacked all of his drawings, in the order that he had executed them.

Smiling at the top picture, she said, "That's Nickie."

"Is that what you see?"

"Isn't it Nickie? It looks just like her."

"But is that *all* you see?"

"What more do you expect me to see?"

"I don't know."

"Sweetie, I'm no art critic."

"There's something about her eyes."

"Something like what?"

"Something . . ."

When Brian set aside the top drawing, revealing the second, Amy said, "A closeup."

"Closer and closer." He paged through the stack of drawings.

"When did you do these?"

"After you dropped me off."

"All these since then? Is that possible?"

"No. It isn't."

She looked up from the drawings.

"It isn't possible," he said. "Not this many drawings, this detailed, in so few hours."

"What're you saying?"

"Damn if I know."

Extraordinary things had happened, were happening, but he lacked the frame of reference to articulate properly what he had

experienced or what he felt about it. Until now he had led an ordinary life in which, with the principles of architecture, he had
striven to impose order on the chaos of existence. Now chaos had
overwhelmed him, and though he sensed a new order under it, he
could not see through the tumult of the moment to the meaning
beneath.

Glancing at the clock, at the drawings, at the clock, at Amy, he
said, "This feeling. Like something stepped into me."

"Into you. What something?"

"And took me outside of time. I don't even know what I mean by
that. I was here in the kitchen. But I wasn't. I was drawing, but it
wasn't really me drawing. I saw something in Nickie's eyes, and my
visitor, whatever stepped into me, was trying to help me portray
what I saw."

"You saw something in Nickie's eyes? What do you mean?
What did you see in her eyes?"

"I don't know. I felt it so strongly. Something." He spread out
the last four drawings, the most abstract of the images, so that
they could be studied together. "What do you see, Amy? What do
you see?"

"Light, shadow, shapes."

"They mean something. What do they mean?"

"I don't know. They're beautiful."

"Are they? I think so, too. But why? Why are they beautiful?"

"They just are."

"You said 'shapes.' What shapes do you see?" Brian pressed.

"Just shapes, forms. Shadow and light. Nothing real."

"It's something real," he disagreed. "I just can't quite draw it. It's
almost there on the page, but it eludes me."

"What else has happened, Brian? What're you so agitated about?"

"I'm not agitated. I'm excited, I'm amazed, I'm mystified, I'm scared, but I'm not agitated."

"Well, you've got *me* all agitated."

"Hallucinations. I guess that's what they must've been. Auditory hallucinations. Because I was exhausted. This terrible sound. I can't describe it. Terrible but at the same time . . . wonderful."

With the mention of hallucinations, he expected her to look at him askance, but she did not. Intuition told him that she had a story of her own to tell.

"And shadows," he continued. "Quick shadows, passing and gone. And no apparent source. My eyes ached. I thought I needed sleep. Come on. I have to show you this."

"Show me what?"

As he took her hand and led her out of the kitchen, into the hallway, he said, "The bedroom. The bed."

"Whoa, whoa there, Mr. Hormones. You're not going to agitate me between the sheets."

"I know that. Who would know that better than me? This isn't about that. This is astonishing." He led her into his bedroom, to the foot of the bed. "See?"

"See what?"

"It's perfect."

"What is?"

"The bed. Perfectly made, neat and tidy, not a wrinkle."

"Congratulations. If I had a merit badge, I'd pin it on you with a flourish of trumpets."

"I'm not explaining this very well."

"Give it another shot," she suggested.

"I was born in Kansas."

"That's really starting at the beginning."

"In Kansas, in a tornado."

"I've heard the story."

"I don't have any memory of that night."

"Birth was boring? You couldn't pay attention?"

"I've heard about it, of course. A thousand times, from Grandma Nicholson and from my mother."

On a windy night, a week before everyone's expectations, Brian's mother, Angela, had gone into labor. Her water broke shortly before midnight, and she woke Brian's father, John. He was dressing to drive her to the hospital when sirens sounded a tornado warning.

Angela's mother, Cora Nicholson, was staying with them, having traveled from Wichita to be of assistance after the birth. By the time she, her daughter, and her son-in-law stepped out of the house, heading for the car, the wind had escalated from gusts to gale.

The sky, as black and evil as a dragon's egg, broke open and spilled sharp electric-white gouts of yolk. In an instant the dusty air reeked of ozone and oncoming rain.

"In the dream," Brian said, "I was an observer. Not part of the action. Have you ever had a dream in which you weren't part of it, you were just observing other people?"

"I don't know. Maybe. Come to think of it . . . maybe not."

"I don't remember having a dream like that before," Brian said.

As Cora, Angela, and John reached the old Pontiac, shatters of rain rattled down on them with such force that the droplets stung the skin and bounced high off the hard earth.

"I wasn't part of the dream, just the audience. I didn't speak to anyone, didn't interact with anyone, and nobody saw me. Yet I was immersed in it with all my senses. I felt the rain snapping against me, the wet of it, cold rain for such a warm night. Scraps of green leaves, torn off trees, kept slapping my face, sticking to my skin."

Behind the crash of the rain rose a greater sound, not thunder, a continuous roar, growing in volume, like a score of passing trains.

"The wall of the tornado, the whirling wall," Brian said, "out there in the blind dark, concealed, approaching, not on top of us yet but not far off."

Their storm cellar was twenty yards from the house, and Cora, who had experience of these things back in Wichita, urged them to forget the car, to run for the shelter.

If Angela was going to deliver the baby in the storm cellar, John wanted clean towels, rubbing alcohol to sterilize the knife with which he would cut the cord, and other items. Cora argued against his returning to the house, but he said he'd be a minute, less than a minute, no time at all.

Brian said, "I ran with Mom and Grandma to an embankment. The grass was slick underfoot, not like in a dream. Intensely real, Amy. Sound, color, texture, smell. There was an open stone vestibule built into the slope. The shelter door stood at the back of it."

Brian had turned to look toward the house, and surprisingly the windows had been still bright with light.

Suddenly lightning broke not in bolts but in cascades, did not step jaggedly down the night as usual, but lashed through the dark like broad undulant whips of chain mail.

Those celestial flares revealed the twister immediately beyond the house, towering over it, the immense black wall churning, like a living beast, as amorphous as any monster in myth, rising up and up and still up, so high into the night that the top of it could not be glimpsed.

All the windows burst at once. The house disintegrated. The funnel seemed to suck up every shard of glass, every scrap of wood, every nail, and John McCarthy, whose body would never be found.

"My mother and grandmother had gone into the cellar and

closed the door," Brian said. "I was outside, watching a tree being pulled up by the roots—such a *sound* that made, a creaking scream—and then I was somehow inside the shelter with them."

At the last moment, Cora had looked back, had seen the house taken and no sign of her son-in-law. She had closed out the chaos and had driven home the six thick bolts that held every edge of the door to the header, jamb, and threshold.

Wind married thunder, birthing ten thousand clamorous off-spring. Previously Brian had heard a sound like a score of trains, but now all the trains in the world were converging on a single inter-section of tracks directly over their bunker.

In that small refuge, brightened by one flashlight, the ceiling and the walls transmitted vibrations from the punished earth above, and dust sifted down, and the hordes of Hell howled at the door and tested the bolts that held it.

Perhaps accelerated by terror, Angela's contractions brought her to the moment of delivery quicker than Cora expected. With the funnel having passed but with the storm still raging overhead, frightened for her unborn child, weeping for her husband, Angela gave birth.

Cora pulled a Coleman lantern from a shelf, lit it, and by that eerie gaslight, she delivered her grandson with a calm and skill that had not been lost with the generations of her family who had first settled the plains above.

"In the dream, I watched myself be born," Brian said. "I was a wrinkled, red-faced, cranky little bundle."

"Some things don't change," Amy observed.

Because not all twisters descend with suddenness, because some storm watches can last hours, the cellar had been furnished with two old mattresses on frames. Angela delivered her baby on one of these, and the cover was wet with amniotic fluid, blood, and afterbirth.

Cora unpacked plastic-wrapped blankets from a shelf, dressed the clean mattress, and encouraged her daughter to transfer to it with the newborn.

As it turned out, the storm had piled a great weight of debris against the shelter door, and they would have to wait nine hours for rescuers to locate and extract them.

"So my grandmother," Brian said, "dressed the mattress with what little she had, but with as much care as if it were a guestroom bed being prepared for an important visitor. When she finished tucking the covers around my mother and me—the infant me— it was a perfect little nest, so neat, so tidy, so cozy. She smoothed the wrinkles out of the blanket, smoothed them with such tenderness, smiling down at my mother. . . ."

The scene still lived in his memory as no scene from a dream had ever before endured.

Amy said, *"And then?"*

"Oh. Yeah. Suddenly I'm not an observer of the dream, I'm a part of it, I'm the baby, gazing up at my grandmother. She smiles down at me and her eyes are amazing, so full of love, so much more vivid than anything else in the most vivid dream I've ever had. And she winks. The last thing I saw was Grandma's wink. Then I woke up. And that's the incredible thing. The bed is like you see it now. Perfectly made. I'm lying on top of the covers, and the bed is neat enough to pass a military inspection."

He expected amazement. She stared at him.

"All right, see, when you hauled me out of here last night to go save a dog from a crazy-drunk-violent guy, I left the bed a mess. And when I crashed for a nap this afternoon, it was still a mess."

"So?"

"Spread hanging over the footboard, sheets tangled, a pillow on the floor. But I wake up, and the bed's been made under me, as if my grandmother in the dream turned around and straightened up *this* one after getting my mother and baby-me settled."

"'Baby-me'?"

"Come on, Amy. You understand what I'm saying."

"Do you ever sleepwalk?"

"No. Why?"

"Maybe you made the bed in your sleep."

"I didn't. I couldn't. That's impossible."

"Yeah. It makes much more sense that your dead grandmother came out of a dream and made it for you."

Eye to eye with her, he chewed for a moment on his lower lip, and then he said, "Why are you being like this?"

"I'm not being like anything. I'm just being practical, prudent, levelheaded, smart, sober, and rational."

He took a deep breath. He blew it out. "What if, okay, what if I believe Antoine the blind dog can drive?"

"The *dog* isn't blind."

Brian put his hands on her shoulders again. "It's not just the bed, Amy. It's the uncanny vividness of the dream, so bright and so detailed, like real life, and being shown the night I was born. It's the way those drawings flowed *through* me, just poured out of the pencil. And the hallucinations—that sound, those shadows— except they were not hallucinations. Amy, something is happening here."

She put one hand to his face, feeling his beard stubble. "Have you eaten anything today?"

"No. I drank a Red Bull. I'm not hungry."

"Sweetie, why don't I make you something to eat?"

"I'm not hallucinating from hunger, Amy. If you could have seen Grandma's eyes, that *wink*."

"I'll make pasta. You have a jar of that terrific pesto sauce?"

Brian leaned closer to her and narrowed his eyes. He could tell that she wanted to look away from him and that she didn't dare.

"Something's happened to you, too," he said. "You *do* have a story of your own. I thought so earlier. What's happened?"

"Nothing."

"Something."

"Just a thing," she said uneasily.

"What thing?"

"It's just the way Nickie is."

"What way is she?"

"Watchful. Wise. Mysterious. I don't know. Actually, it's not even new. Sometimes you get a dog and you think, *This is an old soul.* "

"Come on. What else, Amy?"

"Nothing. Really. Just a bedroom-slipper thing."

She was fingering the cameo locket at her throat. When she saw him take note of it, she lowered her hand.

"Bedroom-slipper thing? Tell me."

"I can't. Not now. It's nothing. It couldn't be anything."

"Now I *am* agitated," he said.

Looking toward the hall, she said, "Where are the kids?"

As she started to turn away from him, he grabbed her by the arm. "Wait. Waking up on top of a freshly made bed isn't the big thing. I haven't told you the big thing."

"What—did Grandma do your laundry, too?"

He felt as though his heart were coming loose in his chest and sliding lower by the moment.

"This is going to be hard. I'm sick to my stomach trying to think how to tell you. It's a wonderful thing and a terrible thing."

A change in her eyes, the steadiness and clarity of her stare, suggested that she knew he needed her as never before and that she was ready.

He kissed her forehead, and with his lips still against her brow, he said, "I love you."

Head bowed, not looking up, as if the words were as solemn as a prayer, she said, "I love you, too."

They had gotten this far months ago, but no further. He had assumed that the next step, which seemed *excruciatingly* overdue, would be consummation, the physical commitment.

No one before her had ever held him in expectation with such exquisite charm.

Now he realized that consummation had never been the next step, could not have been, *should not* have been. The next step must be revelation.

"Come with me," he said, and led her to his study.

All three dogs were waiting there, lying quietly together, as though they knew—or as though one of them knew—that the supreme test of Brian and Amy's relationship would occur in this room.

His apartment study had two wheeled office chairs for those occasions when one of his employees came from downstairs to work here with him. He rolled both behind his desk.

He directed Amy into one chair, and he sat facing her in the other. They were knee to knee.

In their front-row seats, Fred, Ethel, and Nickie watched with grave interest.

When Brian held out his hands, palms up, Amy at once put her hands in his, giving him the courage to speak. "There's something I should've told you, Amy. Long ago. But I thought, the way things were, maybe I'd never need to tell you."

When he hesitated, she did not press him. Her hands had not gone damp in his, or cold. Her gaze remained steady.

"When I was younger, much younger, I was an idiot about a lot of things. One of them was sex. I thought it was easy, women were a kind of sport. God, that sounds awful. But it's the way so many of us came out of college in those days. Life had nothing to teach me. That's what I thought."

"But it never stops teaching," she said.

"No. It's one long lesson. So . . . there were a number of women, too many. I left all the precautions to them, because they seemed to think it was a sport, too. I knew they wouldn't risk pregnancy. They didn't want consequences. They just wanted to get it off. But one of them was . . . different. Vanessa. We weren't together long, but she didn't take precautions. I fathered a child."

His mouth had gone dry. His throat felt swollen, a trap to keep in all his words.

"I think about my daughter every day. I lie awake at night wondering—is she all right, is she ever given a chance to be happy, is she at least safe? With Vanessa . . . she can't be safe. I tried to find her. I couldn't. I've failed as a father, as a man, at the fundamental things."

Amy said, "No failure is forever."

"It feels like forever. I've only seen her once, briefly, when she was an infant. How can I love a child so much when I've only seen her once?"

"The important thing is, you can. You've got that capacity in you."

"She's a Down's syndrome girl," he said. "I thought she looked like an angel, beautiful. I doubt she even knows I exist. I've wanted to see her so bad, for ten years I've wanted to see her, but I never expected to see her again. And now . . . everything is changing."

Amy squeezed his hands and said, "Not everything. There's still you and me."

PART TWO

"The woods are lovely, dark, and deep,
But I have promises to keep"

—ROBERT FROST
Stopping by Woods on a Snowy Evening

Chapter

33

The bedspread is tight and tucked, the pillows plumped. No dust dulls any surface.

Piggy is required to keep her room clean, and periodically her mother conducts an inspection with stern standards and with sterner punishments.

Harrow suspects that the child would keep a spotless room even if she were not required to do so. The threat of chastisement is not what guarantees her cleanliness.

She exhibits a desire for order, for quiet continuity, and a longing for fixity in all affairs. This is evident in the way she marshals the images in her collages and in the classic patterns of decoration that, with thread and needles, she applies to the dresses of the dolls.

"Piggy, you can't eat just the sandwich," says Moongirl. "You don't know what a balanced diet means, but I do. Have some potato salad."

"I will," Piggy replies, but she still makes no move toward the plastic container.

In Moongirl's company, the child seldom raises her head, and she rarely makes eye contact. She knows that her mother wants humility from her, and self-abasement.

As with the yearning for order, humility is not something Piggy learned to please her mother. This quality is as natural to her as feathers to a bird.

Self-abasement, on the other hand, she resists. She has a quiet dignity that should not have survived ten years like those she has endured.

She accepts the scorn, the insults, the meanness that her mother visits upon her, every affront and vexation, as though it is what she deserves, but she refuses to disgrace herself. She can be dishonored by another but never abased.

Harrow suspects that the girl's innate dignity, free of pride, is what has kept her alive. Her mother recognizes this quality in her and wants, more than anything, to destroy it before she destroys the child.

To please Moongirl, this breaking must precede the burning; the spirit must be fatally wounded before the flesh is fed to fire.

Now Piggy opens a lunchbox bag of potato chips, and her mother says, "That's why you're fat."

The child neither hesitates nor stuffs the chips into her mouth defiantly. She proceeds calmly with her meal, head down.

With greater diligence, Moongirl rips out the needlework from the doll's dress.

Piggy is permitted to have these toys only so they can be taken from her as punishment. So it is with all she has.

Each time Moongirl sees that the child has grown fond of one doll above the others, she acts. She seems to have determined that the one on which she now works is such a favorite.

Sometimes, the child cries quietly. She never sobs. Her lower lip trembles, the tears roll down her face, and that is all.

Harrow is certain that often, if not always, the tears are false, summoned with an effort. Piggy knows that tears are wanted, that her mother is a creature who feeds on tears.

This is metaphorically true, but it is also a fact. He has never seen Moongirl kiss her daughter, but twice he has seen her lick tears from the corners of the child's eyes.

If Piggy did not occasionally give her mother a reward of tears, she might be dead by now. The tears have suggested to Moongirl that in time her daughter can be broken; and it is this breaking that she desires more than all else, for which she has been patient.

The pent-up violence in Moongirl is like the megadeath condensed in the perfect sphere of plutonium in a nuclear weapon. When a blast is finally triggered, the explosion will be awesome.

Having cut most of the needlework out of the doll's dress, she now rends the dress itself, not with the scissors but with her bare hands, grinding her teeth with satisfaction as she rips each seam.

Perhaps she has begun to suspect that her daughter's dignity can never be taken from her. This would explain why she might commit to burning Piggy tomorrow night.

Although Harrow is an imaginative man, his imagination fails him when he tries to envision the horrors that this woman will visit on her daughter before setting her afire. After ten years of unslaked thirst for infanticide and then parricide, Moongirl will surely make a memorable spectacle of Piggy's final hours.

At the desk, the child opens the bag of cookies, again passing on the potato salad. She has an instinct for her mother's traps.

Moongirl now holds a naked doll. Its limbs are articulated so that it can be manipulated into almost any position. But when she bends an elbow joint backward, she snaps off one of the forearms.

"Fat little cookie-sucking mouth," she says.

Harrow finds ruthlessness erotic.

"Piggy at the trough."

Power is the only thing that he admires, the only thing that matters, and violence—emotional, psychological, physical, verbal violence—is the purest expression of power. Absolute violence is absolute power.

Watching Moongirl now, he wants in the worst way to take her down into their windowless room, into their perfect darkness, where they can do what they are, be what they do, down in the grasping greedy dark, down in the urgent animal dark.

Chapter

34

I n the sky's distillery, the afternoon light was a weak brandy.
Standing at a study window, Brian said, "She seemed like a free spirit—bold, edgy, but fun. After we'd been together awhile, I began to realize something was wrong with her."

Amy had sampled Vanessa's e-mails. The ten-year collection was large. She got the flavor from a few, and didn't care to read more.

"I wanted to end it, but she had this magnetism." In disgust, he repeated, "*Magnetism*. Truth. She was hot, totally hot, and I knew she was unstable, but I was weak. That's the sick truth."

He had begun this account facing Amy, but even ten years after these events, shame led him to prefer to confess to the window.

She wanted to move behind him, put a hand on his waist, and let him know this changed nothing between them. But perhaps he needed his self-disgust to be able to purge himself of these secrets; she sensed that her affection might weaken his resolve, that he was aware of this, that she must trust him to know when he could face her again.

Fred and Ethel snoozed back to back, bookends without a book. Nickie remained awake, more interested than she pretended to be.

"I never imagined she wanted a child," Brian said. "Of the women I knew back then, she was the least likely to pine for motherhood."

If Amy should not touch him just now, she could stand at another window, sharing the pre-twilight view to which he unburdened himself.

"When she got pregnant, it was an ugly scene. But not how you might expect. She said she wanted my baby, *needed* it, she said, but she never wanted to see me again."

"Don't you have common-law rights or something?"

"I tried to discuss that with her, but all she wanted to talk about was how I took the crown as the world's biggest loser."

"If that's what she thought of you, why did she want your baby?"

"It was weird. She was vicious. Such contempt, loathing. She ripped my taste in clothes, music, books, my financial prospects, everything—some true, some not. I had to get away from her."

The westering sun fired the intricacies of a fretwork of clouds. The majesty of the light and sky was a striking contrast to the base story that he had to tell.

"I expected her to call. She didn't. Told myself good riddance, it wasn't any of my business now. But some things she'd said about me had the sting of truth. I didn't like what I saw in mirrors anymore. I kept thinking of the baby she was carrying, my baby."

Whatever faults he had in those days, he'd grown into a good man. Later, he might want to hear that from her, but not now.

"I needed a month to realize, if I didn't have that baby in my life, then my life would never be right. It would be distorted, more distorted every year. So I called Vanessa. She'd changed her phone number. I went to her apartment. Moved. No forwarding address."

Amy remembered he had once seen the baby. "But you found her."

"Three months I tried mutual acquaintances. She wasn't seeing them anymore. Pulled up all her roots. Eventually I got some money for a private detective. Even he had some trouble tracking her down."

Spilling across the clouds from the tipped snifter of the sun, the light was a richer shade of brandy than before, and the blue sky itself began to take some of the stain.

"She had a huge, expensive apartment overlooking Newport Harbor. A wealthy land developer named Parker Hisscus was paying the rent."

"That's a big name around here."

"She was six months pregnant when I visited her. Gave me five minutes, so I could see the style he kept her in. Then she had the maid show me out. Next morning, a friend of Hisscus came to see me."

"He was that obvious?"

"I don't mean muscle. The guy was unsavory but polite. Wanted me to know Hisscus would marry the lady after the birth of their baby."

"If it was *their* baby, why wait?"

"I wondered. And then this guy offers me a commission—a custom home to design for another friend of Hisscus."

"If it were his baby, he wouldn't try to buy it that way."

"I turned down the commission. Went to an attorney. Then another attorney. Same story from both. If Vanessa and Hisscus say he's the dad, I have no grounds to push for a DNA test."

Threads of self-disgust and quiet anger had been sewn through Brian's voice thus far, but now Amy heard something like sorrow, too.

"I kept trying to find a way, and then one night she came to my place with the baby not two weeks old, born premature. She said . . ."

For a moment, he could not repeat Vanessa's words to him.

Then: "She said, 'Here's what you pumped into me. This stupid little freak. Your stupid little freak has screwed up everything.'"

"So it was over with her and Hisscus."

"I never understood what was going on there anyway. But it was over, it wasn't his baby, and she was out. She wanted money, whatever I could pay for the baby. I showed her my checkbook, savings-account balance. So there I was, made a baby and put it in a situation where it's up for sale, I'm no better than she was."

"Not true," Amy said at once. "You wanted the girl."

"I couldn't get the money till morning, but she wouldn't leave the baby with me. She was crazy bitter. Her eyes were more black than green, something so dark had come into them. I wanted to take the baby, but I was afraid if I tried, she'd kill it, smash its head. She needed money, so I thought she'd bring the baby back for it."

"But she never did."

"No. She never did. God help me, out of fear, I let her walk away that night, take my baby away."

"And she's been tormenting you ever since."

The low orange candle of the sun spread the warm intoxicating light farther across the western sky.

"Unless it's a federal case with the FBI," Brian said, "it's not possible to track somebody from an e-mail address. I can't prove I'm the girl's father. Vanessa's careful what she says in the e-mails."

"And private investigators haven't been able to find her?"

"No. She lives way off the grid, maybe under a new name, new Social Security number, new everything. Anyway, what she's done to me doesn't matter. But what has she done to my daughter? What has she done to Hope?"

By intuition, Amy understood his last question. "That's what you've named her—Hope."

"Yes."

"Whatever Vanessa's done," Amy said, "what's important now is, you might get a chance to make it right."

This was the "big thing" of which he'd spoken earlier, bigger than the drawings that he had done of Nickie's eyes, bigger than the auditory hallucinations and the mysterious shadows he had glimpsed at the periphery of vision, bigger than his dream and waking up on the inexplicably made bed. After ten years, he might be able to get his daughter back.

Amy had read his e-mail to Vanessa, in which he avoided argument and manipulation: *I am at your mercy. I have no power over you, and you have every power over me. If one day you will let me have what I want, that will be because it serves you best to relent, not because I have earned it or deserve it.*

After waking from his dream of storm-racked Kansas, Brian had found a reply from her. He held it in his hand now, as he stood at the window.

You still want your little piglet? You piss me off, there in your cozy life, everything the way you like it, never sacrificed a damn thing. You want this little freak on your back? All right. I'm ready for that. But I want something from you. Stand by.

The quality of light had changed enough to permit upon the pane a transparent reflection of Amy's face.

With his secrets all revealed, and with his own face forming on the glass before him, Brian turned now toward Amy.

She joined him at his window and took his hand.

He said, "She's going to want every dime, everything I own."

Smiling, Amy repeated, in this new context, what she had said earlier. "Not everything. There's still you and me."

Chapter

35

The severed limbs, the headless torso, the eyeless head, and the pried-out glass eyes of the doll are arranged beside the lunch tray on the desk, where Moongirl carefully placed them.

Not once during the dismemberment and beheading did Piggy appear to notice the destruction her mother was committing. Now she ignores the ruins.

Harrow suspects that, this time, Piggy has outwitted her mother. Instead of giving the most elaborate dress of her creation to her favorite doll, perhaps she has given it to her least favorite.

This is a small triumph, but in the child's life, there is no other kind.

If Moongirl realizes that she has been deceived, she will make Piggy pay dearly. Even now, Harrow can see how the woman struggles to contain her fury at the child's indifference to the savaging of the doll.

Like Harrow, Moongirl has the cold intellect of a machine and a body that is machinelike in the perfection of its form and function, but she only pretends to understand and control her emotions as Harrow understands and controls his.

The range of her emotions is limited to anger, hatred, envy, greed, desire, and self-love. He is not sure if she realizes this or if she thinks she is complete.

While she cannot exert iron control of herself, she understands that she empowers herself by *repressing* her emotions. The longer that anger and hatred are unexpressed or only partly expressed, the purer and more poisonous they become, until they make a more potent elixir than any that a wizard could concoct.

She sits beside the desk, glaring at her daughter, and though her long-distilled hatred is lethal, she will not strike a murderous blow yet. She will wait through this night and the following day, until—very soon now—she can have all the deaths that she most wants.

"I bought the potato salad special for you, Piggy."

The blades of light penetrating the cracks in the storm shutters are not pellucid or golden any longer, but a murky orange. The cut-glass vase has gone dark. The auroral glimmer has disappeared from the ceiling over Piggy's head.

Thin spears of orange sunlight touch only the wood surfaces of the furniture, here a decorative pillow, there an oil painting of a seascape.

Yet by some curious mechanism of soft reflection, elfin light twinkles in unlikely corners of the shadowy room: in the glass beads of the shade on the lamp that stands on the far side of the child's bed, in the glass knob on a distant closet door. . . .

"Piggy?"

"Okay."

"The potato salad."

"Okay."

"I'm waiting."

"I had two cookies."

"Cookies aren't enough."

"And a sandwich."

"Why do you do this to me?"

Piggy says nothing.

"You're a little ingrate."

"I'm full."

"You know what an ingrate is?"

"No."

"You don't know much, do you?"

Piggy shakes her head.

"Eat the potato salad."

"Okay."

"When?"

"Later," says Piggy.

"No. Now."

"Okay."

"Don't just say okay. Do it."

The child neither speaks nor reaches for the potato salad.

Diamonds dark at throat and wrist in spite of the desk lamp, Moongirl rises from her chair, snatches up the potato salad, and throws it.

The container strikes a wall and bursts open, splattering the plaster and showering the floor with spit-spiced potato salad.

Bright tears sting Piggy's eyes, and her wet cheeks shine.

"Clean it up."

"Okay."

From the desk, Moongirl seizes the pieces of the ruined doll and throws them hard across the room. She grabs as well the open bag of cookies and throws that.

"Clean it up."

"Okay."

"Every smear and crumb."

"Okay."

"And don't give me tears, you little fat-faced fraud."

Moongirl turns and, diamonds darkling, strides from the room, no doubt to settle herself with her collection of cleansing solutions and emollient lotions for face and body, in a dreamy two-hour regimen that seldom fails to leave her in a better mood.

Perched on the arm of the upholstered chair, Harrow watches the child. As simple as she is, and plain and slow, she has about her a mystery that intrigues him and that seems in some way deeper than the mystery of her mother's madness.

Piggy sits for a minute, unmoving.

As though her tears are as astringent as rubbing alcohol, they swiftly evaporate from her cheeks. In remarkably short order, her eyes are dry as well.

She opens the second lunchbox bag of potato chips and eats one. Then another. Then a third. Slowly she empties the bag.

After wiping her fingers on a paper napkin, she pushes aside the tray and picks up the doll on which she was working when her mother and Harrow first entered the room. She merely holds the doll, does nothing with it other than study its face.

The odd thought occurs to him that Piggy, plain simple Piggy, may be the only person he has ever known who is only and exactly who she appears to be, which may be why she seems mysterious.

And here, unexpectedly, is the Look that Harrow has lately seen subtly transform the child's features, the quality that is not beauty but that might be akin to it. The defining word for the Look still eludes him.

Outside, the wounded day issues a bloody glow that lacks the strength to press through the cracks in the shutters. Only the desk lamp illuminates the room.

Yet elfin lights persist in the crystal beads of the lampshade in the darkest corner, in the glass doorknob far from the desk, in a gold-leaf detail of a picture frame, in window glass that is not at an angle to reflect the desk lamp.

Harrow has the peculiar feeling that he and the child are not alone in the room, though of course they are.

Piggy will not clean up the mess her mother made as long as Harrow remains to watch her. She stoops to such tasks only when she is alone.

He rises from the arm of the chair, stands watching her for a moment, walks to the door, turns, and looks at her again.

Rarely does he say anything to the child. More rarely still does she speak to him.

Suddenly the expression on her face so infuriates him that if he were a man without absolute control of his emotions, he would knock it off her with one hard punch.

Without looking at Harrow, she says, "Good-bye," and he finds himself outside the room, closing the door.

"You'll burn like pig fat," he mutters as he turns the deadbolt lock, and he feels his face flush because this juvenile threat, while worthy of Moongirl, is beneath him.

Chapter

36

The man known as Eliot Rosewater to Vernon Lesley was known as Billy Pilgrim to the associate who had flown the two-engine aircraft to the abandoned military facility in the Mojave.

The pilot, who had worked with Billy on many occasions, called himself Gunther Schloss, and was Gunny to his friends. Billy thought Gunther Schloss sounded like a true name, a born name, but he would not have bet a penny on it.

Gunny looked like a Gunther Schloss ought to look: tall, thick-necked, muscular, with white-blond hair and blue eyes and a face made for the cover of *White Supremacist Monthly.*

In fact he was married to a lovely black woman in Costa Rica and to a charming Chinese woman in San Francisco. He wasn't a fascist but an anarchist, and during one bizarre week in Havana, he had smoked a lot of ganja with Fidel Castro. You could hire Gunny Schloss to kill just about anyone, if it was someone you for some reason didn't want to kill yourself, but he cried every time he watched *Steel Magnolias,* which he did once a year.

After Gunny killed Bobby Onions and Vernon Lesley, he and

Billy stripped the bodies of ID and dragged them to the intersection of the two cracked blacktop roads that served the surrounding cluster of abandoned Quonset huts. They pried a manhole out of the weed-choked pavement and dumped the dead men into the long-unused septic tank.

Even the desert got some rain, and the service-road gutters fed this tank, so the darkness below still stank, if not as bad as it had when the facility had been open twenty years ago, and both bodies splashed into something best not contemplated.

Billy heard movement below, before and after the dropping of the cadavers: maybe rats, maybe lizards, maybe desert beetles as big as bread plates.

When he had been a young man, he would have lowered a flashlight or torch down there, to satisfy his curiosity. He was old enough now to know that curiosity usually got you a bullet in the face.

They worked fast, and after they wrestled the cover onto the manhole, Gunny said, "See you in Santa Barbara."

"Pretty place. I like Santa Barbara," Billy said. "I hope nobody ever blows it up."

"Somebody will," Gunny said, not because he had any proprietary knowledge of a forthcoming event, but because he was an anarchist and always hopeful.

Gunny flew out in the twin-engine Cessna, and Billy walked the scene, kicking sand over the drag marks from the dead men's heels, picking up what shell casings he spotted in the late sun, and making sure they had gathered up all of the major pieces of Bobby Onions's skull.

When the woman disappeared, no one would care as long as she was a nobody named Redwing, living in a modest bungalow, doing nothing with her life except rescuing dogs.

Every week, so many people disappeared or turned up dead in a grotesque fashion that even the cable-news crime shows, with their insatiable hunger for shock and gore, could not cover every case. Some deaths were more important than others. You didn't get killer ratings and book all your ad time at the highest price if your show's philosophy was that the death of any sparrow mattered as much as the death of any other.

Ask not for whom the bell tolls. It tolls for the pretty twenty-something pregnant woman who is clubbed to death by her husband, cut into twelve pieces, packed in a footlocker with concrete blocks, and submerged in a pond. It tolls and tolls and tolls, 24/7, until the only way you can escape hearing it is by switching to Animal Planet.

Amy Redwing's disappearance would merit zero TV time as long as no one knew she had once been someone other than Amy Redwing. Because Vernon Lesley had done a good job of finding the mementos of her past that she had saved, he knew too much about her, and he had to die.

Maybe Lesley had not shared his knowledge with Bobby Onions, but Billy Pilgrim had not been willing to take a chance that Onions was as clueless as he looked. Besides, the moment Onions got out of the Land Rover, with his James Dean sneer and his swagger, Billy wanted to kill him on general principles.

After policing the area for evidence of the shootings, Billy dropped the dead men's ID into the white trash bag that contained what Vernon Lesley had confiscated from the woman's bungalow. With the bag on the passenger seat beside him, he drove out of the desert in the Land Rover and headed west.

Twilight came on like a big Hollywood production, saturated with color—gold, peach, orange, then red, with purple pending—ornamented with clouds in fantastic shapes afire against an electric-blue sky shimmering toward sapphire: the kind of twilight that could almost make you think the day had been important and had meant something.

Billy had a busy night ahead of him. They said there was no rest for the wicked. In fact, there was rest neither for the virtuous nor for the wicked, nor for guys like Billy Pilgrim, who were uncommitted regarding the whole idea of virtue versus wickedness and who were just trying to do their jobs.

Chapter

37

Something unnatural happens to you—judging by the evidence probably something *supernatural*—and at the same time your dead past suddenly comes alive and catches up with you, with the consequence that you have to make the most wrenching confession you've ever made in your life to the one person in the whole world whose opinion of you matters desperately, yet you still have to feed the dogs, walk the dogs, and pick up their last poop of the day.

When Amy had first come into his life and had brought an arkful of canines with her, she had said that dogs *centered* you, calmed you, taught you how to cope. He had thought she was just a little daffy for golden retrievers. Eventually he had realized that what she had said was nothing less or more than the dead-solid truth.

In his pantry, he had kibble and treats for those evenings when Amy came by with the dogs for dinner and two-hand rummy, or to watch a DVD together.

After feeding Fred, Ethel, and Nickie, they walked them through the twilight to a nearby park.

"If this works out," he said, "and Vanessa really will give Hope to me, I'll understand if at some point you decide it's too much."

"Too much what?"

"Some people with Down's syndrome are highly functional, others not so much. There's a range."

"Some architects are highly functional, and some are more dense, yet here I am."

"I'm just saying it's going to change things, it's a lot of responsibility."

"Some architects are highly functional," she repeated, "and some are more dense, yet here I am."

"I'm serious, Amy. Besides the girl's disability, we don't know what Vanessa might have put her through. There may be psychological problems, too."

"Put any three human beings together," she said, "and three of them are going to have psychological problems. So we just cope with one another."

"Then there's Vanessa. Maybe she's had enough of tormenting me, and maybe she just wants to take my money, dump the girl on me, and forget the two of us ever existed. Or maybe it won't be that easy."

"I'm not worried about Vanessa. I can bitch-slap with the best of them."

"If Vanessa decides to be in our lives, one way or another, a Holly Golightly attitude won't work with her."

"Holly Golightly like in *Breakfast at Tiffany's*?"

He said, "If there's a Holly Golightly in *Bleak House*, I'm not aware of it."

"Listen up, nameless narrator, I don't have a Holly Golightly attitude. It's more like Katharine Hepburn in anything with Cary Grant."

"Nameless narrator?"

"*Breakfast at Tiffany's* is told in the first person by a guy who's in love with her, but we never know his name."

They let the dogs lead them in silence for a few steps, and then Brian said, "I am in love with you."

"You said so back at the apartment. I said it, too. We've said it before. We don't have to keep saying it every ten minutes, do we?"

"I don't mind hearing it."

"Dogs know when you love them," she said. "They don't expect you to say it all the time. People should be more like dogs."

"No dog has ever asked you to marry him."

"Sweetie, you've been so patient. It's just that . . . I have some issues. I'm working on them. I'm not just being rotten to you, though I'm sure sometimes it seems like that."

"It never seems like you're being rotten. You're the best. The way you've handled all this with Vanessa, Amy, you're a wonder. It's just . . . nameless narrator never got Holly Golightly."

"He got her in the movie."

"The movie was nice, but it wasn't real. The book was real. In the book, she goes away to Brazil."

"I'm not going to Brazil. I don't like to samba. Anyway, you're not nameless narrator. You're much cuter than he was."

The lampposts brightened as night pressed the last red wine out of the twilight.

Along the pathway, from lamp to lamp, across the grass, from bench to bench and back again, the dogs enjoyed the park entirely as dogs will, sniffing the messages left by legions of dogs before them, alert to the scents of squirrels in trees, of birds in higher branches, and of far places from which stories are carried on the breeze.

"Earlier, when I was doing all those drawings, I sensed—I *knew*—that Hope and Nickie are inextricably entwined, that I can't have Hope without Nickie. There's something so strange happening . . . yet Nickie acts like any other dog."

"Most of the time," Amy said.

She held Fred's and Ethel's leashes in her right hand. With her left hand, perhaps unconsciously, she touched the cameo locket at her throat.

"You want to tell me about the bedroom-slipper thing?" he asked.

"It doesn't mean anything. It can't. Anyway, it wouldn't make sense to you without the backstory."

"So tell me the backstory."

"Sweetie, it's not just a backstory, it's a *big honkin' backstory.* We don't have time to get into it right now. In that last e-mail, Vanessa said 'Stand by.' We should see if she's followed up while we've been out."

When they got back to his apartment, an e-mail from Vanessa was waiting.

Chapter

38

The banks and beds of many rivers in southern California have been paved with concrete, not because the natives considered this more aesthetically pleasing than nature's weeds and silt, but to prevent the course of the waterway from changing over time and to provide flood control. In addition, hundreds of millions of gallons of precious water that might otherwise have poured into the sea were efficiently diverted underground to stabilize the area's water table during drought years.

The rainy season usually began no earlier than December. Now, in September, the riverbed was dry.

In the moonlight, the channel did not appear to be illuminated from above but instead from within its very structure, as though the concrete were radioactive and faintly glowing.

In the Land Rover that had once belonged to Bobby Onions, the headlights extinguished, Billy Pilgrim cruised down the center of the sixty-foot-wide dry river.

Twenty feet above him, chain-link fences prevented easy access to the river. Beyond the fences, on both sides, not visible from his low position, were shopping centers, industrial parks, and housing tracts, where hundreds of thousands of folks were living out versions of the American dream much different from the one that Billy pursued.

Billy had worked in the illegal drug trade, the illegal arms trade, the illegal human-organ trade, and shoe sales.

After high school, he had sold shoes for six months, intending to live in romantic penury in a garret and write great novels. He had soon discovered that looking at feet all day didn't inspire memorable fiction, so he started dealing marijuana, added an ecstasy line, and expanded into a nice little cocaine franchise.

From the start, he declined to take an illegal drug. He liked his brain the way he had originally found it. Besides, he would need every gray cell he had if he was to write enduring novels.

Trading drugs had led to trading weapons, the way shoe sales can easily lead to a broader career in men's haberdashery. Although he had a personal prohibition against the use of drugs, he had never tried a weapon he didn't like.

He had not yet used any of the human organs in which he traded, but if he ever needed a kidney or a liver, or a heart, he knew where to get it.

Somehow he turned fifty years of age. He never saw it coming. They said time flew when you were having fun, and what Billy believed in more than anything else was *fun.*

His love of fun explained why he had given up trying to write important fiction. Writing was no fun.

Reading was fun. All of his life, he had been an avid reader, devouring no fewer than three novels a week, sometimes twice that many.

He had no patience for those few books on the market that sought to find order or hope in life. He liked books steeped in irony. Wry comic novels about the folly of humanity and the meaninglessness of existence were his meat. Fortunately novelists turned them out by the thousands. He didn't care for writers full of brooding nihilism, but rather for those who sweetened their nihilism with giggles, the kind of guys who would be happy operating a weenie stand in Hell.

Books were formative. They had made him the man that he was at fifty: worldly, cheerful, wildly successful in business, confident, and content.

Six years ago, he had gone to work for a man who had taken a family fortune earned in legitimate enterprise and had used it to build a criminal empire, an ingenious reversal of the usual order of things. His current operation was not on behalf of his boss's illegal businesses but on behalf of the boss himself, a personal matter.

As arranged, Georgie Jobbs was waiting for Billy under the bridge. The bridge was six lanes wide and offered a lot of cover for a private transaction.

Georgie stood in the dark beside his Suburban, and as Billy coasted to a stop, Georgie switched on a flashlight, holding it under his chin, directed up over his face, to distort his features and make him look spooky. He knew Billy liked to have fun, and this was his idea of wit.

Occasionally people asked Georgie if he was related to Steve Jobs, the famous software-dot.com-animation-iPhone multibillionaire, which annoyed Georgie because he didn't want anyone to think he would be associated with people like that. Instead of simply denying any relationship, Georgie peevishly called attention to the spelling difference—"Hey, I got two Bs"—which only led to confusion.

Georgie was making faces in the flashlight beam because he liked Billy Pilgrim. Likability was Billy's greatest asset.

People liked him in part because of his appearance. Pudgy, with a sweet dimpled face and with curly blond hair as thin now as it had been when he was a baby, he looked huggable.

And people liked Billy because Billy genuinely liked people. He didn't look down on them because of their ignorance or foolishness, or because of their idiot pride or their pomposity, but *delighted* in them for what they were: characters in the greatest irony-drenched, dark-comic novel of all, *life*.

He got out of the Land Rover and said, "Look at you, you're Hannibal Lecter."

Georgie mangled the line from the movie about eating someone's liver with fava beans and a good Chianti.

"Stop it, stop," Billy said, "you'll have me pissing my pants."

He hugged Georgie Jobbs, asked how his brother Steve was doing, and Georgie said "You crazy sonofabitch," and they threw some playful punches at each other.

The best private investigators had scruples and a regard for the law. Two steps down from them were guys like Vern Lesley and Bobby Onions.

Georgie Jobbs was an entire *flight* down the stairs from Lesley and Onions. He had always wanted to be a PI, but he didn't have the patience to meet the standards and pass the test. He also didn't like the idea of being able to carry only a *licensed* gun, or of giving anyone a legitimate reason to call him a dick.

To his credit, he was a reliable guy, as long as you didn't ask him to do a piece of work that involved algebraic equations or, for that matter, any math at all.

While Lesley and Onions were on their way to the meet in the Mojave, Georgie had burglarized their places of business. Vernon Lesley's place of business had been the crappy apartment in which he lived, and Bobby Onions Investigations occupied a backstairs room above a Thai restaurant.

Georgie had stolen the brains of their computers, their files—which were thin—appointment calendars, notebooks, Rolodex cards, and anything on which they had scribbled notes of any kind what-soever. Together, he and Billy transferred everything from the Suburban to the cargo space of the Rover.

Because Georgie was as thorough as he was thick, Billy was con-fident that when authorities eventually began to investigate the dis-appearances of the two PIs, they would find nothing linking them to a client named Billy Pilgrim.

Billy Pilgrim wasn't his true name, but he used it a lot, and he preferred to be able to go on using it because it had sentimental value to him. Besides, his boss—the wealthy heir turned successful criminal entrepreneur—was adamant about never leaving a loose end, and could not *afford* to leave one.

Georgie had also brought two rigid-wall Samsonite suitcases that Billy had requested, and he handled these with a respect bordering on awe.

"I'd never have thought I'd have so much at any one time, ever," Georgie said.

"It's a day you'll remember," Billy agreed.

"I gotta say, man, it makes me feel good, you trusted me with a delivery like that."

"We go back a long way, Georgie."

"So long I can't count that far," said Georgie, which was nearly true.

After he examined the contents, Billy closed the two suitcases, locked them, and put them not in the cargo space of the Rover, but on the floor in the backseat.

Billy paid Georgie in cash, and while Georgie tucked the money in a jacket pocket, Billy shot him three times point-blank with a silencer-equipped pistol.

He recovered the money and loaded Georgie's body into the Rover with all the other crap. He arranged a blanket over it.

At fifty, he could not manhandle a corpse as easily as he'd done at thirty. He needed every trick he had learned over the years. If he hadn't delighted in his work, he might not have gotten the job done.

After he closed the tailgate on the Rover, he did not bother to search the Suburban. He knew that Georgie Jobbs had not kept an appointment book and had not written any notes to himself, because Georgie couldn't have spelled *Jesus* if that had been the one thing he'd been required to do to get into Heaven.

Georgie might one day have bragged to someone about sweeping the two private detectives' offices on Billy's behalf, but not now. The last tenuous connection between Billy Pilgrim and Amy Redwing had been erased—or soon would be.

Behind the wheel of the Rover, without headlights, Billy cruised the radiant concrete riverbed, happy that he had no agent problems, no publishing deadlines, no literary critics sharpening their knives for him.

Chapter

39

Two e-mails from Pigkeeper were in the box when Brian and Amy returned with the dogs.

The first was succinct: *It will be me.*

Reading the screen over Brian's shoulder, Amy said, "What's it mean to you?"

"Nothing."

He opened the second message: *Did I say STAND BY?*

Brian sent a reply: *Standing by.*

When Amy sat in the second office chair, Fred levered himself off the floor to come prop his chin on her thigh and roll his eyes up at her.

"Good Fred," she said, rubbing his face. "Good, good Fred."

Witness to this, Ethel roused herself from the brink of a nap and came to prop her chin on Amy's other thigh.

"Oh, yes, yes, Ethel is good, too. Good, pretty, pretty Ethel."

Nickie had not settled on the floor when they returned. She sat beside Brian, allowing him the honor of gently scratching her head, but staring at the computer with the intensity that she had brought to the study of a squirrel in the park.

He was looking down at her eyes, which met his directly, wondering why earlier they had driven him to draw obsessively and why they compelled his attention now as well, when the computer signaled the receipt of an e-mail.

He read it aloud to Amy: "'It will be me.'"

"That's it?"

The telephone rang. The caller ID was blocked.

Brian didn't reach for the receiver.

"It's her," Amy said.

"I haven't spoken to her in ten years."

No matter how much he wanted to spring Hope from her mother's control, the prospect of taking another step back into Vanessa's universe was daunting.

The phone rang again, then a third time, and when he picked it up, he said simply, "Yes?"

"Bry, have any of the buildings you designed fallen down yet?"

"Not yet," he said, determined not to let her anger him or frustrate him into a response that might jeopardize his chance to recover Hope.

"It's only a matter of time, Bry. We know what happens when you conceive something."

He had forgotten the extraordinary quality of her voice, an instrument of smoke and steel.

"I think it's time," she said, "for you to take responsibility for the consequences of your funky sperm, don't you?"

He glanced at Amy, but then he felt that somehow he sullied her merely by looking at her when he was on the phone with Vanessa, and he averted his eyes.

"Whatever you want is all right with me, Vanessa. No negotiating on my end. Full transparency of my savings, checking, investments—you'll know I'm not holding back anything."

"I don't want your money, Bry. You live above your offices. If

your folks weren't dead, you'd probably be living with them. Whatever you've got, what would it buy me? A nice coat, some shoes?"

She couldn't have inferred his living arrangements from anything he had said in the e-mails they had exchanged over the years.

"You said you wanted something from me," he reminded her.

"I have this guy now, he's got more money than God. He's even
richer than the creep your baby would have gotten me if she hadn't
been a freak. Money's no problem. You know, Bry, there was a time
when what I wanted was you dead."

"I think I knew that."

"And not slow by cancer. Since then, I've been with some guys
who would've done it for me, and done it good. But I got over that
pretty early."

If his nerves had been piano wires, nothing but high notes could
have been struck from them.

He had taken his left hand off Nickie. He returned it to the back
of the dog's neck—and was surprisingly calmed by the contact.

Vanessa said, "It's been more satisfying to just leave you hanging
out there all these years, taking pokes at you."

"Nobody can play piñata with a man better than you."

He had forgotten that she could laugh and that her laugh had a
throaty and yet appealingly girlish quality.

"This guy I'm with now," she said, "with all his money, when he
has problems with people, he doesn't punch their tickets, he just
deals them out of his way. He's got pockets so deep he can put his
arms in up to his shoulders."

"All I want is my daughter."

"And my guy, he *doesn't* want old Piggy. Other guys, they had
fun watching me tweak her all the time, but not this one. She just
turns his stomach, he wants her out of here."

"So do I. Bring her to me. Or I'll come get her. Whatever."

"Thing is, my guy now, he plays everything by the rules. He's a straight arrow. First one like that since you. Way too horny for his own good, which is why he's so totally *mine,* the poor baby. You remember how that was, don't you?"

"Yes."

"But he wants you and me to sign papers saying that old Piggy is ours, yours and mine, and you found Jesus or something and want full custody, and you don't hold me liable for anything, I've been a really good mother, in fact morally you owe me ten years of child support and you're grateful I'm forgiving you that responsibility, yada-yada-yada."

"I'll sign anything."

"It's like a foot-thick stack of documents, 'cause he doesn't want you coming back on him someday or, worse, he doesn't want to see in the newspaper how he somehow did wrong to a poor little freak girl. He'll even set up a trust fund for her care."

"I don't need that. I don't want money."

"He insists on it, Bry. He worries about his reputation, so he covers his ass at all times. And since I am going to be *Mrs.* Deep Pockets, he's covering my ass, too."

This was a turn of events he didn't like. On the other hand, if anything happened to him, the trust fund would guarantee Hope's care.

He said, "A trust fund needs directors to manage it, invest the money, pay it out. That'll put you in my life, Vanessa, in the girl's life. How would that work?"

"Last thing I want is in your miserable life, Bry, and I've had what fun there was to have with the little freak, I don't want to be in her life anymore, either. The trust needs two directors to start, to sign the documents, then those two can appoint a third later. You will be one director, Bry, and the Redwing bitch can be the other."

He did not trust himself to speak.

After a silence, she let out that throaty, deceptively normal laugh. "I told you my guy covers his ass. He didn't even want to make a deal with you till he knew all about you. He didn't want to set up a trust fund, give you the girl, then it turns out you fondled some six-year-old on a playground. Bad publicity is cancer to him."

"He invaded my privacy, turned loose private detectives on me, something like that?"

"Get the holier-than-thou tone out of your voice, Bry. You're getting what you wanted, so you have to eat some dirt. Knowing what used to get your juices flowing, I have to say I'm surprised you're with Amy. Yeah, she's cute in a Sandra Bullock tomboy kind of way, but are you sure that *she's* sure about her gender?"

"You leave her out of this."

"Can't leave her out of it, Bry. If we're going to do this deal, my guy wants it done right away. You need two directors of the trust. And from what I know about your life—which is mostly everything—Miss Amy is the only candidate. Considering you used to bang anything with a sufficient bra size, she must be witchy, cast a monogamy spell on you. Is she ever going to accept your proposal? She doesn't need to marry you to be a director of the trust. I'm just curious."

He had put himself in this position by his actions as a young man, as he had put Hope where she was now. Actions have consequences. Vanessa was right: He had to eat dirt now, as much as she wanted to feed to him.

"You hate me, don't you?" she asked.

"No."

"Come on, Bry. For this to work, I have to trust you."

"You enrage me sometimes. You scare me. But I don't hate you."

"Bry, I've been blunt with you. I told you, years ago I wanted you dead. I still hate you. If you don't hate me, something's wrong with your head."

He took a deep breath. "All right. I hate you. Why shouldn't I? But it doesn't matter if we get this done. Let's get it done. When do we meet? Where are you?"

"Here's the problem. For years I've been knocking around with our fat-faced little mutant, hooking up with one guy or another who knows how to take care of business, none of them the caliber of what I have now, and every damn time it gets half good, some child-welfare bitch shows up, she's heard about Piggy not being in school and not being treated like the princess of the galaxy, and I have to quick move on, get new ID, find someone new to shack up with."

Given what Hope must have endured, Brian wondered if he would ever be able to redeem himself.

He said, "Sorry to hear about the inconvenience. But what does it have to do with now?"

"So say I give you the address and we make an appointment all businesslike, and you show up with a pack of child-welfare bitches."

"I wouldn't do that. Why would I do that?"

"To embarrass Mr. Deep Pockets, to ruin things between me and him, to get your little freak back without me getting what I want."

"I wouldn't risk it," he protested. "There's no guarantee they'd give the girl to me. The deal you've laid out is good. I don't hate you enough to risk the deal."

"Here's what *I'd* be risking, Bry. Not just all the money I'll ever need. If some child-welfare bitch gets a chance to ask Piggy how does her mommy take care of her, Piggy won't lie. She'll fumble out the truth in her own stupid way, and those bitches won't think what I did with her was as much fun as I thought it was."

He dared not ask for details of the cruelties that she had visited upon their daughter. For the first time, Brian realized that, if he were privy to all the facts, he might be driven to kill this woman. An hour ago, he would have thought that he didn't have the capacity for homicide. Now he was not so sure of that.

"So how do we do this?" he asked.

"You and Miss Amy come to us in baby steps. You don't know the last step, the address, until right before we meet."

"And each step of the way, I figure we're being watched."

She said, "What would really upset my horny rich fella is if you show up with a crew from some tabloid-TV show. He's not a celebrity, but he's a name a lot of people know. He's got the reputation those sickos love to chew up and vomit out coast to coast. First step is, you go to Santa Barbara tonight."

"Think about it one more time," Brian said. "I have everything to lose and nothing to gain by trying to take you down. You have every reason to trust me."

"Every reason? Is that right? Like I trusted you to knock me up with a fine little pink baby, and what you gave me was a freak and ten years of my life ruined. There's nobody I've got *less* reason to trust, Bry."

Her position was irrational, but that didn't surprise him. Any attempt to reason with her about this would be as great a folly as commanding the sea to stop breaking on the shore.

"I have to talk this over with Amy," he said. "I can't decide for her."

"Oh, I'm sure she'll do it. She's so dog nuts. Tell her there's a funky little dog here named Piggy, needs to be rescued. But better e-mail me within an hour."

"An hour isn't enough."

She said, "I've worked this out with Mr. Deep Pockets, but he could turn skittish on me."

Vanessa hung up.

Brian turned to Amy.

"The way you look," she said.

A cold sweat greased the back of his neck. He figured the blood had drained out of his face because his lips felt half numb.

"Like Death," Amy said, "like Death looking for someone to cut down and take away."

Chapter
40

Harrow says, "Cool as ice."

Getting off the kitchen stool from which she had made the call, sitting across from him at the table, she says, "Brian always was easy."

"Dry ice."

As the moon draws ocean tides, so she seems to bend the light of the candles to her by a gravity of her own.

"How much did you prep for that?" he asks.

"No prep. Just played off him."

"Not off him. *Played* him."

She smiles. "Like a piccolo."

"He should know you by now."

"I wasn't this much me, back then."

"You were never less."

"Was I never a child?"

"Were you?"

She does not answer.

"Where did you learn?"

"You mean, to lie like that?"

"You make lying poetry."

"Started learning from Mama's tit."

"You've never told me about your mother."

"She's dead."

"That's it?"

"What else could there be?"

He watches her sip red wine. It looks black on her lips, and then she licks it away.

They are in a new place in their relationship. Anticipation of what is coming gives them a greater sense of shared destiny.

Harrow feels that he can ask questions that were previously off limits. He senses, however, that he cannot yet ask her why she has kept Piggy all these years or why she had a child when she believes, as certainly she does, that nothing matters but the self, the moment, and the thrill.

"What about your old man?"

"He was a liar's liar."

"What did he do?" Harrow asks.

"Nothing he didn't want to."

"My kind of guy."

"He taught history."

"History is lies?"

"The way he taught it."

"Does he still teach?"

"He's dead."

"They both died young."

"Yes."

Harrow takes a shallow sip of his wine. He never drinks to excess in her company.

"Amazing to hear you talk so much on the phone."

"With anyone, a lot of talk always means it's lies."

She is implying that she doesn't lie to Harrow.

He says, "I'm remembering two months ago—Karen and Ron."

"What a fun couple."

They had been twentysomethings, adventurers, backpackers, hiking the coast.

"You were a chatterbox with them," he says.

A guidebook led Karen and Ron to this remote, picturesque cove. They had walnut walking sticks, expensive gear, fresh good looks, and a love of nature.

She says, "Women come on cool to me."

"Because their men come on hot."

Moongirl had done more than open the floodgates of charm. She had posed as a discreet lesbian, and had subtly but repeatedly hit on Karen.

"Poor girl was so flustered."

"But flattered," Harrow says. "She didn't go that way, but she was flattered you wanted her—and relieved you didn't want Ron. You disarmed her."

"We were best pals, me and Karen."

The couple had asked if they could camp the night on the beach, and the four of them had enjoyed a surfside picnic by lantern light.

Karen and Ron didn't notice that their dessert wine and that of their hosts were poured from different bottles.

Later, excruciating pain had awakened them to the indifferent stars, the icy moon, the siren of silver light, and their hostess's eyes as green as an arctic sea.

"Ron was boring," she says.

"He broke so fast."

Harrow participates in such ceremonies only when she asks him to assist her. Just watching, he always has more than enough to keep him entertained and occupied.

She says, "Karen was interesting."

"Quite a marshmallow roast," Harrow agrees.

In his mind's eye, he sees Moongirl on that night, like an Aztec goddess accepting sacrifices made unto her.

"Karen wouldn't give up hope," she says.

"Well, at the end."

"It was a long way to the end."

Moongirl drinks wine without caution. She has no fear of Harrow. Besides, even when she's inebriated, her senses are sharp and her reflexes uncannily quick, as he has seen.

"Why do they hope?" she asks.

"Not all of them do."

"The ones that do hope—why?"

"They have nothing else."

"But hope is a lie," she says.

When she looks at the candles, the flames leap in the red-tinted votive glasses, and she smiles.

He has seen her do this before, and he has asked her how she commands the flames, but she never answers.

Raising her eyes from the candles to Harrow, she says, "Hope is a lie to yourself."

"Most people survive by self-deceit."

"They have nothing."

"Everyone has nothing."

"Oh, *we* have something. We have them."

She regards the candles again, smiles, and ribbons of flame twist, unravel, then ravel back closer to their wicks.

Harrow thinks she does it with a trick of breathing, but he has never seen her nostrils flare or her lips part to betray her.

"One thing is not a lie," he says. "Power."

"Brian is lying to himself right now," she says.

"I'm sure he is. The world always brings you kindling when you need it."

Chapter
41

While driving, Billy Pilgrim put on a soft-brimmed, green-felt Tyrolean hat with a small red-and-gold feather in the band, and he inserted a false gold cap over his two upper central incisors.

When he had found the address he wanted and had parked at the curb, he slipped on a pair of horn-rimmed spectacles with thick lenses of plain glass.

Now that most cell phones were also cameras, you never knew when some meddlesome passerby might take a snapshot of you just prior to or immediately subsequent to a criminal act. Digital technology had contributed to a loss of privacy that he found appalling.

Billy did not consider himself a master of disguise, but he understood the basics of obscuration and camouflage. Only a simple costume was required to foil facial identification from a photograph. A soft-brimmed and somewhat fanciful hat and dark-rimmed glasses went a long way toward changing the look of the face. The gold dental cap gave him a slightly bucktoothed aspect, which made his face seem rounder than it was.

When he got out of the Land Rover, he locked the door. This was a fine neighborhood, but he believed in taking every precaution when he had a dead body under a blanket in his vehicle.

The middle-class to upper-middle homes were in good repair. The landscaping appeared to be well maintained, and landscape lighting set an artful and welcoming mood, with path lamps flanking walkways.

Although the evening was still early and the autumn air warm, no children played in the front yards or bicycled in the street. With predatory pedophiles more numerous by the year and organizing on the Internet to share hunting tips and abduction techniques, parents kept their kids on a short leash during the day and indoors after dusk.

Billy was not a pedophile, but he was grateful to them. Although some biddy might be videotaping him from a window, suspecting him of trolling for toddlers, there weren't half a dozen high-energy kids clustered around him, full of curiosity, asking what was with his hat, was he a mountain climber, did he lose his real front teeth in a climbing accident—which is how it sometimes had been as little as eight or ten years ago.

A guy of about sixty answered the doorbell. He had a face that reminded Billy of certain birds of prey, and he looked as if he had just eaten a couple of live mice that were annoying him by writhing in his stomach instead of being dead.

"Mr. Shumpeter?"

"I don't need any more insurance."

"I'm Dwayne Hoover," Billy Pilgrim said. "I called you earlier today about the Cadillac."

"You looked like cold-call insurance."

"No, sir. My business is organ brokering. One of my businesses."

"You're here about my ad for the car."

"Yes, sir. I called you earlier today. Dwayne Hoover."

"Come on in."

Billy followed Shumpeter into a living room that dazzled with too many floral patterns and fringed pillows.

"You sell a used car to a dealer, they give you piss for it."

"I'm offering cash, Mr. Shumpeter."

"Then they turn around and sell it for a blood price."

"Sometimes, you've got to cut out the middleman," Billy agreed.

"Like I said on the phone, it was my wife's car. She died. Been a widower four months."

"I'm sorry for your loss, Mr. Shumpeter."

"The loss was my first wife. Pauline was my second. Nine years. Left me with all this damn frilly furniture."

"I'm not in the market for furniture, I'm afraid."

Shumpeter seemed to be alone, but Billy couldn't be certain.

"She had to have a Cadillac. Wouldn't let me rest till she got one, then she dies before it's a year old."

"That's so sad," Billy said.

"So I'm hit with big depreciation, and it's hardly been used. Let's be clear right up front—I'm not going to be bargained down."

"I thought your advertised price was reasonable, Mr. Shumpeter."

"Then come take a look at it."

Happily, Shumpeter didn't lead him outside to the driveway, but through the living room, the dining room, and the kitchen, giving Billy a better sense of whether anyone else might be on the premises.

The dining room bloomed with rose, peony, and wisteria patterns: upholstery, tablecloth, wallpaper.

"What's the story with the hat?" Shumpeter asked.

"Tyrolean," Billy said.

"I was a Shriner for years, but a Shriner doesn't wear his fez except at club functions."

"I'm on my way to a club meeting from here," Billy said.

"Never heard of the Tyroleans."

"We're relatively new. We're a social club, but we want to make a difference, too. We're going to find a cure for prostate cancer."

"Tofu," said Shumpeter. "Eat tofu three times a week, you'll never get prostate cancer."

"The guys will be sorry to hear that. We'll have to find another disease. Sir, I gotta say this is a lovely home. Fantastic kitchen."

"I'm selling the place. It was too big for the two of us, but she just had to have it, now it's damned sure too big for just me."

"And it must be hard, alone with all the memories."

"Not going to use a damn real-estate agent, either. They take six percent, and all you get for it is bullshit."

Billy followed Shumpeter through a laundry room—where the widower snared a set of keys from a pegboard—and then into the garage. A new Mercedes stood beside the year-old Cadillac.

Registering Billy's surprise, Shumpeter said, "There was life insurance. The damn IRS doesn't get a cut of life insurance."

Nodding his head at the Cadillac, Billy said, "It looks sweet."

"Full disclosure. She died in it. Massive stroke, gone in two minutes."

"That doesn't spook me, Mr. Shumpeter."

"She didn't lose control of her bowels or bladder, nothing like that, so it's not a reason to bargain."

"I don't want to bargain. Not me. This is just what I'm looking for."

Shumpeter smiled, and his face didn't crack. "Organ broker, you said, Mr. Hoover. Is that like pianos, organs?"

"No, sir. It's like kidneys, livers, lungs."

"Oh. You're a doctor."

"No, just a middleman. But in our aging population, it's a fast-growing business. You yourself are going to need a heart."

Shumpeter's eyes widened. "On what evidence did you come

up with that diagnosis?" He thumped his chest. "I'm sixty, but I've been a vegetarian for forty years, zero animal fat in the diet, rock-bottom cholesterol."

"Well, being an organ broker, I can tell you with authority, statistics show that vegetarians commit suicide at a higher rate than meat eaters."

Shumpeter glowered. "I read that, too, and they say we're more often victims of homicide than meat eaters. That's bullshit. It's the meat industry buying phony research, nothing but propaganda." He fisted his hands and puffed out his chest to proclaim his fitness. "When that Cadillac is ready for the junk pile, I'll still be pleasing the ladies."

"I don't know about that," Billy said, "but I'm sure this would have pleased your wife." He drew the pistol with the sound suppressor and shot Shumpeter through the heart.

He dragged the corpse around to the front of the Mercedes, where it couldn't be seen from the street, picked up the car keys that had fallen from the dead man's hand to the floor, and opened the garage door.

After he backed the Cadillac down the driveway and parked it at the curb, he drove the Land Rover into the garage. He closed the big door in case a pedophile wandered by and saw what he was doing.

He opened the four doors of the Land Rover to vent the initial explosion.

The only thing that he took from the Rover was the white plastic trash bag. It contained everything Vernon Lesley had gathered at the woman's bungalow earlier in the day, as well as the ID for Lesley, Onions, and Georgie Jobbs.

He left the house by the front door, walked out to the street, and got behind the wheel of the Cadillac. He put the bag on the floor, in front of the passenger seat.

At the end of the block, he turned right, then right again at the next intersection. On the street parallel to Shumpeter's street, and behind his property, Billy parked at the curb in front of two houses where other American families were preoccupied with their own joys and problems.

He took off the Tyrolean hat and the horn-rimmed glasses. He pocketed the clip-on gold dental cap. Good-bye Dwayne Hoover.

He got out of the Cadillac, stood on the sidewalk, and withdrew a remote control from his jacket pocket.

Between these two handsome houses, he could see the roof of the Shumpeter residence on the next street to the west. He pointed the remote control, which had plenty of range for the job, pressed the button, and heard the soft *whump* of the initial detonation.

The two suitcases supplied to him by Georgie Jobbs, which he had stored on the floor behind the front seats of the Rover, contained a small initial explosive charge for the purpose of ignition, but held mostly bricks of a ferociously incendiary substance developed by the weaponry wizards of the former Soviet Union, who were currently the weaponry wizards of the new Russia.

Behind the wheel of the Cadillac again, Billy Pilgrim watched the dark roof of the Shumpeter house on the parallel street.

His intention was not to blow up the Land Rover and all of the evidence in it. Rather, he intended to burn everything to ashes and slag: the brains from the two detectives' computers, their files and appointment calendars, and Georgie's corpse.

The incendiary material would produce temperatures as high as 42,000 degrees Fahrenheit, which was less than half as hot as the surface of the sun, not hot at all compared to the eighteen *million* degrees at the core of the sun. Nevertheless, it would be hot enough and sustained long enough virtually to vaporize everything in the

Rover and to reduce the vehicle itself to molten steel from which the make, model, and owner could never be identified.

Of Georgie Jobbs, nothing whatsoever would remain, not even a bone fragment, nothing except Billy's fond memories of him.

On the next street, the night brightened. The first flames broke through the garage roof. They were white with blue edges.

Billy drove out of that neighborhood. The situation there would shortly be untenable.

When Amy Redwing went missing or subsequently turned up dead, nothing in her house would remain to connect her to her previous life; consequently, the authorities would have no reason to suspect Billy's boss of her murder.

Vernon Lesley, who had searched Redwing's house, was dead, and the man whom he had hired for backup, Bobby Onions, was dead, and the man who cleaned out their offices of any possible reference to Redwing was also dead, and all those items from their offices would shortly be smoke and fumes and soot.

If the fire department failed to arrive quickly, houses flanking the Shumpeter residence would either be set afire by traveling flames or, possibly, would be ignited solely by the intense heat of the pyre next door.

In Billy's experience, a truly thorough job usually required some collateral damage.

He drove toward Newport Beach. Although hungry, Billy could wait for dinner until he had done one more job here in Orange County and then had driven to Santa Barbara.

He and Gunther Schloss, who had shot Lesley and Onions, would have a late dinner together, whereafter Billy would kill him. When Gunny was dead, the next to the last connection between Redwing and Billy's boss would have been erased.

The last connection was Billy. This fact had not been lost on him. He had given it much hard thought.

In Santa Barbara, he had booked a luxurious hotel suite in the name of Tyrone Slothrop, a pseudonym that he had not used previously, that he had been saving for a special occasion.

Billy liked extreme luxury and especially enjoyed over-the-top hotels that provided amenities so extravagant that Louis XVI and Marie Antoinette, given a chance to experience such establishments, would have been embarrassed by the comparative grubbiness of their life at the palace.

In Newport Beach, Billy parked around the corner from the building in which Brian McCarthy had both his offices and his apartment.

Chapter

42

Millie and Barry Packard, who had agreed to keep Fred and Ethel for a night or two, lived in a shingle-sided New England-style house on a low rise above the beach.

The front door was unlocked, as Amy had been told it would be. She and Brian followed Fred, Ethel, and Nickie through the house to the back patio, where Millie sat at a teak table, sipping a martini, in the magical light of gas-flame hurricane lanterns with prismatic panes.

Five feet two, slender, with short shaggy blond hair and large eyes, Millie had an air of elfin glamour and looked as if she had just gotten home from playing the lead in a production of *Peter Pan*. She was fiftyish, perhaps too old for the role, though Mary Martin had probably still played the part in Broadway revivals at that age.

"Freddie darling, my adorable Ethel," she exclaimed as the two kids went straight to her, tails lashing, confident of receiving ear rubs and chin scratches. "You're as fabulous as ever, but why didn't you fix your folks a drink before you brought them out here?"

"Don't get up," Amy said, bending to kiss Millie on the cheek.

"Cupcake, I never get up for family, only for people I don't like, so I can mix them weak drinks that make them desperate to go elsewhere."

They were family because they were both board members of Golden Heart and both besotted with goldens.

"Brian, dear, you know where to find the liquor cabinet. We're out of cocktail olives, it's a tragedy of historic proportions, but we're coping because we're Americans."

After bending for a kiss of his own, Brian said, "We can't stay more than a minute, Millie. We have to hit the road."

"My God, you're a handsome young man. It can't be natural. You shouldn't start cosmetic surgery so young. By the time you're sixty, your mouth will be stretched ear to ear."

Amy said, "Where's Barry?"

"On the beach with the dogs. Just for a walk. No romping in the surf. It's too late to be combing sand out of fur, and the dogs would need grooming, too."

Fred and Ethel spotted the trio on the sand below. They hurried to the edge of the patio. As much as they wanted to plunge down the slope to the sea, they wouldn't dash off without permission.

When Millie glimpsed Nickie, her eyes widened with delight. "Oh, Amy, you're right. She's a beauty. Come here, you fabulous creature. I'm your Aunt Millie. Nothing they've told you about me is true."

While Nickie and Millie charmed each other, Amy watched Barry on the beach with Daisy and Mortimer.

Past play, the dogs weaved lazily along the strand, smelling one by one the shells, the driftwood, the knots of weed, the sea urchins, the ocean-smoothed medallions of bottle glass left by the last high tide and to be carried away on the next.

A million fragments of the shattered moon knocked together in the troughs and crests of a low surf, while in the lulls between sets of waves, the jigsaw self-assembled, repairing the silvery sphere, which shimmered in the currents, twisted, and came apart once more.

The rhythms of the sea, the quarter-million-mile light of the moon, and the companionship of dogs inspired a sense of timelessness, of peace, of the profound grace always waiting to be discovered when the noise of daily life subsides.

Amy had the uneasy feeling that this tranquil moment might be the last that she would know for a long time, if not forever.

Perhaps having seen them on the patio, Barry Packard came up from the sea, his dogs preceding him.

Of the Packards' many fine qualities, Amy admired none more than the compassion they revealed in their choice of dogs. They adopted only goldens with special needs, which were the hardest to place in forever homes.

As a puppy only a few weeks old, Mortimer had been found in a Dumpster, thrown away because he had spina bifida and was paralyzed from the waist down. Although treated like garbage, he had been fortunate—considering that he might have been drowned in a bucket before being tossed in the trash.

After examinations by three different vets, Mortimer was judged too severely disabled to be saved. Euthanasia was recommended.

In his expressive face, in his sweet and cheerful demeanor, Amy had seen not an inconvenience but instead a soul as bright as any.

At the start, Mortimer could walk on his front legs but only drag his rear. Surgery to remove his hopelessly deformed left hind leg, followed by weeks of therapy, resulted in an accomplished tripod pup who could not only walk without dragging his butt but also *run* with a gait that was as peculiar as it was swift.

Five years old now, Mortimer was a certified therapy dog. Millie took him to children's hospitals to visit ill and disabled kids who, every one, were inspired by his courage and good cheer.

Daisy was blind. She navigated by sound and smell and instinct, but also by staying close to Mortimer, who was her trusted guide and boon companion.

Steps led up the ice-plant-covered slope, and three-legged Morty and blind Daisy ascended with the enthusiasm of any goldens at the realization that visitors had come calling.

Usually, their rapidly rotating tails would wind them up and wiggle them directly to Amy and Brian. But when they came off the stairs onto the patio, and encountered Nickie, a remarkable thing happened.

Morty froze, Daisy froze, tails suddenly still but not lowered, heads high, ears lifted. Like Fred and Ethel, these two did not rush to Nickie for the usual doggy meet-and-greet.

First Mortimer came forward tentatively, then Daisy. Approaching Nickie, Morty bowed his head, and Daisy did the same a moment later.

Mortimer settled onto his belly and awkwardly crawled forward the last few feet. Daisy, sensing what he had done, followed his example.

When they had reached her, Nickie lowered her head to Mortimer and, as if grooming her pup, began lovingly to lick his face.

Eyes closed, he submitted with a look of ecstasy, tail sweeping the brick patio. His failure to return the kisses was odd behavior.

When after half a minute Nickie had finished with Morty, she turned her attention to Daisy and licked her face, too, as though she were a mother tending to a newborn. Daisy closed her sightless eyes and sighed contentedly.

Fred and Ethel had refrained from greeting their old friends, the disabled Packard dogs, as if in Nickie's presence new protocols applied. They stood nearby, watching intently.

Having come up the steps immediately behind his goldens, Barry Packard witnessed this strange ceremony. A burly, barrel-chested man of reliable good humor, he usually entered with a laugh line followed by handshakes and hugs. Here he stood in silence, intrigued by the dogs' behavior.

Martini forgotten, Millie had risen from her chair to get a better view of these events.

Amy realized that the actions and the attitudes of the dogs were not alone responsible for the extraordinary quality of the moment.

A hush had fallen upon the night, as though a great bell jar had been lowered over the house and patio. The background sounds of which she had been only half aware—faint music from one neighbor's house, soft laughter from another, the spirited singing of shore toads—were silenced. Even the low surf, although no lower or in less frequent sets than before, seemed to dissolve upon the sand with less exuberance, almost in a whisper.

The prismatic lenses of the six gas-fed hurricane lamps had all along sprayed quivering rainbows across the white painted ceiling of the patio and had scattered shimmering coins of light across chairs and tables and faces, but surely the colors had not been as intense as they were now.

Imagination might have accounted for Amy's impression that the air carried a subtle new energy, similar to the freighted atmosphere under storm clouds before the first flash of lightning. But she was not imagining when she felt the fine hairs on her arms and on the nape of her neck quiver as though responding to the silent flute of static electricity.

Mortimer rose to his three feet, blind Daisy to her four. The five dogs regarded one another, grinning, tails wagging, but still in some transported state.

In a voice subdued for him, Barry Packard said, "I knew this kid in college, Jack Dundy. Total party animal. Lived for beer and card games and girls and laughs. Skated through his studies with the minimum of work. Came from money, spoiled, irresponsible, but damn likable in his way."

Whatever story Barry might be telling, it seemed to have no connection to what had just happened among the dogs. Nevertheless, Amy still felt a prickling along her arms, the back of her neck, her scalp.

"One Sunday night, Jack's coming back to college from a weekend home. Just two blocks from the campus, he sees fire in the ground-floor windows of a three-story apartment building. He goes into the place, shouting *fire,* pounding on doors, the place filling fast with smoke."

To Amy, it seemed that even the dogs were alert to the story.

"They say Jack led people out three times before the fire department arrived, saved at least five children whose parents had been trapped by flames and died. He heard other kids screaming, went in a fourth time, even though he heard sirens coming, went back in and up, broke out a third-story window, dropped two little girls to people on the lawn catching them in blankets, went back into that room for a third child but never made it to the window again, died in there, burned beyond recognition."

The night sounds were returning. Faint music from another house. The songs of shore toads.

"I couldn't understand how the Jack Dundy I knew, slacker and party animal, spoiled rich kid, quick to play the fool . . . could have done something so damn heroic and so selfless. For the longest time it seemed to me not only that I hadn't understood Jack Dundy but also that I didn't understand the world at all, that nothing was as simple as it seemed, as if I were an actor just realizing I was in a play, nothing but painted sets around me, and something else altogether behind the stage scenery."

Barry fell silent, blinked, and looked around as though for a moment he had forgotten where he was.

"I haven't thought about Jack Dundy in years. Why did he come to me now?"

Amy had no answer for him, but for reasons she couldn't quite articulate, the story nevertheless seemed appropriate to the moment.

Suddenly dogs were dogs again, each of them seeking the touch of human hands, the sweet-talk that told them they were beautiful and were loved.

The ocean receded into blackness. More blackness lay behind the moon, and still more beyond the stars.

Amy knelt to give Daisy a tummy rub, but because the blind dog could not meet her eyes, her gaze traveled instead to Nickie, who was watching her.

Through her memory, the flock of sea gulls startled into flight with a thunderous drumming of wings, feathers blazing white in the sweeping beam of the lighthouse, sharply shrieking as they ascended, shrieking as if testifying to the terror below, as if crying *Murder, murder!* and Amy with the gun in both hands, standing in the blood-spotted snow, screaming with the gulls.

Chapter

43

Billy Pilgrim walked twice past the building that housed Brian McCarthy's company offices and apartment. The windows were dark on both floors.

The boss had confirmed by phone that the deal was made. McCarthy and Redwing were evidently on the road to Santa Barbara by now.

Billy returned to the Cadillac in which Pauline Shumpeter had died of a massive stroke but had not soiled herself. He boldly reparked it in the lot beside McCarthy's building.

After sheathing his hands in latex gloves, he got out of the car and climbed the exterior stairs to the apartment door.

He needed gloves because he didn't intend to reduce this place to molten metal and soot with exotic Russian incendiary weapons. He would have *preferred* to leave fingerprints and then burn the building because his hands sweated in the gloves, and they made him feel like a proctologist.

With a LockAid lock-release gun, he picked the deadbolt pins in twenty seconds, went inside, closed the door behind him, and stood listening for the sound of somebody he might need to kill.

Billy did not usually kill two people per day and assist in the murder and disposal of two others. If this had been a take-your-son-to-work day, and if he had had a son, the boy would have come to the conclusion that his dad's job was a lot more glamorous than it really was.

Sometimes months would pass between killings. And Billy could go a year, even two years, without having to waste a friend like Georgie Jobbs or a complete stranger like Shumpeter.

Sure, in his line of work, every day required the commission of felonies, but mostly they were not capital crimes that could earn you a lethal injection and burial at public expense.

Episodes of life seldom had the body count of good novels in the everything-is-pointless-and-silly genre, which is why Billy still read so many books even after all these years.

Unnervingly, episodes of real life also were not reliably as meaningless as life was portrayed by his favorite writers. Once in a while, something would happen to suggest meaningful patterns in events, or he would encounter someone whose life seemed to be filled with purpose.

On those occasions, Billy would retreat to his books until his doubts were put to rest.

If his favorite books failed to encourage a full renewal of his comfortable cynicism, he would kill the person whose life had seemed to be meaningful, which at once proved that the meaning had been an illusion.

The apartment remained silent, and finally Billy moved room to room, switching on lights.

He disliked the minimalist decor. Too Zen. Too calm. Nothing here was real. Life was chaos. This decor was not authentic.

Authentic decor was a deranged old lady living with fifty years of daily newspapers and thousands of bags of trash stacked throughout the residence, her husband dead twelve years on the parlor sofa, and twenty-six cats with various seizure disorders. Authentic decor was bombed-out shells of buildings, tenements full of crack whores, and anything Vegas.

Billy loved Vegas. His ideal vacation, which he didn't get to enjoy often enough, was to go to Vegas with two hundred thousand in cash, lose half of it at the tables, win the losses back, then lose the entire bankroll, and kill a perfect stranger chosen at random on the way out of town.

In McCarthy's annoyingly clean neon-free study, Billy unplugged the brain of the computer, carried it from the room, and stood beside the front door. When he headed for Santa Barbara, this logic unit would be in the trunk of his car. Later, he would flood it with corrosive materials and burn it in a crematorium.

The architect had been instructed to take his laptop with him. Billy would have to destroy that machine after McCarthy was dead.

In the study again, he searched the file cabinets and found the printouts of all the e-mails that Vanessa had sent to the architect over the past ten years. Although the waste can was tall, those files filled it to the brim, and he put them by the front door.

Because McCarthy might have saved old e-mail files on diskettes when he updated computers, Billy searched boxes of those but found nothing that, judging by the labels, needed to be trashed.

His purpose here was to eliminate anything that might, in the event of McCarthy's disappearance, lead the police to Vanessa.

In the study and bedroom, he also searched for a diary. He did not expect to find one.

As with literature, authentic decor, ideal vacations, and so many things, Billy Pilgrim had a theory about diaries.

Women were more likely than men to think that their lives had sufficient meaning to require recording on a daily basis. It was not for the most part a God-is-leading-me-on-a-wondrous-journey kind of meaning, but more an I've-gotta-be-me-but-nobody-cares sentimentalism that passed for meaning, and they usually stopped keeping a diary by the time they hit thirty, because by then they didn't want to ponder the meaning of life anymore because it scared the crap out of them.

He did not find a diary in McCarthy's apartment, but he did find scores of art-paper tablets full of sketches and detailed drawings, mostly portraits. This suggested that the architect secretly yearned to be not a designer of buildings but instead a fine artist.

Pencil drawings littered the kitchen table. One of them was a striking portrait of a golden retriever. Some were studies of the dog's eyes in different light conditions. Others were abstract patterns of light and shadow.

Billy became at once fascinated by the drawings because he inferred that during their creation, the artist had been in emotional chaos. Billy was a connoisseur of chaos.

He stood at the table, sorting through the pictures, and after a while he found himself in a chair without remembering having sat down. The wall clock revealed that he had been with the drawings for more than fifteen minutes, when he would have sworn it had been two or three.

Later, still enthralled by the art, he was startled to feel blood trickle down his face.

In no pain, puzzled, Billy raised one hand and felt his cheeks, his brow, seeking the wound, which he could not find. When he looked at his fingertips, they glistened with a clear fluid.

He recognized this substance. These were tears. In his line of work, he sometimes reduced people to tears.

Billy had not wept in thirty-one years, since he had read a huge novel of such stunning brilliance that it had drained him of his last measures of sadness and sympathy for his fellow human beings. People were nothing but machines of meat. You couldn't feel sorry for either machines or meat.

That same novel had made him guffaw so strenuously, for so long, at the folly and bottomless stupidity of humankind that he had also used up his lifetime allotment of tears of laughter.

These new tears perplexed Billy.

They amazed and astonished him.

They also alarmed him.

Dread made his palms clammy.

The nanopowder-coated latex gloves were slimy with sweat, which backed up to the cuffs and leaked out at his wrists, dampening his shirt sleeves.

If his tears were tears of laughter, a preparatory lubricant for gales of giggles, he might have been able to accept them. But he did not feel any laughter building inside him.

His contempt for humanity remained so pure that he knew these could not be tears inspired by the richly comic horror of the human condition.

Only one other possibility occurred to him—that these were tears shed for himself, for the life that he had made for himself.

His alarm escalated into fear.

Self-pity implied that you felt wronged, that life had not been fair to you. You could only have an expectation of fairness if the universe operated according to some set of principles, some tao, and was at its heart benign.

Such an idea was an intellectual whirlpool, a black hole that would suck him in and destroy him if he allowed its fearsome gravity to capture him for another moment.

Billy knew well the power of ideas. "You are what you eat," the nutritionists endlessly hector fast-food addicts, and you are also what ideas you have consumed.

With the thirst of an insatiable swillpot, he had poured down the fiction of two generations of deep thinkers, and he was pickled in their ideas, *comfortably* pickled. At fifty-one, he was too old to be transformed from a dill into a gherkin; he would have been too old at twenty-five.

He did not know why the drawings had brought him to tears.

Heart racing, breathing like a man in panic, he resisted the desire to study them further to ascertain the reason for their extraordinary effect on him.

With his happiness and his future at stake, Billy at once gathered up the drawings, hurried with them into Brian McCarthy's study, and fed them through a paper shredder that stood beside the desk.

Half convinced that they wriggled with life in his hands, he packed the tangled mass of quarter-inch ribbons of paper into a dark-green plastic garbage bag that he found in the kitchen. Later, in Santa Barbara, he would burn the shredded drawings.

By the time he carried the computer brain, the wastebasket full of e-mail files, and the bag of shredded drawings to the Cadillac, where he stowed them in the trunk, his heart rate had subsided almost to normal, and he had regained control of his breathing.

Behind the wheel of the car, he stripped off the disgustingly slimy latex gloves and tossed them into the backseat.

He blotted his hands on his slacks, on his sport coat, on his shirt, and then drove away from McCarthy's den of perils.

By the time he found the freeway entrance, the flow of tears had stopped, and his cheeks had begun to dry.

He suspected that to blot from his mind the entire disturbing incident, the best thing that he could do would be to kill a total stranger selected on a whim.

Sometimes, however, even a random act of murder had to wait for a more propitious moment. Billy was already late setting out for Santa Barbara, and he had to make up for lost time.

Chapter

44

At Amy's house, Brian measured kibble and treats into plastic Ziploc bags, more than they would need, enough for three days. He packed them in a tote with a food dish, a water dish, and other dog gear, while Nickie politely and successfully begged for nibbles.

In her bedroom, Amy selected two days' worth of clothes—jeans and sweaters—and packed them in a carryall with her SIG P245. She included a fully loaded spare magazine.

Since moving to California, she had not used the weapon.

She had no clear reason to suppose that she would need it on this trip. Vanessa was evidently a disturbed, petty, and vindictive woman—even cruel, judging by the evidence of her e-mails—but that did not make her homicidal.

In fact, she seemed too selfish to do anything that would put her liberty—and therefore her pleasures—at risk. To secure a life of luxury and privilege with the wealthy man who evidently thought more with his little head than with his big one, she had good reason to expedite this transferral of custody without a hitch.

Besides, although Vanessa might have been a bad mother, might have been resentful of and mean toward her daughter, she had neither abandoned the girl nor strangled her in infancy. Judging by the news these days, more babies than puppies ended up discarded in Dumpsters. A decade spent looking after the girl, no matter how reluctantly, seemed to argue that at least a faint flame of accountability still lit the final chamber in the otherwise dark nautilus of her heart.

Abandoned in a church at the age of two, with a name pinned to her shirt, Amy could never say for certain who she was or that her birth parents had found her any less repulsive than Vanessa found the girl whom she called Piggy.

By the age of three, she'd been adopted from Mater Misericordiæ Orphanage by a childless couple, Walter and Darlene Harkinson. She had legally taken their name.

She retained only vague memories of them because, just a year and a half later, their car had been hit by a cement truck. Walter and Darlene had perished instantly, but Amy had survived unscathed.

At four and a half, twice traumatized—once by cold rejection, once by loss—Amy had returned to the orphanage, where she lived until shortly after her eighteenth birthday.

Young Amy Harkinson might have been emotionally fragile and even psychologically damaged for life if not for the wisdom and kindness of the nuns. The nuns alone, however, could not have restored her.

No less important had been the golden retriever who had come limping toward her across an autumn meadow, filthy and half starved, only a month after her return to Mater Misericordiæ.

With its charm, the golden earned itself permanent residence as the orphanage dog. And because of its mysterious inclination, it had bonded to Amy above all others and had become no less than a sister to her and the foremost healer of her heart.

Curiously, what now inspired Amy to include the pistol in her bag was not the e-mail witch who had tormented Brian, but this new golden retriever that, less than a day previously, had come into her life with an air of mystery and with a direct stare that reminded her so powerfully of the dog who, long ago, had given her life meaning and who perhaps had even saved her.

She had known terror, loss, and chaos, but always she had found at least a fragile peace after terror, hope after loss, and pattern in the wake of chaos. In fact, it was her eye for pattern that made it possible for her to go on living.

The directness of Nickie's eyes, Theresa's beautiful but bruised purple eyes, Brian's drawings of the dog's eyes, his grandmother's vivid wink in the dream, the bright eye of the lighthouse repeatedly flaring into her memory after all these years, blind Marco in the Philippines (real or not), blind Daisy at the side of three-legged Mortimer: *Eyes, eyes, open your eyes,* the pattern said.

The only physical danger she had faced recently had been from Carl Brockman and his tire iron, and that threat had passed. Yet she read the pattern of these eyes as having urgent and dire meaning.

Among other recent patterns, there were several incidents of strange effects of light and shadow, reminding her that there are both things seen and unseen.

In the scene as now set, something unseen waited.

Until her eyes were fully open or until the patterns proved to be benign and her interpretation proved to be misguided, she believed that packing the pistol and the spare magazine in the carryall was only prudent.

She had told Brian she would bring the gun. He had merely nodded as if to say *Why wouldn't you?*

Likewise, neither of them had questioned the wisdom of bring-ing Nickie. Of all the patterns in the current web, the one that wove through all the others was *dogs*, and this dog in particular.

Although they were using Amy's Expedition, Brian drove be-cause he'd more recently gotten sleep, even if it had been troubled by a tornado, and because Amy wanted to think without the distraction of traffic.

They had put down both rows of backseats, allowing Nickie to lie immediately behind them in the now spacious cargo area.

As Brian pulled away from her bungalow, Amy thought that she glimpsed Theresa's small pale face at a window in Lottie Augustine's house.

She said, "Wait, stop."

Brian braked, but when Amy looked back, a curtain fell across the glass, and the face was gone.

After a hesitation, she said, "Nothing. Let's go."

Block after block, street after street, and up the freeway ramp, she kept checking the side mirror and leaning between the seats to get a better view through the tailgate window.

"No one's following us," he said.

"But she told you we'd be watched."

"They don't need to watch us now. They know we're going to Santa Barbara. They can put a tail on us there."

Rush hour had long passed. Northbound traffic remained heavy, but it moved fast, the freeway a loom ceaselessly weaving from the warp and woof of speeding vehicles a fabric of red and white light.

"Do you think, as bitter and troubled as she is, she really could manipulate some very wealthy man into this, and into marriage?"

"Yes," he said without hesitation. "If he was unfortunate enough for their lives to intersect, Vanessa could turn him off his path and onto hers. It's not just how she looks. She has an instinct for your weaknesses, for finding the buttons that open the door to your dark side."

"You? Even young and stupid, as you described yourself then? I don't think you have a dark side."

"I think most of us do," he disagreed. "Maybe all of us. And the most important thing we can ever do is keep the door shut to it, keep the door shut and locked tight."

P iggy can't keep them out. They can keep her in, but she can't keep them out.

She never knows when the door will open. This is scary.

Let not your heart be troubled.

Sometimes she hears footsteps. But sometimes they make no sound, like your shadow makes no sound when it runs down steps behind you, and they come in quick.

She must never be caught doing the thing she does sometimes, so whenever she is doing the Worst Thing She Can Do, she always listens really hard for the lock squeak.

She cleans up potato salad, all Mother's mess. She bags trash. She washes dirty cleaning rags in her bathroom sink.

Then she goes to the door to listen. Voices. They are far away, maybe as far as the kitchen.

Mother and the man stay awake all through the dark. They sleep when the sun happens.

Doing the Worst Thing She Can Do is safer when they sleep. But right now she wants to do it so bad.

She wishes she had a window she could see out. Sometimes, they live where she can see sky.

Her windows have wood over them now. Sun comes through some cracks, but she can't see out.

If she could see sky, she could wait to do the Worst Thing. Sky makes her feel better.

Sky is best when the dark comes out. It gets deeper. You can see then, and you think what Bear said.

She misses Bear. She misses him worse than all the windows there will ever be or never be. She will always miss Bear.

She will never forget him, never, the way she makes herself forget some things.

She likes moon. She likes stars. She likes shooting stars you can wish on.

If she could see a shooting star, she would wish for a window. But first she has to have a window to wish from.

Bear taught her how star wishing works. Bear knew everything. He wasn't dumb like her.

Let not your heart be troubled, Piggy.

Bear said that a lot.

And he said *All things work out for the best, hard as that is to believe.*

You just have to wait. Wait for a sandwich without a dead bug or live worm or nail in it. You wait and sometimes a good sandwich comes. Wait for a window. Wait.

The kitchen voices are still kitchen voices, you can't hear the words from this far. Maybe she is safe.

The big chair has a cushion. The cushion has a cover. The cover has a zipper.

Inside the cover, under the cushion, the Forever Shiny Thing is hidden.

Forever means all the days there are ever going to be, and then that many more. Bear explained it.

Forever means no start and no finish. *Forever* means every good thing can happen to you, every good thing you can think of, because there's time for all of it.

If there's time for every good thing you can think of to happen, is there time for every *bad thing* you can think of to happen?

She asked Bear her question, and he said no, it doesn't work that way.

Piggy herself is forever. Bear said so.

As soon as she has the Forever Shiny Thing in her hand, Piggy feels better. She feels not alone.

Alone is better than with Mother and the man.

But alone is hard.

Alone is very hard.

Alone is mostly what she ever remembers. She didn't know how bad alone was until Bear.

She had Bear, and then she didn't, and after there was no more Bear, she knew for the first time how hard alone was.

She feels close to Bear when she holds the Forever Shiny Thing in her hand. She holds it now very tight.

Bear gave it to her. A secret. Mother can never know. If Mother finds out, she will get the Big Uglies.

Right here at the chair, where she can quick shove the Forever Shiny Thing into the cushion cover, Piggy does the Worst Thing She Can Do.

Maybe she will be caught, so she is scared. Then not scared.

The Worst Thing always makes her not scared. For a while.

She has to be careful about time. She is not good about time. Sometimes no time at all seems like a lot. Sometimes a lot of time goes by like nothing.

If she forgets about time, she will Drift Away, like she does, and then she'll forget about listening for the lock squeak, too.

She is quiet for a while but says what is in her heart.

Always say what is in your heart, Piggy. That's the best you can do.

She is done. She feels not so alone as before.

"Oh, Bear," she says.

Now and then Piggy thinks if she says his name out loud, he'll answer. He never does. She still tries sometimes.

Bear is dead. But he could still answer.

Bear is dead but Bear is forever, too.

He will always be with her. He promised.

No matter what happens, Piggy, I'll always be with you.

Mother killed him. Piggy saw it happen.

Piggy wanted to be killed, too.

For a long time things were so bad. Very bad. Dark even when there was light.

The only thing that kept the dark back was the Forever Shiny Thing that was her secret.

Now, before shoving it inside the cushion cover, Piggy looks at it one more time.

Silver. Bear said it is made of silver.

It is a word, one of just a few words she can read when she sees it. The word hangs on a silver chain. The word is HOPE.

Chapter
46

They drove through an In-N-Out for cheeseburgers, fries, and soft drinks, and they ate on the road, paper napkins tucked in their shirt collars, more napkins layered on their laps.

Thrusting her head between the seats, licking her chops to take back the drool before it dripped, Nickie suckered Amy into giving her three morsels of hamburger and four fries. She withdrew her head and obediently settled down behind Amy's seat when firmly told "No more, nada, no."

Every road has romance, especially at night, and eating on the fly appeals to the delight in journeying that abides in the human heart. There is an illusion of safety in movement, the half-formed idea that the Fates cannot find us, that they stand on the doorstep of the place from which we recently departed, knocking to deliver a twist or turn that, while on rolling wheels, we will not have to receive.

This false but welcome dream of safety, coupled with the comfort of delicious unhealthy food, put Amy in a mood that made disclosure more imaginable than it would have been elsewhere.

When they had eaten and she had stuffed all their napkins and debris into the In-N-Out bag, she said, "I told you about being abandoned at the orphanage, about the adoption and cement truck and the orphanage again . . . but I never told you about my first dog."

After the accident and the return to Mater Misericordiæ, she had been reduced by her experiences to frequent silences that concerned the nuns, to a poverty of smiles though previously she had been rich in them, and to a desire for distance from others.

One sunny afternoon in October, a month after her return, she had sneaked off alone to the farther end of the play yard from the church, abbey, school, and residence, the buildings that embraced Mater Misericordiæ's quadrangle. The big play yard was on high land, and from it a meadow sloped gently to the valley where the town rose and the river ran and the highway receded.

She sat on the mown green grass just where it ended at the brow of the hill, beneath the spreading boughs of immense old oak trees. After a searing Indian summer, the tall grass of the descending meadow had faded to the color of the sunshine that had stolen the green from it.

The shadows of the oaks began to spill down the slope in early morning, but they seeped uphill once more as noon approached. By this hour, the shadows of other trees at the foot of the meadow steadily inked toward the crest.

Through the shadows, young Amy saw something golden coming, and then through the sunshine it ascended, red-gold in the white-gold grass. When she realized that it was a dog, she rose to her knees, and when she saw that it was limping, she stood.

In those days, she had never been in the company of canines, and she had been naturally wary of this animal. Because the dog limped, favoring its left hind leg, Amy's wariness was tempered by sympathy that encouraged her not to retreat.

The poor thing was in miserable condition, its coat matted and filthy, as though it had been abandoned to fend for itself or as if it had been mistreated. Yet when it came to her, weary and weak and hurting, it smiled.

She didn't know then that it was a golden retriever or that the lovers of the breed referred to this expression as the golden smile, which was easily offered and so different from the false smile of a dog merely panting.

When Amy reached out a hand to the golden, it did not growl or shy away, but instead took another step and licked her fingers in a manner that at once seemed to her to be a grateful kiss.

Halfway across the play yard, leading this four-legged foundling toward the orphanage residence, Amy encountered Sister Angelica, and then for a while there was much bustling about and excitement, with eager children streaming to the yard to see the wounded dog that Amy Harkinson had rescued from the meadow.

Sister Agnes Mary, the abbey's infirmarian, arrived with a medical kit. She found a shard of glass embedded in one of the pads on the dog's left hind foot, extracted it, and treated the wound with an antibiotic solution.

As bedraggled and dirty and flea-ridden and gaunt as the dog was, the children nevertheless were at once of the unanimous opinion that it should be given residence for life as the school mascot.

Mater Misericordiæ had never before enjoyed a mascot, and the sisters were not convinced that it was a good idea. Besides, being nuns and therefore responsible, they intended to attempt to locate the owner of the dog, though it wore no collar.

After assuring the gathered children that the pooch would not be sent to the pound, where it might eventually be put to death if not claimed, Sister Angelica chased everyone out of the yard to dinner in the refectory.

Amy lingered, tagging behind Sister Angelica and Sister Claire

Marie as they, with a makeshift rope leash, led their new charge to the concrete work deck outside the laundry, behind the residence hall. There, they provided water for the dog to drink and devised solemn strategies for giving it a bath.

When Sister Claire Marie noticed Amy, she reminded her that she had been instructed to go to dinner. Reluctantly, Amy retreated.

Although the dog had made no comment on the departure of the other children, it began to whimper as Amy hesitantly walked away. Every time she looked over her shoulder, the dog was watching her, its head lifted, ears raised. She could hear its thin mewling even after she had turned the corner of the building.

Amy had eaten little of the food on her dinner tray when Sister Jacinta—who, because of her sweet high-pitched voice, was secretly called Sister Mouse by the children of Mater Misericordiæ—arrived in the refectory to bring her back to the deck outside the laundry.

The dog had not stopped whimpering since Amy had left. Because of their years of experience with the techniques of manipulation employed by cunning orphans, the nuns were not easy marks. But the dog's mewling was of such a pathetic character that they could not harden their hearts to it.

Instantly upon Amy's arrival, the dog quieted and smiled and wagged its tail.

Through the twilight and into the evening, a gaggle of sisters worked on the dog, cutting the terrible mats out of its coat, giving it *two* baths with shampoo and then a third bath with a flea-killing solution for which Father Leo had made an emergency trip into town.

When Amy strayed more than two steps from the dog, it whimpered, so eventually she participated in the grooming.

Because she was by then hopelessly smitten and desperate to find ways to tie the dog inextricably to Mater Misericordiæ, she decided that they must name it right there, right then, while it was still wet from the bath. Instinctively she knew that a dog with a name would work its way into the sisters' hearts more quickly than would a nameless stray.

She announced that since Christmas was only a little more than two months away, the dog must be an early gift from Saint Nicholas, and therefore should be named for him. Sister Angelica informed her that this foundling was a girl, which set Amy off her stride only a moment before she said, "Then we'll call her Nickie."

Now, almost twenty-eight years later, behind the wheel of the Expedition, Brian glanced away from the road and said, "My God. The same name."

Amy watched him think through the ramifications of this seeming coincidence, and though he returned his attention to the highway, she knew when a shiver of wonder went through him.

"There was a moment in the Brockmans' kitchen last night," Brian remembered, "right before you offered to buy Carl off. You'd been crouching beside the dog, and suddenly you stood up, staring at him so intently. You looked . . . I don't know, not just startled, stricken, but I didn't understand what it was."

"He said her name. Janet hadn't mentioned it on the phone to me. Right away, before any of the rest of this strangeness had happened, I *knew* the name wasn't a coincidence. And don't ask me how I knew or what I mean even now about what *our* Nickie is or why she's here. But I knew . . . no coincidence. Then later, when I asked Janet why they decided to call the dog Nickie, she said Theresa named her."

"The little girl, the autistic girl," Brian said.

"Yes. Autistic or whatever she may be. Theresa said the dog should be called Nickie *because that's what her name had always been.*"

He glanced at her again. "Always?"

"Always. What she meant by that . . . who knows. But, Brian, she meant something."

Twenty-eight years earlier and three thousand miles east of the California coast, on that long-ago bath night, the sisters accepted the name Nickie for the foundling. They had seen that already the dog had brought Amy out of her troubling silence, that she no longer seemed to want to keep herself at a distance, that she had begun to smile again. They wanted to encourage her.

Once Nickie was clean and dry, the nuns decided that she could sleep in the infirmary, where Sister Regina Marie served as the night nurse when patients were in residence.

Although bathed, medicated, fed, and provided with a soft bed of folded blankets, the dog who was an early gift from Saint Nicholas proved not to be content without Amy at its side. The ceaseless and pathetic whimpering began again.

In those days, the concept of a therapy dog might not have been widely in use; but the nuns of Mater Misericordiæ recognized that a bond of some value had formed between the girl and the four-footed waif. Rules were bent if not broken, and although in the best of health, Amy bunked in the infirmary during the week that attempts were made to determine from where the dog had come.

The unrelenting and insistent prayers with which Amy pestered God must have made Him throw up His hands in exasperation and shout "All right already!" in the halls of Heaven, because the sisters failed in their good-faith efforts to locate an owner.

After Dr. Shepherd, a veterinarian, had examined Nickie and had brought her shots up to date, and after it had become clear that the dog was uncommonly well-behaved and housebroken, Mater Misericordiæ yet again lived up to its name—Mother of Mercy—and gave Nickie a forever home.

Although, as official mascot, the dog had free rein of all buildings except the church—and was often invited there, as well—she slept every night in Amy's dorm room. For the next eleven years she was Amy's shadow, Amy's confidant, and Amy's deepest love.

Over those years, of the more than three hundred girls who came at different points in their lives to Mother of Mercy, none became better known than once-shy and silent Amy Harkinson or had more friends, or held more student offices. In each yearbook for more than a decade, no one among them saw her photograph appear more frequently than Amy's—except Nickie, of course, whose grinning mug brightened more pages than not, appearing in class plays and in a Santa hat at Christmas parties, wearing bunny ears for Easter and an American-flag neckerchief on the Fourth of July, always surrounded by adoring girls and beaming nuns.

Amy was sixteen when one day the usual energetic Nickie seemed tired, the next day still tired, and on the third day lethargic. She was diagnosed with hemangiosarcoma, a fast-spreading cancer that was too advanced for a surgeon to strip it all out or for chemotherapy to hold it at bay.

Nickie's decline was swift. Her suffering would be certain if she was not given the mercy that is right for innocent animals; and no one could bear to see her suffer.

Because God is never cruel, there is a reason for all things. We must know the pain of loss; because if we never knew it, we would have no compassion for others, and we would become monsters of self-regard, creatures of unalloyed self-interest. The terrible pain of loss teaches humility to our prideful kind, has the power to soften uncaring hearts, to make a better person of a good one.

Mother of Mercy was a fine school as well as an orphanage. The passing of Nickie, dear mascot to all and sister to Amy, provided an opportunity not only to share but also to learn.

Those girls who felt strong enough—most did—were invited to

assemble at twilight in the quadrangle, where the issue of animals' souls was not debated but quietly accepted, and where prayers were said for Nickie. And during prayers, as twilight faded, candles were raised, hundreds of candles, while at the center of those assembled, Amy knelt beside her best friend to give comfort and to bear witness.

Sister Agnes Mary, the infirmarian, had volunteered to assist Dr. Shepherd, the veterinarian, in the administration of the two injections. The first would be a sedative to convey Nickie into a deep sleep, and the second would be the drug that stopped her heart.

Nickie's favorite recreation-room sofa had earlier been placed in the center of the quadrangle, and Nickie, so weakened, had been carried to it. Amy knelt on the ground, face to face with this first dog that she had ever saved.

Estimated to have been three when she had limped up the meadow to her mistress, Nickie had been fourteen there in the last twilight of her fabled life, but she had still looked like a puppy, with little white in her face.

Only sixteen, Amy found a strength in herself that she had not known she possessed, strength to keep her voice calm and reassuring, even if she could not hold back the tears.

As if to say *It's all right, you're doing great,* Nickie licked Amy's fingers, as she had licked them that first moment they had met in the meadow. A kiss hello, and now a kiss good-bye.

Nickie had always loved to have her face held firmly in cupped hands, thumbs stroking her cheeks, and would submit to this pleasure as long as anyone could be conned into providing it. Now Amy held that always-before comic face in her hands and looked into those expressive brown eyes. She said to Nickie, "You're the sweetest dog who ever lived, and I have always been so proud of you, how smart you are, how quick to make a friend of everyone. I've loved you every moment, I couldn't love a sister more, or my own child, or life," and while she talked, the injections were administered, and Nickie went to sleep looking into Amy's eyes. Amy felt the poor body twitch when the great heart stopped, just stopped, and Nickie went to God while waves of candlelight washed across the walls of the quadrangle and dazzled in windows and glimmered in grief-wet faces, and every flame said the same thing—*A special dog passed this way, who brightened the life of everyone she met.*

Seventeen years later, recounting all of this to Brian, Amy felt a grief almost as sharp as the pain she had felt that awful twilight. Although in the intervening years she had held so many dogs as they were put down, she wept and her voice broke often as she described the scene on the quadrangle.

A week thereafter, Sister Jacinta, "Sister Mouse," had given Amy the locket with the profile of a golden retriever. She had worn it ever since.

Now, in the center of that quadrangle, a flat granite plaque, polished and black, marks where an urn of ashes is buried. A cameo inset in the marker matches the one on Amy's locket. Under the cameo are carved these words:

IN MEMORY OF NICKIE,
THE FIRST MASCOT OF MATER MISERICORDIÆ,
WHO WAS EVERYTHING A GOOD DOG SHOULD BE.

Brian said, "I understand you so much better now—the commitment to dogs, the risks you take. Your life was chaos, and Nickie brought order to it, order and hope. You're repaying that debt."

Everything he said was true, but the story she had set out to tell was not yet entirely told.

What came after that night in the quadrangle took far greater courage to discuss. She had not spoken of the next part to anyone in more than eight years.

In telling him of her first dog, Amy had discovered an intensity of emotion greater than she had expected. Shaken by the depth of that revisited grief, she didn't feel that she could tell him the rest of it now.

She was tired, exhausted. So much had happened in—what?— maybe nineteen hours, and another busy and emotional day most likely lay ahead of them.

Although she had steeled herself to tell it all, she could not proceed to the end. Better to wait now until they had found Brian's daughter and brought her into his life, where she belonged.

Chapter

47

Gunther Schloss, hired killer and pilot and happy anarchist, with a wife in Costa Rica and a second wife in San Francisco, had a girlfriend in Santa Barbara. Her name was Juliette Junke, pronounced *junkie,* which was ironic because she was so adamantly opposed to the use of illegal drugs that she had once castrated two small-time dope dealers who had sold marijuana to her niece.

Juliette Junke did business under the name Juliette Churchill. She was a mortician. She, her sister, and her two brothers owned and operated Churchill's Funeral Home, an elegant and stately facility with four viewing rooms that were frequently in use at the same time.

Although the funeral business turned a profit, the Churchill clan moonlighted by smuggling terrorists—among other things—in and out of the United States in specially designed caskets that contained bottled oxygen and a clever system for collecting and storing the urine of the terrorists therein transported.

Many murderous thugs just hiked across the unprotected border or used international airlines and—wearing T-shirts that proclaimed DEATH TO ALL JEWS in Arabic—breezed through U.S. checkpoints, where highly suspicious federal security personnel strip-searched Irish grandmothers and Boy Scouts on field trips.

Juliette and her family specialized in the smuggling of those terrorists who were so notorious and whose faces were so well known to police organizations worldwide, they couldn't even risk traveling in disguise and must be shipped on missions of jihad while posing as embalmed cadavers. These were the most successful of all terrorists, of course, and therefore the richest, and they paid well.

Arriving in Santa Barbara after viewing hours at the funeral home, Billy Pilgrim met Juliette at the garage entrance. He pulled the Shumpeter Cadillac into an empty bay in the row of black hearses.

Juliette Junke-Churchill was a good-looking woman, terrific-looking for a mortician. She reminded him of a young Jodie Foster: those fine cheekbones and those blue eyes that with just one wink could set your heart racing or, with one tear, break it.

Juliette probably did not cry much—or ever—and she would never do anything as coy as wink. She looked soft, but she was hard. If she claimed to be able to crack walnuts with her thighs, Billy would want to watch but only while wearing goggles to protect against walnut-shell shrapnel.

She greeted him with the nickname she had given him—"Bookworm, you are a sight for sore eyes"—and they hugged because everyone felt they had to hug Billy and because Billy didn't mind hugging someone as delectable as Juliette.

They set right to work unloading the trunk of the Cadillac. Juliette carried the bag of shredded dog's-eye drawings, and Billy toted the wastebasket full of e-mail files.

The funeral home had two superefficient Power-Pak II Cremation Systems, and one of them was ready to be fired up.

Billy left the wastebasket full of e-mails with Juliette, and by the time he returned with the brain to Brian McCarthy's computer, she had fed all the papers into the cremator. He tossed in the bag of shredded drawings, and pointing to the computer logic unit, he said, "I want to pour something corrosive into it."

"Why, if we're going to burn it down to char and twisted scrap?"

"I like to be double sure."

"Billy, I'm having a rotten day, don't bust my chops."

"Well, you know cremators better than I do. You say it'll do the job, that's good enough for me."

Before he could move, she snared the logic unit with one hand, swung it up and into the cremator as if it weighed less than a dead cat. Juliette hated cats, and more than a few of them had most likely gone through this Power-Pak II.

She was a beautiful woman and hard and strong, but she was not a good person.

"What kind of rotten day?" he asked as she closed the cremator door and fired up the burner.

"Gunny wants it to get more serious between us."

The thought of those two in bed seemed, to Billy, to be about as serious as sex could get, except maybe if a grizzly bear tried to get it on with a puma.

"He wants to dump the wife in San Francisco and marry me. She's Chinese, has some connection to China's military-security apparatus, and she collects knives. I don't know what Gunny's thinking."

"Gunny has a hopeless romantic streak," Billy said, which was true.

"Tell me about it. He says, just shacking up with me doesn't fulfill him like marriage would. I'm his destiny, he says."

"I could talk to him."

"I'm nobody's destiny, Billy, except mine. The thing is, I've been thinking of ending it with him even before this, but he's as tight with Harrow as you are, and I don't want Gunny getting pissy and bad-mouthing me to Harrow."

"He's maybe not as important to Harrow as you think."

"Is that right? Well, anyway, he's such a big sonofabitch, he scares me."

"We go way back, Gunny and me. I can talk to him so he doesn't get a mad-on for you."

"Could you? Would you? That would be great. He's up on the top floor, making dinner."

She maintained a large and beautifully furnished apartment above the funeral home.

"I could go up there and see him," Billy said, "or you could get on the intercom and ask him to come down here."

"I just redid the kitchen cabinetry."

"What was wrong with the old cabinets? They were beautiful."

"Too dark," Juliette said. "All that egg-and-dart crown molding. I wanted a lighter, more modern look."

"Are you happy with it?"

"Oh, yeah. It's gorgeous."

"Good cabinetry can bust your bank these days."

"That's what I'm saying."

"So ask him to come down here."

She used the intercom in the garage, just outside the door to the crematorium. "Hey, Big Gun," she said, "are you there?"

Gunny's voice issued from the intercom speaker: "What's up?"

"I've got a really fat dead guy here I need some help with."

"What about Herman and Werner?"

They were her brothers and business partners.

"Viewing hours are over. They went home," she said. "We weren't expecting a stiff."

"I've got to keep an eye on the rack of lamb."

"I just need help getting the stiff into the cooler. One minute. He's a big old hog of a guy or I could do it myself."

"Be right there."

Because it had to accommodate a casket, the elevator was large, but quieter than Billy expected.

When the doors opened, Gunther Schloss looked as big as a steer in a rodeo pen.

He said, "Shit," and Billy shot him three times while he was upright, once while he was falling, and four times as he lay half in and half out of the elevator.

"Is he dead?" Juliette asked.

"He ought to be."

"You want to check for a pulse?"

"Not yet," Billy said, and shot Gunny two more times.

He would have shot Gunny four more times, but no rounds remained in the pistol.

Billy ejected the empty magazine and snapped a full one into the pistol, and during that quarter of a minute, Gunny didn't move.

"Okay, he's dead. I guess that was the easy part, after all."

"It could have gone different," Juliette said.

"It could have, you're right. But I'm fifty now, and the part that's getting not so easy for me is this hauling-them-around part."

"Piece of cake, Bookworm. In this business, I'm always moving dead weight."

She went away and returned in less than a minute, rolling a state-of-the-art hydraulic gurney.

Only the push of a button was required to lower the stainless-steel bed of the gurney until it was two inches from the floor.

With little difficulty, Billy and Juliette wrestled the corpse face-down onto the stainless steel.

She pressed the button again, and the bed rose to its usual height, bearing the cadaver.

"Excellent," Billy said.

They rolled the gurney into the crematorium. Juliette adjusted the height of the bed to match the door on the second cremator, and then the bed telescoped forward, carrying Gunny into the furnace.

Holding a toilet plunger by its long wooden handle, pressing the rubber suction cup against Gunny's head, Juliette held the body in the crematorium while the telescoping bed retracted into its original position.

"That's damn clever," Billy said, indicating the plunger.

Hearing this simple praise, Juliette ducked her head almost shyly. "A technique I developed."

As the woman closed the door and fired up the furnace, Billy said, "Gunny makes the best rack of lamb. Sorry if it's overdone."

"I'm sure it'll be perfect. You want to stay for dinner?"

"I'd love to, but I can't. My day isn't done yet."

"You work too hard, Billy."

"I'm gonna slow down."

"How long have you been saying that?"

"I mean it this time," he assured her.

"All you do is work. You don't take care of yourself."

"I'm having a colonoscopy next week."

"Is something wrong?" she asked.

"No, I'm good. My internist just recommends it at my age."

"Maybe he's some kind of pervert."

"No. He doesn't do the exam. I go to a specialist for that."

"Me, I've got high cholesterol."

"Have an arterial scan. I did. My cholesterol's high, too, but they didn't find any plaque."

"It's all about genes, Billy. If you have good genes, you can eat nothing but fried cheese and doughnuts, live to be a hundred."

"You look like good genes to me," he told her.

From the funeral home, Billy drove the Shumpeter Cadillac to the hotel where he had previously booked luxurious accommodations in the name of Tyrone Slothrop.

He left the Cadillac with the valet, presented his Slothrop American Express card to the registration clerk, and got his key. He carried the white trash bag to the elevator and went up to his suite.

Harrow wanted to see everything in the bag, especially the snapshots from Amy Redwing's previous life. Until Billy could turn the bag over to Harrow, he needed to keep it safe.

The suite consisted of an immense overfurnished living room, two large overfurnished bedrooms, and two baths. The bathrooms were glittering wonderments of marble and mirror.

He didn't need the extra bedroom and bath. He didn't need to drive a Hummer, either, but his personal collection of vehicles included three of them. He had time-shares in a private jet, and never traveled in scheduled airlines.

Billy believed in fun. Fun was the central doctrine of his philosophy. For him, having a giant carbon footprint was essential to having fun.

One of the businesses Billy had a piece of, through Harrow, was selling carbon offsets. He held binding commitments from three tribes in remote parts of Africa, which required them to plant huge numbers of trees and to continue living without running water, electricity, and oil-powered vehicles. The environmental damage they *didn't* do could then be sold to movie stars, rock musicians, and others who were committed to reducing pollution but who were required, by the nature of their professions, to have humongous carbon footprints.

Billy also sold carbon offsets to himself through an elaborate structure of LLPs, LLCs, and trusts that afforded him tremendous tax advantages. Best of all, he didn't have to share any of the carbon-offset income with the African tribes because they didn't exist.

Two locked suitcases awaited him. He had packed them three days earlier and had sent them to the hotel by FedEx.

Also awaiting him were arrangements of fresh flowers in every room, silver bowls full of perfect fruit, a box of superb chocolates, a bottle of Dom Perignon in an ice bucket—and on the nightstand in the primary bedroom, a just-released hardcover novel by one of his favorite writers, which the concierge had purchased at his request.

Billy Pilgrim—now passing as Tyrone Slothrop, a name he had waited literally *decades* to use—should have been in a fine mood, but he was not.

The events at the funeral home should have been fun. They had not tickled him at all.

He wasn't depressed, but he wasn't elated, either. Emotionally, he had slipped into neutral.

He had never been in neutral before. As he sat idling in his luxurious suite, the emptiness inside him—the void where fun had been—made him nervous.

Since the eerie incident with the drawings in Brian McCarthy's kitchen, fun had eluded him. He had been moving at his usual fast pace, as always capering gaily—figuratively speaking—along the brink of the abyss, committing crimes as insouciantly as ever; but the magic was gone.

His life was a novel, a black comedy, a rollicking narrative that mocked all authority, an existential lark. He had just hit a bad chapter, that was all. He needed to turn the page, begin a new scene.

Maybe the new novel on the nightstand would shift him out of neutral. One of the suitcases contained clothes and personal effects, but the other one was packed with weapons; maybe playing with guns for a while would get him in gear.

He sat in an armchair in the bedroom, alternately staring at the book and at the suitcase filled with lethal devices.

He worried that if he tried the book and it didn't lift him out of his funk, and then if he disassembled and reassembled the weapons with no improvement of mood, he would be at an impasse.

An impasse was a terrible place to be, a dead end, but in a truly existential life, it should be an *impossible* place to be. Since only he made the rules by which he lived, he could make new rules if the old ones began to bore him, and off he would go again, zipping along, having fun.

He was thinking too much, making himself nervous.

All that mattered were the motion and the act, not any meaning in the motion nor any consequences to the act. No meaning existed; no consequences were important.

He tried the book. That was his first mistake.

Chapter

48

At a few minutes past two in the morning, Amy woke from a
dream full of the sound of wings. Her breath caught in her
throat, and for a moment she did not recognize her surroundings.

An end-table lamp draped with a towel served as a night-light.

Santa Barbara. The motel. They had found accommodations that
accepted dogs, one room that had not been taken for the night.

Brian had finally gotten her into bed; but it was her own bed, one
of two in the room. And a watchdog slept with her.

As she had shaken off sleep, she had thought that the thrumming
of wings was in the room, not in the dream. That could not be true
because both Brian in the other bed and Nickie beside her remained
asleep.

She remembered nothing of the dream, only the sound of pinions
plying the air. In sleep, she must have returned to Connecticut, and
the gulls must have been startled into flight yet again.

According to psychologists and sleep specialists, you could never
see yourself die in a dream. You might be in prolonged high jeop-
ardy, but at the penultimate moment, you would wake. Even in

dreams, they claimed, the human ego remained too stubborn to admit to its mortality.

Amy, however, had seen herself die in dreams. Several times, always in that Connecticut night.

Perhaps subconsciously she had a death wish. That didn't surprise her.

On that winter night almost nine years before, she had fought for her life and survived. Then for a while, ironically, she'd had no compelling reason to live.

In the days immediately after, she wondered *why* she had fought back. Death would have been easier than living. The pain that nearly tore her apart could have been avoided by submitting to the knife.

Even in her darkest moments, she would never have committed suicide. Murder included self-destruction.

Her faith got her through, but not faith alone. Her ability to see patterns in chaos, when others saw more chaos, served her well.

Patterns implied meaning. No matter how inscrutable the meaning might seem, no matter that an understanding of it might forever elude her, she was encouraged by the perception that meaning existed.

She read the patterns in life the way other people might read tea leaves and palms and crystal balls. But her interpretation wasn't guided by a code of superstitions.

Intuition alone determined for her what the patterns meant and what they suggested she should do. To her way of thinking, *intuition* was a word for perceptions that were received on a level far below the subconscious. Intuition was seeing with the soul.

Plugged in and charging on the nightstand, her phone rang. She disliked all the musical tones and the cartoon-voice tones and the raucous sounds with which phones "rang" these days. Hers just burred quietly.

Surprised to get a call at this hour, she snatched up the phone before it could wake Brian, and said softly, "Hello?"

No one responded.

Although Brian continued to sleep, Nickie had awakened. She raised her head to watch Amy.

"Hello?" she repeated.

"Oh. Is that you, dear? Well, yes, of course it is."

The sweet, high-pitched voice was unmistakable. Amy almost said *Sister Mouse*, caught herself, and said, "Sister Jacinta."

"You've been in my thoughts so much lately, Amy."

Amy hesitated. She thought of the slippers. She felt now as she had felt then, when Nickie insisted she take the slippers. "Sister . . . You too. You've been in my thoughts."

Sister Jacinta said, "You're always in my heart of course, you were one of my very favorites, but lately you're in my thoughts all the time, all the time, so I thought I better speak to you."

Emotion tied a knot in Amy's vocal cords.

"Dear? Are you all right with me—I mean, the middle of the night like this?"

Speaking hardly above a whisper, Amy said, "Just tonight I told Brian, a friend . . . told Brian about back then, our mascot Nickie."

"That wonderful, wonderful dog."

"And the locket you gave me."

"Which you still wear."

"Yes." With her forefinger, she traced the contours of the canine cameo.

"This friend, dear, do you love him?"

"Sister, I'm sorry, but I'm kind of . . . struggling here."

"Well, love is or it isn't. You must know."

Amy merely murmured now. "Yes. I love him."

"Have you told him?"

"Yes. That I love him. Yes."

"I meant have you told him all of it?"

"No. I guess you know. I haven't yet."

"He needs to know."

"It's so hard, Sister."

"The truth won't diminish you in his eyes."

She could barely speak. "It diminishes me in my own."

"I'm proud you were one of my girls. I say, 'See her, she was one of my Mother of Mercy girls, see how she shines?'"

Amy had come to tears again, quiet tears this time. "If only I could believe that was true."

"Remember to whom you're talking, dear. Of course it's true."

"I'm sorry."

"Don't be sorry. Just tell him. He very much needs to know. It is imperative. Now get some sleep, child, get some sleep."

Although Amy heard no change in line tone, she sensed that they had been disconnected. "Sister Jacinta?"

She received no reply.

"Oh, Sister Mouse, sweet Sister Mouse."

She placed the phone on the nightstand.

She turned on her side, toward Nickie. Face to face, Amy put one arm around the dog. Those eyes.

Amy shuddered, not because of the call itself, but because the call must mean that something terrible was coming.

Sister Jacinta, Sister Mouse, had been dead for ten years.

Chapter

49

A writer who had never failed to excite Billy Pilgrim's contempt
for humanity, who had reliably made him laugh uproari-
ously at those cretins who believed in human exceptionalism, had
this time failed him utterly and had raised in him not one giggle in
forty pages of text.

Billy twice studied the photograph on the back of the jacket, but
the face was familiar. The piercing eyes that challenged you to read
the savage truth between these covers. The slight sneer that said *If
you don't laugh at this poisonous satire, you're a self-deluded fool who will
never be invited to the best parties.*

The writer had changed publishing houses, but that could not
account for the collapse of his standards, the loss of his narrative
voice. This publisher had released a number of books that Billy had
found enormously appealing. It was a highly credible house.

No publisher hit home runs all the time or even the majority of
the time, but this colophon on the spine had always previously been
a mark of quality.

As Billy stared at the colophon, a chill prickled at the crown of his
head and spread outward in concentric shivers, to the limits of his

receding hairline and beyond, down his unsmiling face, down the back of his neck, to the base of his spine, to the pit of his gut.

A stylized sprinting dog served as the colophon. Although not a golden retriever, it was a dog nonetheless.

He had seen this colophon a thousand times, and it had never unnerved him before. It unnerved him now.

He was tempted to click on the gas-log fireplace and consign the book to the flames. Instead, he put it in the nightstand and closed the drawer.

The memory of the tears that he had shed in McCarthy's kitchen remained vivid, mortifying and frightening. In his line of work, if you started weeping for no reason—or even for a good reason—you were on a slippery slope.

In the living room, he opened the Dom Perignon and poured the champagne not into one of the handsome flutes but instead into a drinking glass. He selected a miniature bottle of fine cognac from the honor bar, opened it, and spiked the champagne.

Pacing through the wonderfully cavernous suite, he sucked at his drink, but by the time he had drained the glass, he felt no better.

Because he would be seeing Harrow in the afternoon and could not afford a hangover, he dared not risk a series of such concoctions.

The only other solace at hand were the weapons in the second suitcase. They were new purchases, gifts to himself. Other men indulged themselves with golf clubs, but Billy didn't golf.

He returned to the bedroom and put the suitcase on the bed. With the smallest key on his chain, he disengaged the locks.

When he opened the case, the firearm and accessories were there in the left half, as he had packed them.

In his current mood, he had half expected that the always before reliable FedEx had confused his bag with an identical one belonging to, say, a vacationing Mormon dentist or a Bible salesman, and that the contents would give him no fun at all.

The right half of the case contained a second gun, but on top lay a sheaf of papers. The first was McCarthy's pencil drawing of the golden retriever.

Billy didn't remember exploding out of the bedroom, but in the living room, the bottle of champagne rattled against the rim of the glass as he poured.

He needed ten minutes to decide that he had to go back into the bedroom and examine the drawings—which, damn it, he had shredded in McCarthy's office, bagged, and later tossed into the cremator at the funeral home.

If the drawings could survive the cremator and show up in his luggage, there was no argument against the possibility that Gunny Schloss, shot ten times and consigned to the fire, might be waiting in the bathroom when Billy went in there to piss.

He approached the open suitcase with caution—and discovered that the sheaf of papers were not torn from McCarthy's art tablet. They were the pages of a monthly tabloid-format newspaper published for hunters, target shooters, and other gun aficionados. He had packed the publication himself three days previously.

The reappearance of the drawing had been entirely the work of his imagination. This discovery was an enormous relief. And then it wasn't. A man with Billy Pilgrim's responsibilities—and with his associates—could not survive long if he lost his nerve.

Chapter

50

Piggy sits at the desk with magazines. Piggy likes pictures.
She cuts them out of magazines.

She can't have words.

Mother says Piggy is too dumb to read words. Reading words
is for people with brains in their heads.

*Piggy, poor baby, if you try to learn to read, your fat funny little head
will explode.*

Piggy can read *hope* when she sees it. She can read other words,
a few.

Her head is okay. Maybe it will go bang with one more word.
Probably not.

Mother lies. A lot.

Mother lives to lie, and she lies to live. Bear said so.

*Piggy, your mom doesn't just lie to you and everybody else. She also
lies to herself.*

This is true. Weird but true.

Here's one way Piggy knows it's true: Being told lies makes you
unhappy. Her mother is always unhappy.

Lying to herself gets your mom through the day. If she ever faced the truth, she'd fall apart.

Sometimes on a star, sometimes no star, Piggy wishes Mother wouldn't lie.

But she doesn't want her mother to fall apart, either.

Maybe Mother sometimes feels she will fall apart, so she tears a doll apart instead. Something to think about.

Here's another way Piggy knows Mother lies to herself: She thinks nothing bad can happen to her.

Something bad already happened to her. Piggy doesn't know what bad thing happened to her mother, but you can tell it happened. You can tell.

Bear knew Mother always lies. But Mother lied to Bear, and Bear believed some of her lies.

Weird but true.

Mother and Bear were together to Make Some Money. Everyone needs to Make Some Money.

Piggy and her mother are always going new places, meeting new friends. All friends, everywhere, talk how to Make Some Money.

Usually they talk guns when they talk money. You Make Some Money with guns.

Piggy does not like guns. She will never Make Some Money.

So Bear wanted to Make Some Money, but he was different. Bear saw Piggy. Mostly they see Piggy but don't really see her.

Bear was a mess, but he wasn't as big a mess as Mother.

Piggy, I'm a mess, I'm weak and I'm foolish, but I'm not as big a mess as your mother.

She didn't like Bear saying bad things about himself. Because she knew Bear didn't lie to her.

Mother promised Bear when they had money, then she would give Piggy to child-welfare people.

Piggy doesn't know who child-welfare people are. Bear made them sound nice. He made them sound not like the usual friends with guns.

After they had money, Mother broke her promise. No child-welfare people for Piggy.

Bear and Mother are laughing, and Mother sits on his lap.

This was back on the day it happened.

Mother sits on Bear's lap, laughing, and takes the big knife out from between sofa cushions, where it never was before.

Piggy remembers like it's right now, like it's not back then.

Mother makes the knife go all the way through Bear's neck, front to back.

Then everything gets very bad, worse than anything ever.

Let not your heart be troubled.

Let not your heart be troubled.

Mother says she didn't kill him to take his money. She says she killed him because he was Piggy's friend.

Mother says, *My friends are mine, you fat-faced little freak. My friends aren't yours. What's mine is mine. You're mine, Piggy Pig. You belong to me, Piggy Pig. Nobody takes what's mine. He's dead because of you.*

This would make Piggy sad forever if it was true Bear was dead because of her.

Here's one way Piggy knows it isn't true: Mother always lies.

Let not your heart be troubled.

Here's another way Piggy knows it isn't true: Dying, Bear looks at her, and his eyes aren't afraid or angry.

His eyes just say *Sorry, Piggy.*

And his eyes say *It's okay, girl, you keep on keepin' on.*

Piggy can read eyes. She can't read words, but she reads eyes real good.

Sometimes when she reads her mother's eyes, Piggy feels her head might go bang.

The lock squeaks.

Piggy doesn't hide the magazine. She keeps scissoring pictures. She is allowed to cut pictures.

The magazines are Mother's, but old ones she doesn't want.

Piggy is allowed to cut lots of pictures and paste them together to make bigger pictures. Mother calls the bigger pictures some name Piggy will never read and can't remember.

Piggy doesn't call them any name. She just sees how some pretty things can be put with other pretty things in ways so all the things are even more pretty because of how they're put together.

The most pretty things Piggy makes, her mother burns. They go outside, and Mother burns the best put-together pictures.

This is one of not many things you can say for sure makes her mother happy.

Here's another way Piggy knows Mother lies even to herself: She thinks she is *always* happy.

The lock squeaks. The door opens. Mother comes in.

The man stays in the doorway, leaning there, arms crossed.

Mother and the man have been drinking. You can tell.

Mother sits on the desk. "What're you doing, baby?"

"Makin' stuff."

"My little artist."

"Just pictures."

Mother has a knife.

Not the Bear knife, but like the Bear knife.

She puts it on the desk.

Piggy thinks maybe she forgot to zip the chair-cushion cover after she put away the Forever Shiny Thing.

If Mother sees an open chair-cushion cover and finds HOPE on a silver chain, then here come the Big Uglies.

Piggy glances at the chair. Cover is zipped.

"Big day coming, Piggy."

Cover is zipped, so just keep working the scissors.

"Your daddy is coming to get you, baby."

Piggy makes a mistake. She cuts off a pretty lady's head. So she pretends she only wants a head, and she cuts the head out very carefully.

"I've told you about your daddy, how you made him sick to his stomach, your stupid fat face embarrassed him, so he dumped you on me and split."

"Sure," Piggy says, but just to say something.

"Well, he's got religion all of a sudden, wants to do the right thing, so he's coming to take you home with him, where the two of you will live happily ever after."

This is bad. This is as bad as bad can be.

Maybe it is a lie her father is coming.

If it's a lie, why say it? Only to make Piggy hope and then, no, it doesn't happen, but some really really bad thing happens instead.

And if her father really is coming, they won't go and be happy ever after. No way.

What's mine is mine. You're mine, Piggy Pig. You belong to me, Piggy Pig. Nobody takes what's mine.

Her nice Bear dead and all the blood and her mother whispering *You're mine, Piggy Pig.*

And here on the desk is a knife like the Bear knife.

If Piggy's father comes, Mother will kill him.

She wants Piggy to know what will happen. That's why the knife on the desk. So Piggy will know.

Mother wants Piggy to know there is a chance of getting away but, no, not a chance after all, because nobody takes what belongs to Mother. She wants Piggy to have hope, then steals it from her.

But Mother doesn't know, whatever happens, Piggy has HOPE Bear gave her on a silver chain.

"My guy here, Piggy, he wonders why I ever had you in the first place, a little mutant like you."

She means the man standing in the doorway. Piggy is afraid of this man more than others who were before him. He makes Mother worse. Mother is much worse since him.

"There was this big rich guy, he built homes, name was Hisscus. He couldn't make babies, he had bad seed."

Piggy looks her mother in the eyes. She reads Mother's eyes, and in there with all the scary, Piggy sees some truth.

So she can't look at Mother's eyes anymore, Piggy works the scissors on another picture.

While she cuts, she listens close, not understanding half, but when Mother tells truth, it's a big thing because she never does.

"Hisscus, he wasn't married, but he wanted a baby in the worst way. Didn't want it officially. Wanted an unofficial baby."

From the corner of her eye, Piggy sees Mother glance toward the man in the doorway.

"Hisscus knew this doctor who was like him, would deliver the baby at home, no birth certificate, no record."

Mother laughs at something the man in the doorway does.

Piggy keeps her head down.

"So I had your daddy knock me up," Mother tells Piggy.

This doesn't mean anything to Piggy. She listens closer.

"Didn't have an ultrasound scan to determine sex or anything."

The closer Piggy listens, the less sense Mother makes.

"If I gave him a girl, Hisscus would keep it. If I gave him a boy, he knew people who wanted the same kind of candy he did, but who liked the opposite flavor, so he could trade it to them for a girl."

In the doorway, the man whistles very soft and low. He says, "What's colder than dry ice?"

"Me, baby," Mother tells him.

Neither of them is making any sense. Ice is wet.

"Hisscus had this second house, cool place, up the coast. I was going to live there, get a big fat paycheck every month, whatever I wanted. When the maid came in to clean, she wouldn't know about the secret cellar."

Piggy doesn't understand what her mother is telling her, but she knows for sure, without knowing *how* she knows, that whatever she does right now, she must not look in Mother's eyes, because what's in them now is scarier than anything before.

"Then, Piggy, you pop out of me, stupid fat-faced little Piggy Pig, and the whole deal falls apart. He doesn't want a little Piggy Pig in his secret cellar, not even if he's got me, because I wasn't what he wanted most to begin with."

"Blackmail?" says the man in the doorway.

"That's why I kept the little bitch," Mother says. "I tried to play that angle. But I didn't have proof. He'd been totally clever. He tried paying me off with chump change, and I took it, but I kept pushing for a year—and then it turned out he knew how to push back hard."

"After that, why didn't she end up in a Dumpster?"

"By then," Mother says, "I thought old Piggy Pig owed me big-time, and I like to be paid what I'm owed."

Mother picks up the knife.

"Piggy's been paying me good interest, but it's about time I get my principal back."

Mother gets up from the desk.

"Piggy, my guy and me just had a bonding moment." To the man, she says, "Now you know it all, you think I'm too nasty for you?"

"Never," he says.

"So are you nasty enough for me?"

"I can try to be," he says.

She laughs again. Mother has a nice laugh.

Sometimes, no matter what happens, Mother's laugh makes you want to smile. Not now.

They leave and lock the door.

Piggy alone.

She doesn't know what any of it meant. But whatever it meant, it didn't mean anything good.

She puts down the scissors.

She says, "Hey, Bear," but though Bear will always be with her, he does not answer.

Mother and the man talking, voices fading. They are going away awhile to do something, she doesn't know what, but she can tell.

When Mother comes back, she will have the knife. The knife is going to be with her from now on. Until she uses it.

All things work out for the best, hard as that is to believe.

That's what Bear said. And Bear knew things. Bear wasn't dumb like Piggy. But Bear is dead.

PART THREE

"The woods are lovely, dark, and deep,
But I have promises to keep,
And miles to go before I sleep,
And miles to go before I sleep."

—ROBERT FROST
Stopping by Woods on a Snowy Evening

Chapter

51

The first one out of bed, at a quarter to six, Amy showered and dressed. She fed Nickie and took her for a walk while Brian prepared for the day.

The sun hadn't appeared with the dawn. Gray clouds smeared the sky. They looked greasy.

In the oceanside park, the immense old palm trees barely stirred in a breeze as languid as the ocean off which it came. As if wounded, colorless waves crawled to shore and expired on sand ribboned with rotting seaweed.

When you believe life has meaning and can glimpse patterns that seem to suggest design, you risk *seeking* signs instead of waiting to receive them as a grace. Omens seem to be scattered as extravagantly as litter in the wake of a wind storm, and in the rain of reckless imagination, portents spring up in mushroom clusters.

After the telephone call from Sister Jacinta, Amy did not trust herself, for the time being, to recognize the difference between a true pattern and a fancy, between a significance and an iffiness. The coincidence of Nickie's name, her behavior, the business with the slippers, Theresa's reference to wind and chimes—all of that had been peculiar, suggestive, but not clearly evidence of otherworldly forces at work. A phone call from a dead nun, however, qualified as a higher order of the fantastic, and you tended thereafter to see portentous messages in every face that Nature turned toward you.

Movement drew her eye to a rat that scurried up the bole of a great phoenix palm and disappeared into the fringe of folded dead fronds beneath the green crown.

A rat was a symbol of filth, decay, death.

Here, on the sidewalk, a large black beetle lay on its back, legs stiff, and swarming ants fed on the leakage from it.

And here, beside a trash can with a gated top so loose that it creaked even in the sea's faint exhalation, lay an empty bottle of hot sauce with a skull and crossbones on the label.

On the other hand, three white doves arrowed across the sky, and seven pennies were arranged on the rim of a drinking fountain, and on a bench lay a discarded paperback titled *Your Bright Future.*

She decided to let Nickie's instincts guide her. The dog sniffed everything, fixated on nothing, and exhibited no suspicion. By the golden's example, Amy found her way to a less fevered interpretation of every shape and shadow, and then to a disinterest in signs.

In fact, skepticism crept over her, and she began to question whether the conversation with Sister Jacinta had actually occurred. She could have dreamed it.

She thought she had awakened from a nightmare of wings moments before the phone rang, but maybe she only moved from a dream of Connecticut to a dream of a dialogue with a ghost.

After the call, she had faced Nickie, put her arm around the dog, and had gone to sleep again. They had awakened together in that cuddle. If the call only happened in a dream, she had merely turned to Nickie in her sleep.

By the time Amy returned to the motel room, she had decided not to tell Brian about Sister Mouse. At least not yet. Maybe when they were on the road.

Before he had gone to bed the previous night, Brian had sent an e-mail to Vanessa. While Amy had been walking Nickie, Vanessa sent a reply.

She gave the address of a restaurant in Monterey at which she wanted Amy and Brian to have lunch.

They grabbed breakfast at a fast-food joint and ate on the move again, northbound on Highway 101. They should be in Monterey by noon.

For the first three hours, Brian drove. He said little, and most of the time he stared at the road ahead with a grim expression.

Although he was eager to gain custody of his daughter, he must be worried about the condition in which he would find her and about how much she might hold him responsible for her suffering.

Amy tried more than once to lure him out of the glum currents of his thoughts, but he rose to the conversation only briefly each time, and then swam down again into brooding silence.

Forced by his introspection into some self-analysis of her own, she admitted to herself that skepticism had not been the real reason she hesitated to tell Brian about the telephone call from Sister Jacinta. Her dismissal of the visitation as just a dream had been insincere.

The truth was that relating the content of her conversation with the nun would require her to tell Brian the rest of the story she had been too exhausted and too emotionally drained—too gnawed by guilt—to finish the previous night. She had broken off that narrative with the death of Nickie at Mater Misericordiæ; she tried to summon the courage to tell the rest of it.

After they parked in a lay-by to stretch their legs and to give Nickie a potty break, Amy drove the last two hours to Monterey.

She had to keep her eyes on the road now. She had reason not to look at him directly while she talked, and this gave her confidence to return to the past.

Nevertheless, she could still only approach the monstrous event obliquely, and in steps. She began with the lighthouse.

"Did I ever tell you, I lived in a lighthouse for a few years?"

"Wonderful architecture in most lighthouses," he said. "I would have remembered your lighthouse years."

His tone implied that he knew she also would have remembered having told him, and that he recognized the false casualness of her revelation.

"With satellite navigation, many lighthouses aren't in service anymore. Others have been automated—electricity instead of an oil brazier."

"Some are bed-and-breakfast inns."

"Yeah. They renovate the caretaker's house. Some even offer a room or two in the lighthouse itself."

This lighthouse had stood on a rocky promontory in Connecticut. She had been twenty when she moved there, twenty-four when she left.

She did not explain what brought her to that place or mention whether she had been there alone or with others.

Brian seemed to sense that questions would inhibit her and that the wrong question, asked too soon, would halt her altogether.

She spoke of the rugged shore and the thrilling seascapes, of the spectacular views from the lantern room at the top of the tower, and of the charming details of the lightkeeper's house.

She dwelt at length on the beauty of the lighthouse itself, the walnut paneling of the round vestibule, the ornate fretwork of the circular iron staircase. At the summit, in the lantern room, waited the marvelous Fresnel lens, oval in shape, with integrated series of prismatic rings at bottom and top, which reflected the rays of a one-thousand-watt halogen bulb to the center of the lens, amplifying them. Thus concentrated, the light was beamed outward, across the dark Atlantic.

They arrived at the restaurant in Monterey as she finished telling him that, in the early nineteenth century, Fresnel lenses were so heavy, the only way to turn them—and make the beam sweep the coast—was to float them in pools of mercury. Extremely dense, mercury will support great weight and reduce friction to a minimum.

Mercury is highly toxic. Gradually, mercury flotation was phased out in favor of clockworks and counterweights, which were subsequently replaced by electric motors.

Before then, however, some lightkeepers were driven insane by mercury poisoning.

Chapter

52

Billy Pilgrim flew as the lone passenger in a chartered Learjet from Santa Barbara to Monterey.

The steward wore black slacks, a white coat, a white shirt, and a black bowtie. He had a British accent.

Airborne at ten o'clock, Billy was served a late breakfast of strawberries in clotted cream, a lobster omelet, and toasted brioche with raisin butter.

He'd left his suitcase of clothes at the hotel in Santa Barbara because, sometime in the evening, when everyone who needed to be dead was dead, he intended to resume his vacation as Tyrone Slothrop.

He had brought the second suitcase containing the guns. The first was a Glock 18 with thirty-three rounds in its magazine. The second was a disassembled sniper rifle.

Before leaving Santa Barbara, he had taken the tabloid newspaper for gun aficionados out of the suitcase and had left it on the living-room coffee table. He was not concerned that the publication would once more transform itself into Brian McCarthy's drawings of the dog. That had been a hallucination born of weariness. Billy was rested and past all that. He merely wanted to save the paper for reading later in the week. Nothing more. Just that. He felt fine.

The steward brought him an array of glossy magazines, and when he opened one, the first thing he saw was an advertisement for high-end men's suits. In the double-page spread, three well-tailored young men were walking three golden retrievers.

Billy closed the magazine and put it aside. The photo had meant nothing. Coincidence.

Suspecting that the same two-page spread might appear in many publications, Billy did not leaf through the front matter of the next magazine, but opened it to the middle, where he was more likely to encounter editorial content than advertising. The story in front of him concerned a dog-loving celebrity and her three golden retrievers.

In the opening photograph, all three dogs were looking directly into the camera, and something in their eyes suggested to Billy that months ago, when the photo shoot occurred, the dogs had known that he, Billy Pilgrim, would many weeks later be looking at them as he was looking at them now, in a state of agitation. The three dogs were grinning, but he saw no laughter in their eyes, quite the opposite.

Billy dropped the magazine and went at once into the bathroom. He didn't throw up. He felt good about not throwing up. Not throwing up indicated that he had pretty much regained control of his nerves.

He looked in the mirror, saw that sweat beaded his brow, and blotted his face with a towel. After that, he looked good. He wasn't pale, but he pinched his cheeks anyway, to get more color in them. He looked fine. He hadn't wept a single tear. He winked at himself.

In Monterey, when Brian McCarthy and Amy Redwing arrived, Billy had the restaurant under surveillance from a rental car parked across the street.

He knew that she rescued goldens and owned them. But he had not expected her to bring one with her on a trip like this. They didn't know their ultimate destination. They didn't know how far they were going or where they might be staying, or what situation they would find on the other end. Taking the dog with them made no sense. It made no sense. He couldn't see any way it made sense.

The restaurant didn't accept dogs, so they locked the golden in the Expedition with the windows cracked. The SUV was parked at the curb. They went inside, and after a minute, Billy saw them in one of the windows. They had taken a table from which they could watch over the dog.

Billy telephoned Harrow to report that the pair had arrived in Monterey.

"Do they have a shadow?"

"If they're suspicious and they came with backup, it's way discreet. I'd bet my ass, no, they're alone. Except they brought a golden retriever."

Harrow surprised him by saying, "Kill it."

To be sure he made no mistake, Billy said, "Kill the dog?"

"Kill it good. Kill it hard. That's what she wants."

"Who wants?"

"Vanessa. Kill the dog. But not until they get here. They're flying on good feelings, coming to get his precious child. We want to keep them in a 'What-me-worry?' mood."

Harrow hung up.

Billy watched the golden watching McCarthy and Redwing in the restaurant window. They occasionally looked up to check on the dog.

The Glock 18 featured a selector switch on the slide with which he could convert it from a semiautomatic to a full automatic that cycled at thirteen hundred rounds per minute. When the time came, he could pump twenty bullets into the dog in like one second. That seemed to qualify as *kill-it-good-kill-it-hard*.

The dog was watching Billy.

It had been intently focused on the restaurant window where McCarthy and Redwing were eating lunch, but it had turned around.

From across the street, Billy stared right back at it.

The dog seemed to have lost all interest in its owners. It appeared to be fascinated with Billy.

Not in the least intimidated, Billy narrowed his eyes to pull the golden retriever into even clearer focus.

The dog raised its nose to the two-inch gap at the top of the open window. It was getting Billy's scent.

At once, Billy started the rental car. He drove back to the airport. He had a schedule to keep. He needed to get moving. Nothing more. Just that. He felt fine.

Chapter

53

In the restaurant, Amy did not return to the subject of the light-house. Brian sensed that she didn't want to talk about that period of her life within earshot of anyone but him.

He realized that she must be leading to some disclosure that she was loath to make, to that ringbolt in the past to which he had long suspected she was tethered.

His own revelation surely had helped her. For ten years, he had failed the child whom he had fathered. Whatever Amy had done was not likely to have burdened her with the weight of guilt that Brian felt he had earned.

Vanessa phoned during their lunch. "You'll be going through San Francisco and across the Golden Gate Bridge."

"I didn't realize it would be this far."

"You're going to whine at me, Bry?"

"No. I'm just saying."

"Ten years of my life are crap because I had to take care of our Piggy Pig, and now you're going to whine about one day on the road?"

"Forget I said anything. You're right. Once we cross the bridge, what?"

"Stay north on 101. I'll call with details. Anyway, Bry, you couldn't have flown to San Francisco and driven from there. Not on short notice, not with the dog."

He glanced out the window at Nickie in the Expedition. "So you really are watching us."

"My nervous little rich boy says what if the dog's wired by some scandal-crazy tabloid-TV show. You believe that? The *dog*?"

"I told you, I won't risk blowing this deal."

"I know you won't, Bry. His security people were going to do an electronic sweep of you, your SUV, soon as you got here. Now they'll also sweep the dog. Maybe there's a microphone built into its collar. Maybe there's a power pack up its butt. Isn't that hysterical?"

"If you say so."

"See you soon, Bry."

She terminated the call.

Brian picked at the second half of his meal, and Amy seemed to have lost her appetite, too.

"I want it over," he said. "I just want Hope away from her."

"Then let's hit the road," Amy said.

Back at the Expedition, Nickie got out to take a pee and then graciously accepted two cookies as a reward for having been such a patient girl.

After the dog sprang into the back of the SUV once more and turned to Brian as he stood at the tailgate, he met her stare and held it. On this clouded day, Nickie's warm-molasses gaze was not brightened by refracted sunshine, but full of shadows, steady and direct and dark.

For a moment, he felt nothing strange, but then the centripetal force of these eyes seemed to pull him toward them. He felt his heart quickening, and his mind was bright with a perception of deep mystery and with the desire to understand it that had led him to draw so many studies of her eyes with such obsession.

In his memory rose the complex and enfolding sound: hiss, whizz, soft clicking, rustle and flump, deep throb and ruffle, *crumpcrump-crumpcrump—*

The sound stopped abruptly when the dog turned away from him and went forward into the cargo area.

Brian became aware of the traffic noise in the street rising slowly from the hush into which he had not until now realized that it had fallen.

He closed the tailgate and went around to the front passenger door. Amy had expressed the desire to drive.

In the car, on the open road, they would have privacy. Secrets could more easily be shared.

On the interstate, bound for the storied city, she was silent for a while but then said, "When I was eighteen, I married a man named Michael Cogland. He probably intended to kill me from the day that I accepted his proposal."

Chapter

54

The previous evening, when he had shot Gunny Schloss, Billy had killed his third person since dawn, having also assisted in two other homicides. When he should have been full of merriment, all the fun had gone out of the day and all the frolic out of him.

As he drove away from the restaurant in Monterey, feeling the dog's stare on the back of his head even after he turned the corner, he decided the problem might be that he had killed those people solely for business reasons. He hadn't wasted any of them just for a lark, simply as an expression of his conviction that life was a parade of fools marching to no purpose.

Shumpeter had not been a business associate, but he had not been killed as an act of meaningless violence, either. Billy blew him away for his Cadillac and to use his house as a furnace in which to obliterate multiple life-sentences worth of incriminating evidence.

To his chagrin, Billy realized that he had lost his way. He had gotten so consumed by business that he'd strayed from the philosophy that had given him such a happy and successful life. He had become so *serious* about the illegal drug dealing, arms dealing, organ dealing, and other enterprises that he had succumbed to the idea that what he did *mattered*. Other than the fact that everything he did to earn money was illegal, he could not see one lick of difference between himself and Bill Gates: He had committed himself to *building* something, to a *legacy*! .

He was embarrassed for himself. He had become a counter-culture bourgeois, seduced by the illusion of purpose and accomplishment.

The previous night, driving away from Brian McCarthy's place after the inexplicable crying jag, he had told himself that the tonic most certain to improve his mood would be the ruthless murder of a total stranger selected on a whim, thus confirming the meaningless and dark-comic nature of life.

He had been correct. A moment of clear seeing. But he had not yet acted on his own good advice more than half a day later.

With the Learjet, he could leapfrog over McCarthy and Redwing, and be waiting at the interception point long before they arrived. He had time to put his life back on track.

In a Best Buy parking lot, Billy opened the weapons case. He snapped the thirty-three-round magazine into the 9-mm Glock 18 and screwed on the sound suppressor.

Then he cruised.

During the next half hour, he encountered numerous excellent targets. A sweet-looking elderly woman walking a Maltese. A girl in a wheelchair. A beautiful young woman, demurely dressed, getting into a Honda bearing bumper stickers that urged JUST SAY NO TO DRUGS and ABSTINENCE ALWAYS WORKS.

When he failed to work up the energy to pull the trigger on a young mother pushing two infants in a tandem stroller, Billy knew he was having a midlife crisis.

In a Target parking lot, he unscrewed the silencer from the Glock, ejected the extended magazine, and returned everything to the molded-foam niches in the suitcase.

He had never been so scared in his life.

When he completed the current job, he would take off longer than a few days, perhaps a month. He would live the entire time as Tyrone Slothrop, and would reread all the classics that had liberated him in his youth.

The problem might be that the current generation of alienated, bitter, ironic, angry, nihilistic writers with a comic bent were not as talented as the giants who had come before them. If he had been sustaining himself on weak tea, mistaking it for white lightning, he could have unwittingly been starving his mind.

He returned to the airport, where the Lear waited.

At Billy's request, the steward with the British accent prepared Chivas Regal over cracked ice.

Lunch, served high above the earth, was a chopped salad with breast of capon and quail's eggs.

Billy sipped Scotch, ate, and brooded. He did not pick up any magazines. He went to the bathroom once, but he didn't glance at the mirror. He did not worry about the dog getting his scent through the open SUV window. He did not weep. Not a single tear. His malaise was just a bump in the road. Nothing to worry about. A bump. In the road. Hi-ho.

Chapter

55

Driving toward the city where so many people had claimed to have left their hearts, Amy unburdened hers.

In her senior year at Misericordiæ, she won a scholarship from a major university. Because it was partial, she had to support herself.

For two years in high school, she had worked part-time as a waitress. She had liked the job and had earned good tips.

When she went away to university, she landed a job in an upscale steakhouse. There she met Michael Cogland, a regular customer, when he was twenty-six, eight years her senior.

He was charming and intense, but when he asked her out, she did not initially accept the invitation. He proved to be indefatigable.

Amy thought she knew what she wanted: a first-rate education, including a doctorate, a career as a professor, a quiet academic life with many friends, and an opportunity to enrich the lives of students as the sisters of Misericordiæ had enriched hers.

Michael Cogland not only persisted until he swept her out of her waitressing shoes, but he also swept her into a world of wealth that she found irresistibly seductive.

Later she would realize that being abandoned at the age of two with only the clothes she wore, having lost the Harkinsons and the solid middle-class life they would have given her, and having been raised in an orphanage, she had grown up with a thirst for security that had not been quenched by all the love that the sisters had rained on her. She had gotten along for eighteen years without more than a few dollars in her wallet, and she had thought that poverty— and the comfort with which she lived in it—inoculated her against an unhealthy desire for money.

Cogland had recognized her subconscious yearning for security and, with subtlety and cunning, had presented her with a vision of a cozy future that she could not resist.

Because she was a modest Catholic-school girl, he treated her with respect, too, and delayed a physical relationship until they were married. He knew precisely how to play her.

They were engaged two months after they met, and were married in four. She dropped out of university and into a life of leisure.

He wanted a family. Soon she was pregnant. But there would be a nanny, maids.

Only much later did she learn that although Michael was a rich man by most standards, his greatest wealth was held in trust. By the terms of his grandfather's will, those funds would pass to him only on two conditions: Before his thirtieth birthday, he must marry a girl acceptable to his parents, and he must father a child by her.

Apparently his grandfather, if not also his parents, had seen in him, even when he'd been a boy, a tendency toward bad attitudes and ill-considered actions. As the Coglands had been a scandal-free family of faith, whose wealth had been built with a strong sense of community service, they believed in the power of a good wife and children to settle a man who might otherwise indulge his weaknesses.

Amy gave birth to a daughter when she was nineteen, and for a while all seemed well, a long life of privilege and joy propitiously begun. Michael came into his inheritance—and still she didn't know that she had been the vehicle by which he obtained it.

Gradually, she began to see in him a different man from the one whom she had thought she married. The better she knew him, the less that his charm seemed genuine, the more it appeared to be a tool for manipulation. His warm manner wore thin, and a colder mind at times revealed itself.

He had a goatish streak, and he jumped the fence to more than a few other women. Twice she found evidence, but in most cases she knew the truth not from facts but from inference. He had a temper, well concealed until the beginning of their third year.

By the time they were married two years, Amy had begun to stay more often and longer in their vacation home, a stunning oceanfront property on which a handsome residence had been expanded from the lightkeeper's house. The lighthouse itself, while owned by the Coglands, had long been automated; it was serviced once a month by Coast Guard engineers who flew to the site in a helicopter.

Michael was content to remain in the city. He visited as seldom as he could while maintaining the appearance of a marriage, but his desire for her faded so that even during his visits, he often slept in his own room. He seemed to view her with a contempt that she had not earned and could not understand.

She remained married to him solely for the sake of their one child, whom Amy loved desperately and whom she wanted to raise in the stable family environment that characterized the Coglands, generation after generation. In truth, she told herself that she remained for no other reason, but she engaged in self-delusion.

Although she yearned for a genuine husband-wife relationship, and though she suffered loneliness, she liked the lifestyle, liked it perhaps too much: the magisterial aura of old money, the peaceful rhythms of daily life without struggle, the beauty of her property.

Now, years later, having become a far different Amy from that young woman, she braked behind traffic crawling along the approach to the Golden Gate Bridge.

Without glancing at Brian, she said, "He wanted to name our daughter Nicole, and I was pleased with that, it's a lovely name, but by the time she was three, I called her Nickie."

Chapter
56

When the dark goes away outside the windows, when Piggy is pretty sure Mother and the man are sleeping, she sleeps, too.

If she sleeps when they don't sleep, she might wake and see her mother watching. She is scared to have Mother watching her sleep.

Sometimes, she wakes and Mother has fire. A lighter. Her thumb turns the fire on. Then off. Then on. Over and over. Mother watching Piggy sleep and making fire.

Piggy dreams of Bear. He has a sock puppet on each hand. The sock puppets are so funny, like they were when Bear wasn't dead.

Then Mother is in the dream. She touches fire to the sock puppets. Bear's hands are all fire.

In the dream, Piggy says *No, no, this isn't how, not fire, it was a knife.*

Now Bear's hair is all fire. He tells Piggy *Run. Run. Run, Piggy, run!* Bear's mouth spits fire, his eyes melting.

Piggy sits up in bed. Throws off covers. Gets out of bed. She stands hugging herself, shaking.

She feels so alone. She's afraid. She's afraid alone is forever, all the days there are ever going to be, and then that many more.

She hurries to the big chair, lifts off the cushion. Cushion has a cover. Cover has a zipper.

With the Forever Shiny Thing in her hand, Piggy does the Worst Thing She Can Do.

It is really a good thing. It makes her feel not so alone. Makes her remember Bear not all fire, no knife in him, just Bear smiling.

Bear calls it the Worst Thing She Can Do because Mother will get the Big Uglies, maybe bigger than big, if she catches Piggy doing it.

When the Worst Thing She Can Do is done, the Forever Shiny Thing put away, Piggy washes, dresses. She is Ready for Anything.

Bear says when you have HOPE, you are Ready for Anything.

She eats broken cookies from yesterday. She saves food when she can. Food won't always come when you want it.

She thinks what Bear said in her dream. *Run, Piggy, run!*

He means not just in her dream but now. Bear is warning her.

She remembers what she read in Mother's eyes last night, Mother with the like-Bear knife, her eyes so ugly.

Run, Piggy, run!

If Piggy looks at the bottoms of her feet, she will see what you get when you try to run. That was long ago. But the marks are there, you can see them.

What you get when you try to run is hurt, you get hurt. You hear a click, then you hurt.

Mother's thumb turns fire on. Then off. Then on. If you try to run.

Piggy sits at her desk and takes a box out of a drawer.

In the box are pictures. Lots and lots. They are all the same but different.

She has been cutting them from magazines a long time, not for all the days there are ever going to be and then that many more, but a long time.

She will paste them together in a way that makes her feel good. She has saved them and saved them from so many magazines. Now she has enough. She is ready to start.

The pictures make her smile. They are so nice. Lots and lots. Standing and sitting. Running and jumping. Dogs. All dogs.

Chapter
57

An infinite army all in white marshaled in the west and rolled eastward on silent caissons, seizing the great bridge without shout or shot.

Golden Gate was the name not of the bridge but of the throat of the bay, and the bridge was orange.

The stiffening trusses, the girders, the suspender cables, the main cables, and the towers began to disappear into the fog.

As Amy drove north toward Marin County, there were moments when she could see nothing of the surrounding structure except vertical cables, so it seemed that the bridge was suspended from nothing more than clouds and that it conveyed travelers from the white void of the life they had lived to the white mystery beyond death.

"In those days," Amy said, speaking of her years of marriage to Michael Cogland, "although I had been raised to believe, I wasn't able yet to *see*. Life was vivid and strange and at times tumultuous, but in the rush of days, I was oblivious of patterns. A wonderful dog named Nickie had come to me when I was a girl . . . and now into my life had come this girl whose nickname became Nickie, and I thought it amusing and sweet, but nothing more."

As her husband grew more remote and as Amy became increasingly estranged from him, Michael began to travel more frequently and to remain away for longer periods, sometimes in Europe or Asia, or South America, supposedly on business, but perhaps in the company of other women.

Her daughter, Nicole, her second Nickie, at five years of age, had recently begun having bad dreams. They were all the same. In sleep, she found herself wandering in a snowy night, lost in dark woods, alone and afraid.

The woods were those behind their house, thickets of various evergreens, where the great beam of the lighthouse did not sweep.

Amy suspected that Nickie's dreams were a consequence of having been all but abandoned by her father, who had at first charmed her and won her heart as he had charmed and won her mother.

One night, in her pajamas and sitting on the edge of the bed, Nickie had asked for slippers.

Mommy, last night I was barefoot in the dream. I have to wear slippers to bed so I won't be walking barefoot through the woods in my dream.

If it's just a dream woods, Amy replied, *why wouldn't the ground be soft?*

It's soft but it's cold.

It's a winter woods, is it?

Uh-huh. Lots of snow.

So dream yourself a summer woods.

This night was in the winter. The first snow of the season had fallen the previous week, and just that afternoon, the sky had salted two fresh cold inches across the coast.

I like the snow, said Nickie.

Then maybe you should wear boots to bed.

Maybe I should.

And thick woolen socks and long johns.

Mommy, you're silly.

And a mink coat and a big mink Russian hat.

The girl giggled but then sobered. *I don't like the dream, but I don't like the barefoot part the most.*

Amy had gotten a pair of slippers from the closet and had put them under Nickie's pillow.

There. Now if you dream about the woods, and if you're barefoot again, just reach under your pillow and put them on in your sleep.

She had tucked her daughter in for the night. She had smoothed Nickie's hair back from her face, kissed her brow, kissed her left cheek and then her right, so her head wouldn't be unbalanced by the weight of a kiss.

Then Amy had spent the evening reading and had gone to bed in her own room at half past ten.

Now, in the passenger seat of the Expedition, Brian said with awful tenderness, "Maybe I should drive."

Having crossed the Golden Gate Bridge, they were heading north on Highway 101.

The clotted mass of fog that smothered the bridge had boiled off into a thin milk as they had come somewhat inland.

"No," she said. "It's better if I drive, something for my hands to grip."

That winter night, wind had awakened her, not with its own moan and whistle, but with the disharmony that it rang from the collection of wind chimes on the balcony off the master bedroom.

Amy looked toward a west-facing window, expecting to see the fairy dance of falling snow against the glass, but there was only the darkness and no snow.

Although the chimes usually appealed, something in their jangle disturbed her. In her years here, this was the first wind that was not a good musician.

As she came fully awake, instinct told her that not the chimes but some other sound had awakened her and stropped her nerves. She sat up in bed, threw aside the covers.

A separate house was occupied by the couple—James and Ellen Avery—who managed the property and made sure that their employers' every need was met. In addition to being a good manager, James was a strapping man, and responsible.

In their own wing of the main house were private rooms for Lisbeth, the maid, and Caroline, the nanny.

Each night a perimeter alarm was engaged. The breaking of a window or the forcing of a door would trigger a siren, and James Avery would come running.

Nevertheless, Amy was impelled by animal suspicion to remain standing beside her bed.

Head lifted, she listened intently, wishing that the wind would declare an intermission and let the chimes fall silent.

Her bedside lamp featured a dimmer switch. She fumbled for it and eased the palest light into the room.

Only weeks before, she'd done something that, at the time, had seemed impulsive, excessive, even foolish. Because several stories of grisly murder had recently filled the news, she had bought a pistol and had taken three lessons in its use.

No. Not because of murder in the news.

That was a self-deception that allowed her to go on believing her life had merely encountered a length of bad track, that it had not derailed.

If her fear had been of homicidal strangers, she would have told someone, at least James Avery, that she had purchased the pistol and had taken lessons. She would have left the weapon in her nightstand, where it would be easy to reach—and where the maid would have seen it. She would not have hidden it in an unused purse, in the back of a bureau drawer that held a collection of purses.

Feeling as though she moved not through the waking world but in a dream, with just enough light to avoid the furniture, she went to the bureau and withdrew the purse that served as holster.

As Amy turned from the bureau, she heard the faint creak of the doorknob, and gasping she turned in time to see him enter, his eyes shining in the gloom, like ice on stone in moonlight. Michael.

Supposedly in Argentina on business, he was not due back for another six days.

He did not speak a word, nor did she, for the circumstances and his eyes and his lurid sneer were phrases in an infinite sentence on the subject of motive and violence.

Fast he was, and brutal. He hit her, and she rocked backward, the knobs of bureau drawers gouging her back. But she held on to the purse.

He clubbed her with one fist, striking at her face but hitting the side of her head, and she fell to her knees. But she held on to the purse.

Grabbing a fistful of her hair, Michael hauled her to her feet, and she was conscious of no pain, so totally was she in the thrall of terror.

She saw the knife then, how big it was.

He was not ready to use the blade, but twisted her hair to turn her, and she turned like a helpless doll.

When Michael shoved her hard, she stumbled away from him and fell, and almost struck her head against a dresser. But she held on to the purse.

She tore at the zipper of the purse, reached within, rolled onto her back, and worked the double action as she had been instructed.

The shot shattered something, missing Michael, but in shock he shrank from her.

She fired again, he fled, and as he passed through the doorway between the bedroom and hall, he cried out in pain when the third shot nailed him. He staggered, but he did not go down, and then he vanished.

In self-defense and in defense of the innocent, killing is not murder, hesitation is not moral, and cowardice is the only sin.

She went after him, certain that he was not mortally wounded, determined that he would be.

Into the hallway, light spilled from Nickie's room.

In the clockworks of Amy's heart, the key of terror wound the mainspring past the snapping point, and the scream that came from her was silent, silent, her lungs suddenly as airless as the world around her seemed to be, a vacuum in a vacuum.

With the pistol in both hands and held stiff-armed before her, she went into Nickie's room, and Michael was not there.

He had been there earlier, and what Amy saw was aftermath, a sight from which she reeled in horror and in instant crippling grief, a sight that almost compelled her to put the pistol in her mouth and swallow her fourth shot.

But if in that moment she did not care whether she sent herself to Hell, she was *determined* to send him there.

Into the hall, down the stairs, she seemed not to run but fly, and in the entry hall found the front door standing open.

Impossible that she was still alive, that she was not dead from her own ardent wish to be dead, and yet she moved out of the house, across the porch, down the steps, into the night.

To the east, beyond the house, the concentrated light beamed out from the high lantern room, as powerful and silent as her still-silent scream, warning sailors in transit on the deep Atlantic.

Because its arc was constrained to 180 degrees in respect of inland dwellers, the lighthouse failed to brighten the night here in the west. Only a faint ghost pulse of its sweeping beam played upon the snow, so weak that it could quiver up no shadows.

Scanning the night, seeking Michael, she could not see him—and then did. He was running for the woods.

She squeezed off her fourth shot, and sea gulls thrashed into flight from the eaves of the high catwalk of the lighthouse, flew west in confusion, but then over her head wheeled east and high into the sky.

Michael was beyond the reach of the pistol, and she ran after him, holding her fire until she had gained ground.

She closed on him as she knew she would, because he was wounded and she was not, because he ran in fear and she ran in fury.

As Michael reached the woods, Amy fired again, but he did not fall, and the trees crowded around him and welcomed him into their dark.

Now it seemed to her that this was a fulfillment of her sweet girl's dream, Nickie's dream that she would be lost in the woods. Her father had not only taken her life but her soul, and he would cast it away in the forest, where she would wander forever, barefoot and afraid.

Crazy as that thought was, it compelled Amy ten steps into the woods, twenty, until she halted. Before her were a thousand pathways through the night, a maze of trees.

She listened but heard nothing. Either he was laying for her in this labyrinth or he had fled far enough along a trail he knew that she could not hear him running.

Were he lying in wait, she would risk being taken by surprise, because she might kill him anyway, in the struggle.

If on the other hand he had gone deep into the woods, if he had left a car on the farther side, along the county road, her pursuit of him would only ensure his escape.

Reluctantly, desperately, she retreated from the trees and ran back toward the house, to call the police.

She was almost to the front-porch steps when she realized that her gunfire had brought no one out of either house. Neither James nor Ellen Avery, nor Lisbeth, the maid, nor Caroline, the nanny.

They were all dead, and she the sole survivor.

Chapter
58

Harrow stands on the rocky brink above the beach, watching the wall of fog advance across the sea.

In a sufficient desolation of fog, when above the lower mist the sky itself is plated with black clouds and sunlight therefore doubly curtained, the automated lighthouse is programmed to beam forth even before darkfall.

Although the Coast Guard engineers are unaware of it, Harrow has learned to confuse the sensors and to prevent the light show from starting early in this weather. There will be no high flare to warn their incoming visitors.

Having waited nine years to finish the hard work of that night, he is impatient to show Amy the whetted knife, which is the same he used then. He hopes that she will recognize it and know, as he slips it in, that her daughter's fate is hers, after all.

She may know the knife before she recognizes him. During the two years that he lived in Brazil, much work was done on his face.

Rio is the world capital of plastic surgery, boasting the finest collection of cosmetic surgeons to be found anywhere. People travel there from every continent to be made young and recuperate.

When after two years he returned to the States with a different name and a different face, he had begun to search for Amy. He was a busy man, with numerous lieutenants, and though he gave them orders for the most part indirectly and from a distance, he could not make the search his full-time job. He made of it instead his primary avocation.

He'd had to be discreet. Expressing an interest in her fate to anyone with access to sealed court records would bring him under too much scrutiny.

For a long while, both his own wits and private investigators had failed him. She had gone deep into her new life.

Only nine months ago had he thought of the locket she wore and of the sentimental story she had told about the dog that had walked out of a meadow, starving, and into the hearts of nuns and orphans.

She had always so admired golden retrievers. She had said that when Nicole was eight or nine, old enough to be responsible for a dog, she would buy a golden for the girl.

Also she had given money—*his* money—to a local golden-retriever rescue group. He had seen their publication and had wondered why they bothered. Dogs are dogs, and men are men, and they all die, and none of it matters if it isn't you.

He suspected that, when adopting a new identity, she had kept her first name. Most people did, even in the witness-protection program, when the mob was hunting them.

Besides, after that winter night, she'd had not much left except her name. Needy orphan that she is, she would not want to be shorn of both her Christian name and her surname. Even more than most people, she has always needed something of the past to which she can hold tight.

The Internet had failed him and the investigators he had hired, but only for the lack of the right search string. With the words *Amy, dogs, golden, retriever,* and *rescue,* he made another try.

He located more than a few dog-loving Amys, but none other that had founded a rescue group. Her photograph did not grace their web site, but the more he read of the rescue accounts that she posted there, the more he recognized the voice of the woman he had married.

An investigator named Vernon Lesley had been able to obtain a photo of her, which confirmed that she was, indeed, the mother of Michael Cogland's child, Harrow's child.

He could have moved against her then, aggressively, but he did not know how wary she might be. He took his time. He did research.

When he discovered she was dating McCarthy, he paid Vernon Lesley to do a sweep of the architect's apartment. From that, he had learned of Vanessa, had read the e-mails she sent to Brian, and had become fascinated by her.

When he tracked her down—using sources more illegal than any available to McCarthy—and saw what she looked like, and met her face to face, he knew that his life had changed. Exploring the body, mind, and heart of Moongirl became more important to him, for a while, than finishing his business with Amy.

Now the day has come.

Chapter

59

For the moment, Amy could not talk any more, and she could not drive. She parked the Expedition on the shoulder of the highway.

Without another word, she walked into a meadow of stunted yellow grass, gray weeds. The land sloped but only slightly, and far out at the low crest, no oaks waited, but only more struggling grass and weeds, and beyond the crest an ashen sky, bearded and blind.

She stopped after she had gone twenty feet and looked at her hands, the palms and then the backs of them, and the palms again.

The memories were not stored only in her mind, but in her hands as well. The skin of her palms retained the memory of the last time she had touched her living child, the softness of her girl's skin and the texture of her clean glossy hair as Amy had smoothed it back from her face, the warmth of the breath from her delicate nostrils.

Amy could feel all that and more—the sweet sweep of Nicole's jaw line, the curve of her cheek, the tender lobe and helix of her ear—detailed sensations as real to her now as when the touch had occurred, sensations that she would carry with her all the days of her life, that could rush back to her both summoned and unsummoned, to devastate her when she least expected.

She walked farther into the meadow with no destination in mind, as she had proceeded for almost nine years, toward nothing concrete, seeking only a solution to her loss, all the while knowing that no solution was possible, that the meaning of her loss was an equation that could not be solved in this life.

In another twenty steps or a hundred, she dropped to her knees, but could not even maintain that posture, and went to her hands and knees, all fours, as if she were a child reduced to crawling, but she didn't have the strength to crawl, or anywhere to go.

After she had stopped being Amy Cogland and could not return to being Amy Harkinson, as Amy Redwing, she had never told the story of that night to anyone. After so many years of husbanding her emotion, tending to it in the dark and quiet nights of sleepless recollection, she discovered that telling it to Brian had torn her down harder and farther than she had expected.

Knees and hands against the earth, she hung her head, for it was heavier than stone, and the sounds she made were more efforts to draw breath than they were sobs. She had wept when recounting the death of Nickie, Misericordiæ's mascot. Now tears seemed not to be an adequate expression of the loss of her second Nickie. Perhaps the only way to honor such a loss would be to have died that night with her daughter.

She sat on the yellow grass, legs crossed, almost in the lotus position, except that she clutched her knees with her hands and still hung her head. She rocked slowly back and forth.

Once she had read that meditation was the path to serenity; but she never meditated. She knew that inevitably meditation would lead every time to contemplation of that night, to the same unanswerable questions, the one *why* and the thousand *what-ifs*.

She had prayer instead, and it sustained her. She prayed for her daughter, for James and Ellen, for Lisbeth and Caroline. She prayed for the dogs, all the dogs, for the amelioration of their suffering.

After a while, Amy looked up and saw Brian standing awkwardly forty feet away, with Nickie on a leash. Clearly, he wasn't sure that giving her time to herself was the right thing, but of course it was.

She loved him for his occasional awkwardness, his hesitations, his doubts, his self-consciousness.

Michael Cogland had been always self-assured and smooth and confident in any context. But what had seemed to be a natural grace had been in fact the sociopathic gloss of a man who had never been inhibited by so much as a scintilla of humility.

Now Brian released the golden from the leash, and that was also the right thing. The dog raced into her arms.

After a hesitation, almost as gawky as a boy, Brian came to her and sat beside her.

Following an awkward silence, he said, "Dogs' lives are short, too short, but you know that going in. You know the pain is coming, you're going to lose a dog, and there's going to be great anguish, so you live fully in the moment with her, never fail to share her joy or delight in her innocence, because you can't support the illusion that a dog can be your lifelong companion. There's such beauty in the hard honesty of that, in accepting and giving love while always aware it comes with an unbearable price. Maybe loving dogs is a way we do penance for all the other illusions we allow ourselves and for the mistakes we make because of those illusions."

Dear God, she heard nothing awkward in that. In that was the perfect truth of her eight years in rescue, as she could never have put it into words.

For a time they didn't need to speak, and they lavished on the dog, on this living Nickie, the affection they felt for each other.

"Michael fled the country," she said at last, needing to finish the account. "They never found him. Although he didn't go back to Argentina, he had established quite an alibi in Buenos Aires. His friends there *swore* he'd been with them on the night. Of course that wouldn't work after I'd seen him and survived. What kind of people were they, swearing to a lie *known* to be a lie, when swearing to it didn't matter anymore?"

Having claimed his inheritance by marrying and by fathering a child, Michael had no further use for a family. By law, a wife had a claim on a portion of his wealth, as did a child. Amy and Nicole were not assets, but liabilities, and he needed to purge them from his books.

He could have hired someone for this little accounting job, but he must have worried that a paid killer would have no scruples about engaging in blackmail. The savagery of the murders suggested that Michael had done the deed not solely to avoid being vulnerable to extortion, but also because killing gave him pleasure.

The police discovered he had prepared for the possibility that he might become a suspect in spite of his tightly woven alibi. In the three years preceding the night, he had gradually transferred most of his fortune out of the United States, moving it through a complex series of investments and entities designed to launder it and fold it away under an alternate identity that could never be traced.

Devastated by the actions of their son, the senior Coglands had been kind to Amy; they would have treated her as if she were their daughter. But her taste for luxury had been lost, and the lifestyle in which she once delighted now appealed to her no more than would have a diet of vinegar and ashes.

Amy had cashed out what comparatively little equity Michael had left in such mortgaged assets as their houses. Even that felt too much like blood money, and she knew she would have to find something to do with her life that would make her funds clean again.

Michael's cold calculation and the extreme brutality with which he had treated his victims argued that he would not remain safely on some tropical island, lazing in the sun with piña coladas for the rest of his life. By fighting back, she had forced him into hiding; worse, literally and figuratively, *she had wounded him*.

When a man has no humility, pride is the thing that fills the void. He might feel that the wound she'd dealt to his pride required payback, and in time he might come looking for her.

Consequently, her attorney was able to convince the court that the government needed to assist her in the creation of a new identity and forever seal the records involving her name change.

She had lived as Amy Harkinson since she was three, and she had all but forgotten the last name pinned to her shirt when she'd been abandoned in the church at Mater Misericordiæ. *Redwing*.

She was quite sure she had never mentioned it to Michael. Her history of tragedy embarrassed her, as if she were a waif imagined by Dickens. Rather than the full truth with all the melodrama of her abandonment, and rather than present herself as a woman of unknown parentage, she had preferred a white lie of omission, allowing him to believe she had been the Harkinsons' child and had gone to the orphanage only after their death.

Her attorney and the judge preferred she create a new name from whole cloth, but she had suffered panic attacks at the thought of a life without *any* touchstones to her past. The nuns at Misericordiæ cooperated by redacting the name *Redwing* from their records, and as best they could from memory.

She had, then, also lost the sisters who had raised her. Until Michael was found, if ever he was, Amy dared not return to Mater Misericordiæ for a visit.

She had come west. She bought a little bungalow. She became a bone to grief, gnawed thin, and a prisoner of loneliness, who for most of a year could find no way to escape her cell.

Then one day, slipping her locket around her neck, remembering sweet Nickie who had come to her out of an autumn meadow, she knew what she must do. She found a good breeder. She bought two puppies.

Fred and Ethel had brought hope back into her life. With hope she could again consider what meaning her life might have, and so she founded Golden Heart.

Now in the withered meadow, Brian's cell phone rang. Vanessa had further directions. They were less than an hour from bringing Hope back into Brian's life.

Chapter

60

The single-lane blacktop led half a mile off the county road before arriving at the simple, painted steel-pipe gate that barred passage.

If the pearly fog grew thicker, even in daylight the white gate might be hard to see in spite of the red reflectors affixed to it. In the headlights, a line of those ovals glittered as if the gate were a trophy rack mounted with the heads of giant rattlesnakes.

Billy Pilgrim put down the driver's window and pressed the button on the call post.

After only a short delay, Harrow replied. "Who's there?"

"It's Billy."

Harrow knew him by a few other names, as well, though not by the name Tyrone Slothrop.

"You're cutting it tight," Harrow admonished.

"I saw this beautiful young girl in a car with a bumper sticker that said ABSTINENCE ALWAYS WORKS, and I didn't kill her."

After a silence, Harrow said, "You always make me laugh, Billy. But not now, okay?"

"Juliette Junke says I'm working too hard. Maybe that's it."

"We're gonna talk workloads *now*?"

"No. I'm just saying."

"You have the bag of stuff from Amy's house?"

"Yeah, but I'll bring it to you later."

"Later when?"

"Like you said, I'm cutting it tight. I've got to get set up. I'll bring the bag when I bring you the bitch and McCarthy."

"Are you all right?" Harrow asked.

"After this, I'm taking some time off. Do some reading, see if I can find that young mother with the two kids in the tandem stroller."

"Young mother who?"

"Listen, I'll get set up right away. I'll bring the bag of stuff from Redwing's house later."

The gate swung open, and Billy drove through.

In the event of clear weather, he had the sniper rifle, which would have allowed him to conceal himself at a distance and shoot out a couple of tires on Redwing's Expedition at the designated point in the road, taking them by surprise. They wouldn't have had a chance to see him with a gun and throw the SUV in reverse, backing out of sight at high speed.

In this fog, however, Billy didn't need the rifle. He could wait closer to the road. He would use the Glock machine pistol to blow the tires, to persuade Redwing and McCarthy to get out of the Expedition, and to shoot the dog through the side window.

Past the gate, the road rose and fell and curved for nearly a mile before it topped a final rise and descended the last two hundred yards to the lighthouse.

Harrow wanted Redwing to cross this crest, see the lighthouse, and realize that she had been lured to her death, and to worse than death. At that moment, Billy would disable the Expedition.

Right now, fog shrouded much of the lighthouse, but the tower was huge, and it *loomed* even in this murk.

Billy pulled off the pavement, drove among a cluster of hillside pines, parked, switched off the headlights, and killed the engine.

When he marched Redwing and McCarthy to the caretaker's house, quite a program would unfold. The boss had showmanship.

After the pair were chained in the kitchen, Harrow would no doubt tell Billy to wait for him in the lighthouse. That was where they discussed business, not in front of Vanessa.

Because Billy was the last man left who could link Redwing and McCarthy to the boss, Harrow would kill him in the lighthouse.

Billy wanted his midlife crisis to *be* in the middle of his life, not at the end. He wouldn't wait in the lighthouse to be killed.

Instead, he would go to the garage and remove the spark plugs from both of Harrow's vehicles. Then he would return to his rented SUV and drive out of there, around the gate in the road, away.

No more Billy Pilgrim. Done, over, finito. He would be Tyrone Slothrop for a week, a month, perhaps for the rest of his life.

He would not be able to continue criminal activity in California, Arizona, or Nevada, or in select South American countries, because he was well known there in too many circles as an associate of Harrow.

Everybody liked pudgy balding Billy and wanted to hug him, but they feared Harrow and wanted to kiss his butt. Fear always trumped affection, and it was Billy's experience that most human beings also preferred butt-kissing to hugging.

Once it was known that Billy had fallen from Harrow's grace, every old friend he met would want to kill him right away, to please Harrow. Friendship wasn't worth the heart it was written on, as

Billy himself had proved many times, as when he had shot Georgie Jobbs. A heart was just meat, people were meat, meat didn't care. Did a filet mignon care about a pork chop? No.

As Tyrone Slothrop, he would have to go somewhere Harrow and his crowd would never travel. Like Oklahoma or Utah or South Dakota. This would be a hardship, but he would find lots of crime to commit in his new turf; and there were people to kill no matter where you went.

He would have to lose weight, grow a mustache, cut off an ear. If a friend of Harrow's *did* cross Tyrone's path in Pierre, South Dakota, he would maybe do a double take, but then say *Nah, it can't be Billy. Billy had two ears.* As a disguise, cutting off an ear is better than a Tyrolean hat and fake gold teeth combined and cubed.

Maybe he was getting his groove back. His life was beginning to seem meaningless and brutal and comic again, just like the fiction he admired.

He got out of the rented SUV with the plastic bag of crap from Redwing's house and the Glock 18. He had taken the silencer off the Glock. The boss wanted to hear the bang.

He walked up the slope and chose a position just below the crest, at the edge of the small copse of trees.

The fog imparted a pleasant chill to his exposed face and his bare head, and it suppressed most noises. He could barely hear the surf breaking, which sounded like ten thousand people whispering in the distance.

Thinking in similes and metaphors was a not always welcome consequence of being formed by literature.

Like ten thousand people whispering in the distance.

It wasn't a very good simile, because why would ten thousand people be gathered anywhere to whisper?

Once the simile was in his head, he couldn't cast it out, and it began to annoy him. Annoyance phased into uneasiness, and soon uneasiness became a deep disquiet.

As improbable as the image was, the thought of ten thousand people whispering together began to creep him out.

All right. Enough. It was just a damn simile. It didn't mean anything. Nothing meant anything, ever. He was doing fine. He was back in his groove. He was just swell. Hi-ho.

Chapter
61

They turned toward the coast and were eventually found by fog again, which didn't creep around them on little cat feet but prowled forward with no less menace than a pack of lions.

Vanessa called Brian three times at fifteen-minute intervals, with additional bursts of directions, as her wealthy paranoid fiancé tried to thwart any tabloid-television crews that might be tailing them with or without their knowledge.

The absurdity of it seemed to confirm the reality of Vanessa's story, and by the time they reached the white gate, Amy wanted to believe that the document signing, while awkward and unpleasant, would not be an intolerable ordeal.

Even with fog lights, they almost didn't see the gate. The red reflectors were nearly defeated by the curdled mist.

When Brian, who was driving, pushed a button on the call post, Vanessa answered. "It's a mile and a half past the gate, Bry. Piggy's packed and I've got Dom Perignon on ice. Let's get this done. I'm so happy the little freak is getting out of here, I might pee myself."

Amy had not heard the woman before. She was struck that, even through the cheap speaker on the call post, the voice was throaty yet strong, and uncommonly seductive.

The gate swung open, and they passed through, and as the barrier swung shut again, Nickie growled.

The dog stood behind them in the cargo space. She looked left, right, and then forward through the windshield. The growl was low but not brief. She held it in her throat, then let it deepen, as though warning something off that didn't take the first growl seriously enough to suit her.

Braking to a stop, Brian said, "Maybe the fog spooks her."

"Maybe," Amy said. "Where are the security people Vanessa said would sweep the car, us, and Nickie?"

"She said it's still a mile and a half to his place. There's probably a more formal guardhouse somewhere ahead."

The car drifted forward. Amy said, "Wait." Brian stopped again.

Amy turned in her seat, said "Move" to Nickie, and snatched her carryall from the back. She opened a zipper, withdrew the SIG P245.

"If it's feeling funky to you," he said, "we can turn around, drive past the gate. The open ground's rough but passable."

"I don't know how it feels. I have to trust furface here."

At the sight of the pistol, the golden stopped growling.

Amy said, "We know Vanessa's sick. How sick, do you think?"

"She's too in love with herself to do anything too stupid."

"That's the calculation I made when I wondered whether I should bring a gun. I decided I didn't need it. Yet here it is in my hand."

He nodded. "Let's go back."

"No."

"You just said—"

"Here's the thing. There's a pattern. I lost a girl, and you lost a girl. Mine is gone forever. Yours isn't, but she may be soon."

Nickie whined, as though to suggest urgency and to add emphasis to Amy's use of the word *soon*.

"But they want us to take her," Brian said.

"The pattern includes things unseen. That night, Michael wasn't in Argentina, he was right *there*, I didn't know. The alarm system appeared to be engaged, a secret override disarmed it."

Phantoms of fog shaped all the monsters of myth.

"Vanessa's rich boy is waiting with documents, a fat checkbook," Amy continued. "But he's a thing unseen, maybe he doesn't exist."

"We agreed her story made sense."

"The pattern is clearer now. In Connecticut, I thought I might get a golden. If I'd had one, it would have warned me, saved us."

As if on cue, Nickie growled again.

"We have a golden now," Amy said. "And not just any golden."

"For sure, not just any. She's . . . something."

"I had a phone call from a dead nun."

"Is this a Marco-and-his-blind-dog moment?"

"The dog isn't blind. I told myself *Just a dream.* I knew better. Sister Jacinta said tell you about my girl, how I lost her."

"Okay, that's it, we go back to the county road, call the cops."

"No. Vanessa expects us in a few minutes. The fog explains a short delay, not a long one. I've got a bad feeling, Brian."

"Yeah. It's infectious."

"Truth is, I've had a bad feeling the whole way here."

"You didn't say."

"Because it was maybe the only chance to find your girl. Let's go a little farther."

The amorphous white tissue of the late afternoon parting as if to the thrust of a blade, healing at once behind, enfolding on every side things unseen . . .

Amy said, "If something about this *does* stink, and she thinks we smell it, she'll kill Hope."

"Where do you get that from?"

"Intuition. Pattern. What Theresa said."

"Theresa?"

"She told her mother the dog's name was always Nickie. Always."

In the deep swamp of fog, half-seen trees, bearded and strange, prehistoric and insectile, looming then gone . . .

Amy said, "You and me forever, Brian. Isn't that where we are?"

"God, I hope it is. It's what I want."

"So if it's you and me, and Hope is yours, then Hope is mine, too. *Our* daughter. I couldn't save my own girl. Not back then." Her voice pulled tight, didn't break. "But two nights ago I saved her."

"Amy . . . ?"

"I saved her, and now she's helping us save Hope."

He coasted toward a stop. "Amy, you don't mean . . ."

"Keep moving." She held the pistol in both hands, palms dry, ready. "Whatever I mean, this is a second chance for both of us. If we fail to take it, the levels of Hell don't go deep enough to give us what we'll deserve."

Into the last white-blind minutes before twilight, when the mist will darken to murk . . .

Brian said, "So it's this again."

"This?"

"Tagging after you into crazy-violent, tire-iron, jumping-on-the-table places."

Chapter

62

ike ten thousand people whispering in the distance.
Standing with his back to the fissured trunk of a pine, Billy strove to silence the sea, but the sea had no respect for Billy.

Not only had the stupid simile changed how he perceived the sound of the surf, but it also led him to the further conviction that those ten thousand people were whispering his name.

Everybody liked Billy. Likability had always been his most valuable asset. But the ten thousand people out there in the fog, down on the shore, were not whispering his name in a friendly way. The muttering multitudes were angry, hostile, and *eager.*

He didn't know what they were eager for, and he refused to think further about it, because they weren't people, damn it, just waves.

What he needed to do was come up with a simile that would push his stuck mind on to a more pleasant image.

Muffled by fog, the breaking surf sounded like . . .

Muffled by fog, the breaking surf sounded like . . .

A condensation of fog soaked his thin hair and beaded on his face. Just fog, not a cold sweat.

Muffled by fog, the breaking surf sounded like ten thousand of Billy's friends whispering about what a great guy he was.

Pathetic. He might be having a midlife crisis, but he was still the old Billy, a tough guy, a funny guy, a guy who embraced the truth of truths, that nothing matters, nothing except how to get what you want.

He had read all the great deathworks, he had read *Finnegans Wake* three times, *three times,* he had decanted all those brilliant beautiful scalding ideas into his head, thousands of volumes of deathworks, and because you are the ideas you pour into yourself, he had in a sense been killed by what he read, was already dead to any truth except the truth that no truths exist. Having died in this way, he had no fear of death, no fear of anything, and he certainly did not fear *breaking surf that sounded like ten thousand people whispering in the distance!*

With one hand he wiped at his wet face.

How could a drawing of a dog give a guy a midlife crisis?

He cocked his head and listened for the sound of an engine.

He thought that he heard the Expedition approaching. Then the fog stole that sound, though it kept paying out the susurrations of the sea.

Nickie growled, Amy said "Stop," and Brian braked on the rising road.

Denser than any waves before it, a tide of fog poured down from a crest unseen, as formless as dreams, as weightless as air yet as solid as alabaster, pressing the vehicle as if to encapsulate and fossilize it.

Here in a snowless whiteout, where nothing beyond the

Expedition could be seen, where nothing layered upon nothing, Amy Redwing was perhaps at an ultimate place, deep in the immortal primordial, where faith mattered so much that she dared rely on nothing else.

Nickie let out a faint sigh, and Amy felt the equivalent of a sigh in the centrum of her soul, an expelled breath of resignation to the power of fate.

"How far yet?" she asked.

"Just over half a mile."

"She's lying. We're close."

"Why would she lie about that?"

"I don't know. But I know."

Billy again heard the engine of the Expedition, and this time it did not fade, as before, but grew louder by the moment, until he could no longer hear the surf crawling on the shore.

Although no headlights brightened the fog at the crest, the SUV appeared, ten feet away, like the specter of a vehicle, ghost ship on wheels.

Puzzled by the lampless arrival, but happy to be back in action, Billy rushed from the shelter of the trees.

Because the sea held the fog close to itself before flinging it at the land, the high catwalk and lantern room of the lighthouse were visible above the slowly churning curdled mass that hid the rest of it, though at the brink of twilight, the halogen beam did not yet stab out from those summit windows.

As expected, at the sight of the lighthouse, the Expedition braked to a stop, and at the same moment, Billy arrived beside it, squeezing a short burst from the Glock 18, blowing out the front portside tire.

He would have stooped and fired under the vehicle, popping other tires, before pointing the gun at the driver's door and shouting *Put the window down*, but after he blew one tire, nothing went as planned.

Brian drove slowly up the hill, and Amy walked behind the SUV, concealed by it, left hand on the vehicle to steady herself on the slick pavement, the SIG P245 in her right hand.

From the cargo space, solemn Nickie peered out at her through the tailgate window.

For some reason, for luck, for a blessing, Amy raised her hand from the tailgate handle, to which she had been holding, and put it on the glass, in front of Nickie's face.

Twice Amy glanced around the side of the Expedition, but she could see nothing more than streaming fog.

With the headlights off, the taillights were off as well, and therefore did not prematurely reveal her.

She could not clearly express to Brian the purpose of this tactic, but she had no doubt that it was what she needed to do. Intuition is seeing with the soul.

She knew they reached the crest when she felt the front of the Expedition cant downward.

A moment later, as the back of the Expedition crossed the crest and Amy with it, the brake lights flared red, and she moved at once around to the driver's side.

She saw a figure rush through the fog only twelve feet or so in front of her, saw muzzle flashes, heard a stutter of shots, the pop of a tire, ricochets off metal.

Her heart knocked against her ribs at the thought of Brian shot.

Sideways to Amy, the shooter started to turn his head, but she had the pistol in a two-hand grip.

In self-defense and in defense of the innocent, cowardice is the only sin.

Scared, she was scared, all right, but she stopped, squeezed off a pair of rounds, and when he rocked as if hit, she fired two more as she moved toward him.

Headlights bloomed, and the driver's door flew open.

Brian got out, not a ghost in the fog, a ghost still safely in his skin, his explosive breath stirring the mist.

The man down, the shooter shot, lay on his back, as sweet-faced as a favorite uncle, bleeding from the abdomen, bleeding from his nostrils, eyes wide and lashes lush.

He blinked at Amy, said, "Do you know me? I'm Leopold Bloom, I'm Wallace Stevens. My name is Gregor Samsa," and then closed his eyes.

When you shoot a man dead, even when it's a righteous shooting, your attention tends to fix on him, and Amy's was riveted, so that Brian had to say her name urgently twice, before she looked up and saw the lighthouse.

The lighthouse in Connecticut was made of limestone, this one of painted brick, and the stone tower's catwalk was encircled by an ornate iron railing, this one by a plainer wooden railing painted red.

Materials didn't matter, nor details, nor a distance of three thousand miles. Only the iconic form mattered, a symbol for death and for the love of death, for faithlessness and lies and vows taken with a stifled laugh.

Michael was here. He had found her at last; and through her, Brian; and through Brian, Vanessa.

She didn't know how, didn't know why such indirection, but she had no doubt that he meant to finish his blood sacrifice. She was a better woman than she had been on that distant day, and now she was being given the chance to save an innocent if she could be wise and brave and quick. Even if she died trying, there was redemption in that kind of death.

"Get Nickie," she said, but as she turned, she saw that the dog had clambered across the console, onto the driver's seat. She leaped out of the Expedition, to Amy's side.

Somewhere in the dismalness below stood a caretaker's house, probably two hundred yards away, judging by the position of the lighthouse. Maybe the flow of fog across its roof and around its corners suggested the lines of the place—*there*—or maybe not.

Michael might be in the house. Or anywhere. If he had been waiting for them to be brought to him at gunpoint, the different voices of the two weapons might have alerted him to trouble.

Brian picked up the dead man's gun.

Somewhere in the fog, Michael was coming.

She said, "Keep Nickie back."

Leaning into the SUV, she shifted it out of park.

Brian had engaged the emergency brake. She released it, and jumped out of the way as the car began to roll.

"Something to distract him."

The blown tire began to shred, but the grade was too steep for the vehicle to be stopped or even much slowed by that friction. The Expedition pulled to the left as it descended, the bared wheel rim shrieking on blacktop, chunks of rubber torn loose and knocking against the undercarriage.

Fog licked thick tongues around the SUV, then swallowed it whole, and there was only the glow of its lights going down the

gullet. Rattles and clatters rose as small obstructions were encountered and plowed aside.

"If he's coming, he's coming here," Amy said.

As if she understood, Nickie led them across the road, onto the
slope north of it, into scattered trees and universal fog.

Chapter

63

Waiting for the gunfire that will signal the game has begun, Harrow stands in the open kitchen door, fog seething past him and into the house.

He would have assisted Billy except for two reasons, the first of which is that, for this kind of work, Billy is the best man Harrow has ever encountered. Billy is a machine. A perpetual-motion machine, free of friction. He reliably functions flawlessly.

Billy is also brutal, without an instant's hesitation in his brutality, utterly without remorse or second thoughts. Yet unlike most other men with these qualities, he is highly intelligent *and sane*.

Billy is a jewel, a treasure, irreplaceable. Harrow regrets the necessity of killing him later.

The other reason Harrow does not want to participate in the early stages of the action is because he has a program written for the evening, one that he has refined for months. He wants the full enjoyment of realizing the show as he conceived it.

He prefers to delay his entrance, giving Amy an hour or more to anticipate his arrival. She must be humiliated, emotionally broken, and in a state of terror before he appears.

Harrow will see his ex-wife after she has been reduced to the condition of a caged breeder dog in those puppy mills against which she crusades. Then he will prove to her that worse horrors exist.

At gunpoint, she and the architect will undress. They will be chained to chairs.

Then Billy will leave, and Harrow will listen from an adjoining room as Moongirl breaks down Amy.

He will enter when she can't stop sobbing, and all that he will do at first is fix open her eyes so she cannot close them.

He wants her to see what Moongirl will do to Brian. The father of the freak will end the evening as a eunuch.

No transgression exists that won't be committed here this night.

Harriet Weaver would be proud of him. She'd been his nanny, who from the cradle quietly schooled him to understand that the values of his family were repressive, that the world was a more exciting place for the transgressors than for the submissives. They had shared such thrilling secrets from the earliest days of his memory.

At Harriet's instruction, he exhibited behavior problems that she convinced the family could be resolved by home-schooling, with her as the only tutor, and when all his time was spent with her, he obliged by behaving much better. She hated the Coglands and all their kind, and she was right, for in the end he hated them, too.

The incoming fog carries a chill and the fecund scent of the sea. Harrow is invigorated by it, and by anticipation.

At the first burst of gunfire, he steps across the threshold, out of the house, onto the brick deck, alert, standing tall and stiff with expectation.

An answering weapon, of a different character from the first, damps his excitement but does not greatly discourage him.

He stands motionless, listening. Perhaps Billy moved in on them with a gun in each hand, Old-West style. Billy does have flair.

When half a minute passes, a minute, with no further gunplay, it seems that the two-gun theory might be correct.

Then the engine roar swells, as if Billy is driving them down to the house when he was instructed to walk them, cuffed together. But with the engine noise comes others: a banshee shriek of tortured metal, a series of small collisions that suggests a runaway vehicle.

Harrow backs off the deck, into the open doorway.

Headlights dimly announcing it, the Expedition careens through the fog, across the corner of the deck, and across the rocks toward the oval yard.

Because the SUV passes so close and because the interior lights are on, Harrow can see that no one is behind the wheel.

The yard is lost in fog, and when he hears the Expedition come to a violent stop, he can only assume that it has crashed into the giant Montezuma pine.

He steps into the kitchen, leaving the door open behind him.

At the table, Moongirl has been arranging surgical instruments. The commotion outside has caused her to pause in her preparations.

"Trouble," he says.

"Watch out for the dog."

"You're the one afraid of it."

"I'm not afraid. It can't smell me."

He can make no sense of that.

"I just want it dead," she says.

"I think it is."

She stares at him.

Harriet Weaver had such eyes, though gray, not bottle-green.

He says, "Amy and Brian are probably dead, too."

"Billy? Why would he?"

"We had a weird conversation earlier."

She waits.

"He was testing me somehow."

"That could get him dead."

"I gave him all the pieces of this. I should have split it up."

"It's over just like that?"

"Billy figured out he's the last link between me and Amy, no future in that. So he kills them to show me no hard feelings, but he's not coming down here."

"You'll find him."

"He's going 'on vacation.' Which means new name, new look, and he'll do it right."

"They got off easy."

"I'll check the Expedition. Maybe they're not dead on the floor. Maybe he just wounded them for us."

"I'm sick of this place."

"We'll go to the desert."

"I hate the gulls and the damp."

"You'll like the desert."

"Not with Piggy."

Her elegant fingers move across the blades on the table, but she seems unable to decide upon a favorite.

He says, "You want to do her tonight?"

She nods. "Tonight."

"How?"

"Hard, the little freak. Real hard."

She leaves the room without a scalpel.

Chapter

64

Daylight had begun to fail; and the white mist silvered.

After they had gone twenty yards north, staying pack-close in the fog, Amy and Brian followed Nickie downslope, sixty or eighty yards, out of the trees, onto open ground.

At a distance stood a door in the fog, dimly defined by light in a room beyond.

Out of pistol range, a woman came through the door, carrying something, turned west, and at once vanished in the murk.

"Vanessa," Brian whispered.

As the sky tarnished and the silvering mist developed a darker patina, the automated-lighthouse program engaged. The lantern room high in the night brightened with a thousand watts of halogen glare. The rays were reflected by the prismatic rings of the Fresnel lens, amplified, concentrated, and beamed out into the Pacific.

A part of Amy was in the past, on another coast, where the sweep of such a light had been the sharp scythe of Death. And a vision of aftermath flashed through her mind, Nickie dead at her father's hand.

Her heart, so steady through so much, steady even through

the killing of the shooter, slammed now, and her soaring blood pressure muffled her hearing until she stretched her jaw, cracked her ears.

Brian said, "Wait," but she ran toward the lighted door, which was already fading in a thicker current of fog.

High overhead, the bright signal swept 360 degrees. It seemed to pulse as it passed out of each quadrant of its arc and into the next.

The fog—an optical construct with a million lenses, a billion bevels, infinite prisms—stole a minute fraction of the beam and shattered it through the night. From the dark trough of each pulse the fog took shadows, which chased the phantasms of light, which in turn chased the shadows.

She had never seen this phenomenon before and supposed it must be particular to this Fresnel lens, this landscape, and the unique nature of this fog.

At the periphery of vision, figures leaped, flew, fell. They were shadows from the lantern room, the consequence of the arc pulse, not cast by anything at ground level, though something malevolent and real might be moving in their cover. They chased directly in front of her eyes, too, and frequently flew up from the ground, as if they were dark gulls.

By the time she reached the building with the open door, the fast-waltzing dancers of shadow and light inspired dizziness that turned her in a half-circle with her last two steps. She found the wall with a soft thump.

Nickie followed at her heels, Brian close behind, and the dog padded past her, along the wall to the doorway, into the light.

Trusting the golden's nose, Amy boldly followed, and found herself at the threshold of a garage. The place seemed deserted.

"She might come back," Brian whispered.

"Then kill her."

Amy started west, in the direction the woman had gone, but Brian grabbed her arm. He wanted her to be less reckless, to keep in mind the danger of blundering into a murderous burst of gunfire.

She didn't want to waste time, but instead of pulling away from him, she turned, face close to his in the whirling harlequin parade, and whispered fiercely, "They're killing Hope."

This was not a fear, but a presentiment, not merely the dread of failing another child, but a knowledge that came to her from wherever this new Nickie had come.

Indeed, the dog was trotting west, receding into the fog, and now both Amy and Brian ran after her.

Cautious in this treacherous weather, carrying an eight-battery flashlight with a five-inch lens, Harrow crosses the slippery rock formations to the oval yard, searching for the Expedition.

He is accustomed to the disco dazzle that the great signal light generates in certain fog conditions. In fact, he is weary of it. He, too, is ready for the desert.

The SUV hit the Montezuma pine, skinned significant bark off the south side of the trunk, and kept going. It sits on the rocks beyond the grass, its undercarriage hung up on a thrust of granite.

Somehow, it got turned around, most likely after the collision with the tree, and now faces inland. The headlights are shattered, and one door is sprung open.

The garage was not attached to the house, but the structures stood close together. When Amy rounded the corner, she saw lighted house windows flanked by dark shutters, lamplight behind curtains.

The dog led the detail along the wall of the house, hesitating at a corner, peering around, then venturing forth.

As the door stood open at the garage, so another stood wide at the house, billows of cold fog swarming into warm rooms beyond.

On another coast, in another year, Amy had chased Michael out of the house, into the night. This was worse: out of the open into confinement, the short sight lines and the many corners and the closed doors of a house, a strange house, but not strange to *him*.

When the dog crossed the threshold, they were committed as well, and followed her into a kitchen.

Polished steel glittered on the table, a variety of blades so sharp they seemed to slice the fluorescent light that fell on them, not the usual cutlery of a kitchen, but the kind that, after being used, were placed in an autoclave instead of a dishwasher.

Past an open door, back stairs led up to a landing and turned out of sight. Nickie appeared to be interested in them, but then not.

One closed door, maybe to a pantry. They wouldn't be hiding in a pantry. Too bold to hide, both of them.

Incoming fog, cold on her neck, chilled Amy into a frightened turn, but nobody had followed them out of the night.

An open door, a hallway beyond. Nickie liked that route.

Brian motioned Amy ahead. He wanted to bring up the rear.

Archway to the left. Living room. Archway to the right. A study.

Every deserted room meant that the next one was more likely to be occupied.

Gun in both hands, muzzle jumping. Amy needed to get control of herself. Hold the muzzle down. It would kick up on recoil. Shoot them in the head, not over their heads.

Now a closed door on the right, two on the left. They could go through the doors like movie cops, low and fast, stepping away from the hinges after crossing the threshold. Although maybe that was just movie crap, and if you were a real cop, you laughed at it.

Nickie showed no interest in these rooms, and though Amy was nervous about proceeding past those spaces without checking them, leaving closed doors at their back, she followed the dog's lead.

A vestibule ahead. The main stairs to the right. The front door flanked by French-pane sidelights, strobe-lit fog pressing against the glass.

To the left, a final door was ajar. Beside the door stood a red utility can marked GASOLINE.

Nickie sniffed at the gap between door and jamb. She pressed her head through the gap, pushed the door open wider with her body, and disappeared inside.

Amy found a bed-sitting room brightened by a desk lamp and a nightstand lamp with a glass-bead shade.

A girl in a gray sweatsuit knelt at an upholstered chair, half turned away from the door. Hope. It must be Hope.

She was talking, her speech slightly slurred. She seemed to be in distress, speaking fast.

Nickie stood at a distance, staring at the girl, as if not wanting to intrude.

Amy motioned Brian ahead of her. Quietly she closed the door to the hall, stepped away from it. She stood where she could both see the girl and cover the only entrance.

"You caught me, I don't care, I don't," the girl said. "I have to say what's in my heart, that's the best you can do, say what's in your heart. You can burn my feet again, I don't care, I don't. I'm gonna say what's in my heart again."

Brian went to his knees beside her.

The girl looked up, surprised. Clearly, she hadn't known they were here. She had been talking to someone else.

Someone who had stepped out—and would be back.

Chapter

65

Harrow quickly ascertains that his ex-wife and the architect are not in the SUV either dead or wounded.

The back wheels of the Expedition overhang the edge of the cliff, forty feet above the beach, and the tailgate has sprung open.

He must therefore assume that the bodies were in the cargo space and were pitched out of the back when the vehicle came violently to a halt. In that case, they have been cast down to the beach below.

In this fog, in the last of the dying daylight, he will be wasting time and taking risks for nothing by trying to survey the terrain below from the slippery edge of the granite escarpment.

A set of old concrete stairs with a rusted iron railing lead down to the beach. He can descend by those.

He's not keen on searching the strand, but if the bodies are down there, he needs to know. Before morning, the tide could carry them out to sea and move them farther along the coast.

The police are clever about coastal currents and tide charts. Upon finding a corpse and, by forensics, determining the length of time that it has been in the water, they can calculate its point of origin with disturbing accuracy.

The kneeling girl's hands were folded, entwined by a silver chain, with perhaps a pendant hidden between her palms.

She was beautiful, as she'd been beautiful as an infant. Beauty has more faces than beaches have grains of sand; and this was the beauty of innocence, humility, gentleness.

Her eyes were blue, Brian's shade of blue, and clear. They widened with wonder, but then a shyness came into them, and she looked away.

Brian wanted to put a hand to her face, lift her chin, raise her eyes to him. He wanted to put his hand over her hands.

That she might know who he was, that she might flinch at his touch, that she might ask where he had been all these years: The fear of rejection prevented him from touching her.

"Let's go, come on," Amy whispered.

"Honey," he said softly, "do you know who I am?"

Eyes still averted, the girl nodded.

"Will you come with me?"

"Mother has a knife."

"I'm not afraid of her."

"She kills you sometimes."

He trusted inspiration. "Not with our attack dog."

Following his gesture, she saw the golden for the first time. Her face brightened, and her eyes. "Doggie."

Considering this an invitation, Nickie went to the girl, plumed tail celebrating the making of a new friend, and Hope flung her arms around the dog in a display of instant and total trust.

Brian glanced at Amy, and she motioned him to her.

Amy worried that even if they could find keys for Michael's vehicles, they couldn't drive away. The engine would be heard. They would be shot down as they backed out of the garage.

At any moment, they might encounter Michael or Vanessa. They had been in the house maybe three minutes. They were already overdue.

"We can't hunt them with Hope. The dog will keep her safe."

She saw the anguish in his eyes as he said, "That would make sense if you were right about . . . what Nickie is."

"My daughter will take your daughter to safety." As Hope petted Nickie, the pendant on the chain hung visible. "Look."

The silver word stunned him.

"Believe what you know," Amy urged.

She crouched to hug Hope, who was awkward about the affection, though she had been easy with the dog.

"Honey, you're going outside with Nickie. Hold her collar. Stay with her. She'll keep you safe. Don't be afraid."

Smiling at the dog, Hope said, "I'm not. She's a Forever Shiny Thing."

With a glance at Brian, Amy said, "Yes, sweetie, she is."

The hall was deserted. They went to the nearby front door. Fog entered, and Hope left with Nickie.

The dog hesitated on the stoop, testing the air, then led the girl quickly away into the fog.

Harrow on the beach searches sand, fog, and surf foam for any sign of the bodies, when belatedly he realizes that he saw no blood in the Expedition.

He feels deceived, not only by his quarry but also by his own expectations.

Amy got lucky once, back in Connecticut, but she's a submissive, not a transgressor, just like her architect, and it is an affront to Harrow's deepest-held views to imagine that she could get the best of a killing machine like Billy.

He hurries back to the steps and climbs two at a time, clutching at the rusty iron railing.

He is not worried about Moongirl, only about missing something that she might do to them if she finds them in his absence.

Vanessa catches the little freak doing it, mumbling over a HOPE pendant as though it's a fragment of the Lord God Almighty's toenail, hallelujah, smell that toe-jam residue!

She always thought this would be long and slow when the time came. Thought she might like to take a couple of days breaking down the little freak before burning her.

Now she just wants it over. Tonight. Right now.

She has a gallon of gasoline for the third act.

The second act is just going to be punching Piggy. Except for the burns on the bottoms of her feet, Vanessa never marked the little creep before. You have to be careful: all the meddlesome bastards who see one bruise and they're on to child welfare. She really wants to hit her. She's got a lot of years of hitting saved up.

The first act is some little pretend-drowning in the big bathtub upstairs. Tie her up, do some dunking, see how long she can hold her breath. If it's good enough to get some answers out of terrorists, it's good enough for Piggy, who doesn't even have any answers to give.

Vanessa has just finished filling the tub with cold water, as cold as she could draw it. She's selected and set out some scarves she doesn't want anymore, to tie up the little freak.

She has wasted ten years with this. Ten years. She has never gotten from it the level of satisfaction she expected.

It's very difficult for a pleasure in reality to be equal to what you work up first in your imagination. The world is always failing her. Pleasure is the only thing, everything, and yet it is never what it ought to be.

Maybe she'll find something better in the desert. She likes the heat of the desert, the barrenness, the emptiness.

There's too much nature here on the coast. She just wants sand and heat and white sky and silence.

She bought a book, *The World Without Us,* she wants to read it in the desert, someplace isolated, where there's just her and Harrow, and then maybe not him.

Death is the only thing that satisfies. It's the only thing that is *complete,* everything you expect it to be. The dead never fail you.

She is descending the front stairs when, just as she's about to turn onto the landing, she hears whispering in the vestibule. She stops, puts her back to the wall, and eases to the corner.

She's just in time to see Piggy going out the door with a dog. What the hell is *that* about?

Amy Redwing looks after the girl for a moment, then closes the door and turns to Brian.

Vanessa eases back from the corner, for fear they'll glance up at the stairs. She hears fragments of their quick exchanges: *search . . . kitchen . . . back stairs.*

She retreats to the second floor and races across it, as light-footed as always. She descends the back stairs.

They have guns, and she just has the knife she was going to use to mess with Piggy's mind a little, the old Bear knife. She doesn't care if it's a challenge. She doesn't even care if she dies. But she won't die, precisely because she doesn't care. It's when you care about dying that you hesitate, and when you hesitate, Vanessa cuts you down.

Redwing and Bry want to live. They'll hesitate, which makes a knife faster than a bullet every time.

She is very excited. She has wanted him dead a long time.

Off the back stairs, across the kitchen, where fog creeps through the open door, toward the pantry, but instead into a narrow broom closet. The closet contains only a mop, no broom, and Vanessa has just enough room to close the door. It's like standing up in a coffin.

Returning from the front of the house, Amy and Brian searched the rooms that they passed by earlier when Nickie led them through the place. As it turned out, the dog's disinterest in those spaces proved to be wisdom at work, because they were all deserted.

In the kitchen, the pantry seemed unlikely to yield either one of the charming couple, but Amy yanked open the door while Brian covered it with his pistol.

The hinges creaked on the pantry door, and behind Amy other hinges creaked almost simultaneously, and she started to turn, but the knife took her in the back and went deep, and the air went out of her, and the strength.

Amy made a small bird cry, and Brian turned to see Vanessa behind her, and Amy's face as white as the whites of her eyes.

Running horses on stone could have clopped no harder than his heart, and he hesitated to shoot because Amy was blocking Vanessa.

His hesitation coincided with movement glimpsed from the corner of his eye, and he saw a man, surely Michael, coming through the open kitchen door, a pistol in his fist.

Brian wasn't familiar with the gun that he had taken off the shooter earlier, but he didn't hesitate to fire before being fired upon. The weapon was a machine pistol; a quick squeeze pumped out five, six rounds.

Michael went down, but maybe not because he was hit, maybe only for cover, and as Brian turned back to Vanessa, he saw her stab Amy a second time, with another down stroke, and then she surprised him by shoving Amy toward him and surprised him again by coming at him as Amy fell forward between them. She might have half climbed over Amy to slash his face, but he emptied the gun at her, and she was done.

Quaking with terror, he threw aside his gun, dropped to his knees beside Amy, whose face had darkened from white to pale gray, and took her pistol.

Looking under the table, he saw Michael across the room, lying in blood, looking as if his shade had already left his flesh and was boarding the Hellbound train. His arm was stretched out in front of him, his pistol pointed at Brian, and enough of a quiver of life remained in him to pull the trigger.

The round hit Brian in the abdomen, knocked him off his knees, and onto the floor beside Amy, where his left hand fell into her upturned right palm.

If he was going out for good, he wanted to squeeze her hand, but he didn't have the strength, and neither did she.

The pain was so fierce, a furious white heat, that his vision blurred, but he nevertheless saw Hope toddering through the back door, trying to stay on her feet as Nickie dragged her with all the power of a team of sled dogs. In fact, as Brian began to go blind, in the strange euphoria accompanying massive blood loss, he saw Nickie fly over the table, toward them, and Hope flying, too, one hand clutched around the dog's collar.

Chapter

66

A my and Brian agreed that they were not cut out to kill people. They just didn't have the right stuff.

For one thing, they regretted having to pull the trigger even on certifiable sociopaths like Philip Marlowe. That turned out to be the born moniker of Billy Pilgrim et al., a name he never used because he hated all that it stood for.

Their regret did not go as far as maturing into remorse. But when they thought about pulling the trigger on Billy and Michael and Vanessa, they sometimes felt a little sick to their stomachs, though Alka-Seltzer usually helped, also Rolaids Softchews.

Another thing they were not good at anymore was skepticism in spiritual matters. Amy always had been a believer with an open mind, although stories about phone calls from dead nuns would once have tested the limits of her credulity.

Brian traveled a greater arc than she had; now he acknowledges layers of mystery in the world, and he recognizes that what he saw in Nickie's eyes was the light of a divine presence, perhaps the innocent soul of Amy's murdered daughter empowered to return for a brief time and a limited purpose, or an angel.

He is certain now that the sound he heard in his apartment, when he obsessively rendered Nickie's eyes, had been the laboring of enormous wings, which argued for the angel answer. Amy's view is that, since the job-assignment and promotion policies in celestial realms are not known to any living person, there is every reason to assume that the entity in Nickie was *both* her lost daughter and an angel, which were one and the same.

A thing Amy and Brian *were* good at was dying without serious consequences. They had been mortally wounded in the kitchen of the caretaker's house. They entertain no doubt about that, yet here they are, not only alive but without scars.

The way Hope tells it—and she does not lie—Nickie dragged her into the kitchen and *flew* with her over the table. Hope had seen dead people often enough, but she had never flown on a dog before. She let go of the collar and "sat down plop and said *Whoa*."

Nickie spread herself over the wounded Amy and Brian as if she were a furry blanket. Their pale faces regained color, their eyes fluttered open, a few minor blemishes unrelated to the shooting and stabbing cleared up, Brian's beard stubble vanished, Amy remembered where she had misplaced a recipe for fudge a year earlier, Brian found he'd regrown the wisdom teeth he'd had pulled years ago, and all the blood on their clothes and on the floor just "kinda went somewhere some way."

Hope also says Nickie did a "really silly lot of face licking" during the first few minutes of the healing, which explains why Brian's first complaint after resurrection was that his lips tasted funny.

Neither Amy nor Brian has any doubt that in addition to physical healing, they received psychological and emotional healing, for they have found peace sooner than their experiences would seem to allow. Likewise, considering how well-adjusted Hope is after the ten years of hell in her mother's care, she may have received a similar grace.

Hope has learned to read and write at a seventh-grade level. She has not called herself dumb in many months. She has to give back a dime of her allowance every time she does.

Having experienced a number of those small supernatural moments that can arguably be explained away with psychology or science—such as still having a pencil in your hand every time you put it down—they were also parties to a genuine miracle, with the result that they have become more aware than ever of the mysterious patterns in life. This does not mean that they cope with life any better because of their perceptions. Seeing a pattern and making sense of it are different things, and maybe the only people who make sense of the patterns *and* properly shape their lives to them are saints in the making or the pleasant kind of lunatics. Hi-ho.

Fred, Ethel, and Nickie continue to share life with Amy and Brian, and they are a happy bunch of kids. Three days after the events that September, the winged Nickie in the furry Nickie went back to her forever home. After a particularly long and sweet cuddle on the sofa, she signaled her departure with a joyous sound of wings that reverberated from one end of the bungalow to another. Now Nickie, bought for two thousand dollars—a bargain—from a crazy drunk guy, is just a good dog, nothing more, though a good dog is one of the best of all things to be.

Millie and Barry Packard's blind dog, Daisy, regained her sight one day after the visit by Nickie, but three-legged Mortimer did not grow a fourth. So it goes.

Golden Heart thrives. The estate of a man named Georgie Jobbs (no relation to Steve Jobs), who was thought to have been a person of modest—and mysterious—means was settled entirely on Golden

Heart, to the tune of $1.26 million. No one knew he admired goldens until, in his last will and testament, he said that the only person in his life who ever loved him was a golden named Harley. Amy's dream center for goldens may someday be built.

Too many dogs continue to be abused and abandoned—one is too many—and people continue to kill people for money and envy and no reason at all. Bad people succeed and good people fail, but that's not the end of the story. Miracles happen that nobody sees, and among us walk heroes who are never recognized, and people live in loneliness because they cannot believe they are loved, and, yes, Amy and Brian were married.

About the Author

DEAN KOONTZ, the author of many #1 *New York Times* bestsellers, lives with his wife, Gerda, and the enduring spirit of their golden retriever, Trixie, in southern California.

Correspondence for the author should be addressed to:

Dean Koontz
P.O. Box 9529
Newport Beach, California 92658